THE LAST GIRLS STANDING

Also by Jennifer Dugan

Hot Dog Girl
Verona Comics
Some Girls Do
Melt With You

With Kit Seaton

Coven

THE LAST GIRLS STANDING

JENNIFER DUGAN

G. P. Putnam's Sons

G. P. Putnam's Sons

An imprint of Penguin Random House LLC, New York

First published in the United States of America by G. P. Putnam's Sons,
an imprint of Penguin Random House LLC, 2023

Copyright © 2023 by Jennifer Dugan

Visit us online at PenguinRandomHouse.com.

Library of Congress Cataloging-in-Publication Data | Names: Dugan, Jennifer, author.
Title: The last girls standing / Jennifer Dugan. | Description: New York: G. P. Putnam's, 2023. |
Summary: As the only two survivors of a summer camp massacre, Sloan and her girlfriend Cherry form a seemingly unbreakable bond, but as Sloan discovers more about the attack, she begins to suspect Cherry may be more than just a survivor. | Identifiers: LCCN 2022060794 (print) |
LCCN 2022060795 (ebook) | ISBN 9780593532072 (hardcover) | ISBN 9780593532089 (epub)
Subjects: CYAC: Psychic trauma—Fiction. | Murder—Fiction. | Lesbians—Fiction. |
LCGFT: Thrillers (Fiction) | Novels. | Classification: LCC PZ7.1.D8343 Las 2023 (print) |
LCC PZ7.1.D8343 (ebook) | DDC [Fic]—dc23
LC record available at https://lccn.loc.gov/2022060794
LC ebook record available at https://lccn.loc.gov/2022060795

Printed in the United States of America

ISBN 9780593532072

1st Printing

LSCH

Design by Eileen Savage | Text set in Arno Pro

To Joe, for always letting me pick the movie

THE
LAST GIRLS
STANDING

ONE

IT HAD TAKEN sixteen sutures to close the wound on the underside of Sloan's forearm.

Sixteen threads, woven in and out of her skin by careful hands wrapped in latex, while whispered words had promised, "It's okay. You're safe now." As if anyone could really know that.

Sloan remembered the way the pain had dulled down to a useless ache as the doctors worked, a pressure and tug that she knew should hurt, would hurt, *had* hurt before everything faded to a blur of sirens and lights and hospital antiseptic.

Sixteen stitches holding her together when she could not do so herself.

"Sloan," a voice said, sounding far away and underwater. Sloan ignored it, instead staring down at the puckered pink line running down her arm. She traced the scar with her finger, paying special attention to where it bit into the peculiar patch of raised skin above her wrist. Her mother called it a birthmark, but Sloan had never seen a birthmark like that before.

Not that either of them really knew. When the Thomas family adopted her at the age of four, the mark, whatever it was, was already there. Her social workers were no help, and her biological parents were long gone—a single Polaroid picture and an urgent, whispered "remember who you are" were all they left in their wake. There would be no asking and no answers for anyone.

"Sloan," the voice said again.

This time Sloan snapped her attention to the woman sitting across from her. "Beth," she said, matching her therapist's tone. If you could really call her that. Beth was some new-age hypnotherapist-slash-psychic her mother had dug up when Sloan refused to talk to the doctors the hospital social worker had sent them to. She wasn't even sure if Beth was accredited. She wasn't even sure if hypnotists *could* be accredited.

"Where were you just now?" Beth asked, trying very hard to keep her face neutral. Beth was always trying to keep her face neutral, and it rarely worked. Sloan had never met a therapist with so many tells, and she had met a lot of them in those first few weeks after the "incident."

Sloan flashed her patented smart-ass smile. "Here, in this chair, wondering how much more of this beautiful day I have to spend stuck inside your office."

Beth frowned. "Is that all?"

"Does there always need to be more?"

Beth leaned back in her chair. "It would be helpful to your recovery if there was, at least occasionally, more."

Her recovery. That was hilarious. What recovery? It felt more like a countdown from where she sat. They had been waiting and watching her for a while now. Waiting for her to snap. To break down. To tell anyone other than that first police officer what she remembered. What it was like. What she saw. To put the few memories of that night she could manage to scrape up on display for them to dissect like a science experiment.

Her parents, Beth, and all the therapists and gurus and life coaches before her all claimed to want to "help" her process what she'd been through. They wanted to understand. But nobody could, not unless they'd been there too. Sloan glanced out the window to where Cherry's truck sat glinting in the September sun. As if she could sense Sloan looking, Cherry opened the door and slid out, her long brown hair flipping up in the breeze.

Sloan drank in the sight of the other girl, her entire body relaxing as the person she loved most leaned against the truck with crossed arms. Cherry was safety, warmth. She didn't pry because she didn't have to. She was there when it happened, when everyone died except for the two of them: the last girls standing.

Sloan's loss was her loss. Sloan's wounds were her wounds. They didn't need therapists or police or parents wandering around inside their heads—they had each other for that.

"You need to talk about what happened. Let me help you."

Sloan sighed. It wasn't that she didn't like Beth—she did. Or that she didn't think Beth meant well—she did. Sloan just didn't see the point. "Help with what?" she asked softly.

"Your mother says your nightmares are getting worse. We could start there—do a longer session and try to reprocess whichever memories are affecting you most. We might be able to take some of the bite out of them. Many of my clients have had a lot of luck with this approach in the past, but you have to work with me. I can't do it for you."

"I'll think about it," Sloan said, and then they lapsed back into silence.

She was relieved when Beth's phone alarm chimed, signaling the end of the visit. The truth was that Sloan wasn't sure she wanted to "take the bite out" of her memories. To reprocess them or share them with anyone else. Because what she remembered most from that day wasn't fear. It wasn't the sticky scent of warm blood, although that remained thick and cloying even in her dreams. And it wasn't even the pain of the cut in her skin.

No.

What she remembered most was love.

TWO

CHERRY PULLED OPEN the driver's side door before Sloan was even down the concrete steps of the Smith Medical Building. It was home to an urgent care, a massage therapist, four empty suites, and, of course, Beth McGuinness, holistic hypnotherapist specializing in traumatic response therapy.

"How was the headshrinker?" Cherry teased as Sloan slid across the long bench seat of her old F-150. Sloan didn't know anything about trucks, and she gathered Cherry didn't either, given that the passenger's side door had been stuck shut for as long as Sloan had known her. The truck had originally belonged to Cherry's dad, and her mom had passed it on to her when he died a few years back. Sloan didn't know if it was a sentimental thing or a money thing that kept them in that truck. Maybe a little of both.

"Shrinky," Sloan answered.

"I don't know why your mom keeps making you go." Cherry shifted the truck into drive and slowly pulled out of the parking lot.

Sloan threaded her fingers between Cherry's and let all the

tension bleed from her body. "Probably because if I had to write an essay about what I did on my summer vacation, it would say 'survived a mass murder,'" Sloan said, attempting to make air quotes with her free hand. "You know it freaks her out."

"Then maybe *she* should see someone and leave us alone for once."

Sloan liked the way Cherry said "us." The way she always combined them into one now. Nothing happened to Cherry or to Sloan; it only happened to both of them, as if what happened that day at camp had fused them somehow.

"Oh, she does," Sloan said, twisting in her seat. "I'm pretty sure me going was actually *her* therapist's idea. Or maybe her guru's. I can't keep them all straight anymore. You'd think she was the one who had to get sewn back together."

Cherry made a little tsking sound. "Sounds like a conspiracy to me."

"Yeah, a real conspiracy: protecting my mental health."

"You know I'm always here for all your protection needs." She puffed out her chest, and Sloan smiled back at her.

"Yeah, I noticed that with the whole hiding-me-from-masked-men-with-machetes thing."

"Oh yeah, that clued you in? Good," Cherry said with a laugh.

It didn't use to be like this.

The lightness, the teasing, it was new. Just since Cherry moved to town with her mother a few days ago. Now it was like Sloan could breathe again. Like there was a reason to want to smile.

It was a fluke they had both ended up at Camp Money Springs—two girls on opposite sides of the state just looking for a fun summer job and a way to earn some cash that didn't involve fast food or retail. They were both fresh high school graduates, and while Cherry was planning on taking a gap year to "find herself"—aka use up her friends' goodwill to couch surf her way across the country—Sloan was just trying to earn some spending money for her first semester at NYU starting that fall.

They had almost nothing in common. Cherry loved punk and grunge bands from the '90s; Sloan would die for Olivia Rodrigo and Doja Cat. Cherry was sure that they didn't need to worry about global warming because nature would heal itself, getting rid of people the way it had gotten rid of dinosaurs. Sloan thought they should all use metal straws anyway, just in case.

They shouldn't have worked, but from the second they met, painting old boats and then clearing weeds at the archery range to prepare the camp for summer, Sloan knew they were meant to be. And to her delight, so did the other girl.

Fate, Cherry had called it, eating slushies made from ground-down ice and cheap syrup by the fire. She had tasted like sugar the first time they kissed.

She had tasted like blood the next.

"Your mom home?" Cherry asked, pulling Sloan from her head.

She had a knack for doing that, and it was especially useful after a session with Beth—even if Sloan barely talked, it was still somehow exhausting. Like it knocked things around in her mind, leaving everything slightly off-kilter. Beth kept poking into the things Sloan couldn't remember—like that gap of time between Cherry finding her and the police arriving. It was just *missing*. Like her brain had deleted it. Like it was a detail as unimportant as the color of the socks she had worn on the first day of school. There was fear, and then nothing, and then blood in her hair. It felt very matter-of-fact without the middle bits.

Without the important bits.

Cherry had filled her in, of course; they'd gone over it dozens of times. That was good enough for Sloan. She wished it were good enough for Beth. Sloan knew she would likely have another nightmare that night. She always did after Beth poked around in the missing places.

"Sloan," Cherry said again. "Is your mom home?"

"Yeah." Sloan frowned. "She wants me to go to Simon's baseball game later. She thinks we need 'family time.'"

"Right." Cherry sighed. "It would be nice if Allison could at least set the mandatory emotional manipulation aside after your therapy sessions. Let me guess, she turned your little brother loose on you?"

Sloan liked that Cherry called her mother Allison. Sometimes she did too, secretly in her head or when it was just her and Cherry.

"Yep," Sloan said. "It's hard to call her out on it when Simon's standing there with his big, round eyes all 'Sloany, please come.'"

"I love that 'family time' is just code for 'Cherry's not invited.'"

And it was. It was. Both girls knew it. It was Allison's latest invention to keep them separated.

Before, when they were still living hours apart, Sloan's mom had imposed a curfew even on weekends. She claimed it was because she needed Sloan in her sight after what happened; it was just a coincidence it was early enough for Sloan to visit Connor and Rachel, her former best friends, but there was never, ever enough time for her to make it to Cherry's house and back.

"You'd get over this sooner without a constant codependent reminder of what you went through," Allison had shouted at Sloan, while clutching her latest homeopathic calming tea.

Clearly, Beth needed to work on the recipe.

Thank god Cherry had a truck and a mom who was quick to look the other way, and more often than not she'd climb through Sloan's window at night like a stray cat that had been fed once and formed a habit.

Eventually, Allison gave up and asked Cherry to "at least use the door instead."

It was better now that Cherry lived nearby, streets away instead of counties, an entire year for themselves stretched out in front of them ever since Sloan had sent in her deferral letter to NYU. It would be good year, a reset, a fresh start. Even the boxes yet to be unloaded from the bed of Cherry's truck, battered and sliding around with every turn, seemed somehow hopeful.

If only the rest of the world would leave them alone.

Other people were the worst, even the ones Sloan used to be close to—especially them, maybe. They talked about Sloan and Cherry, and around them—worse yet, they wanted them to share the gory details over lunch or in an interview. They didn't understand that Sloan and Cherry's experience—and it was *theirs* because sometimes it was hard to tell where Sloan ended and Cherry began—was not carrion for scavengers to pick through. It was their *life*.

Even Connor, Sloan's best friend since third grade, had tried to get the scoop under the guise of "being there" for Sloan. But Rachel, his girlfriend, was the worst, demanding Sloan "get over it already" because she was "freaking everyone out." Sloan had stopped replying to her texts after that. She had stopped replying to *all* their texts after that.

How was she supposed to explain that she'd hidden while someone else's blood pooled hot and sticky around her hair? How she couldn't get the smell out for days even though her mother swore the only thing she could smell was the lavender shampoo.

(That was one memory she wished her brain *had* deleted.)

"Almost there," Cherry said, as if it hurt her to be away from Sloan as much as it hurt Sloan to be away from her.

But that was impossible.

Sloan cursed the ride home for being so short—just a blink-and-you-miss-it burst of freedom between Beth's office and mandatory family time.

Cherry parked in the driveway but kept the truck running. She was quickly learning to choose her battles with Sloan's mom. Respecting their family time would mean less chance of a fight when she slipped into Sloan's room that night, curling tightly around her like a snake.

"I'll see you later?" Cherry asked.

"You better." Sloan leaned forward for a kiss—strawberry lip gloss, her favorite—and her belly twitched and ached. Goodbye kisses were stressful—being away from Cherry at all was stressful—but she didn't have a choice. She slid over Cherry's lap, knocking their teeth together with one last kiss, before hopping out the door.

Sloan walked to the house with a little wave, disappearing through the door with a frown. She tried to ignore the cold sinking feeling in her stomach that took up residence whenever the girls were apart. It was okay. She could do this. She just had to get through the next little while.

Cherry's truck would be at the ball field, just out of her mother's sight, waiting, watching, keeping her safe from afar.

"Sloan?" her mother called from the kitchen. "Come eat!"

"Coming, Mom," she chirped brightly, pasting the perfect smile on her face.

She was fine.

She was fine.

THREE

THE TOOTHBRUSH WAS hard and heavy in her hand. Her fingers curled around it so tightly that it might snap, would have snapped, should have snapped, if she had been anywhere except in a dream.

And Sloan knew it was a dream. A nightmare, really, although Sloan knew the real nightmare wouldn't begin until she opened the door to her cabin. Until she saw the blood running in rivulets, following the same divots in the wood and grass that the rain had the day before. But she could never get that far. Not anymore. It was as if her mind was working backward, clearing out the memories from the end to the beginning, leaving her with confusing flashes of half memories—all without order or context.

But the dreams still came like clockwork. Every night, pinned to her bed, she relived the final moments before it all went to shit, before she opened the door. Beth had suggested that if they could break the pattern, if Sloan could get the door open before the dream ended, maybe they could make some real progress. Whatever that meant.

Still, Sloan hoped this night, this dream, this nightmare, would be the one.

If she had to open that door, she would rather do it on her own terms, in her own bed, instead of sitting on an oversize armchair in front of Beth.

She looked at the toothbrush in her hand, looked at the wide-eyed reflection of herself in the cabin mirror, and tried to sink all the way inside herself. Deep, deep, until she was drowning in the sensation. Until she felt fused with the body looking in the mirror, until her past and present melted together into one word, one thought: now.

Sloan had been in the bathroom when she'd heard the first scream, and so the bathroom was where she always started, caught in a time loop in her head every night like a rabbit in a snare.

She had just changed into her pink-striped pajamas. Because she knew Cherry liked them best and had been expecting, hoping, waiting for her to visit for one of their late-night talks. Cherry had made it a habit to show up out of the blue, and Sloan wanted to be ready.

Thus, the cute pajamas, the toothbrush heavy in her hand. They had kissed earlier, and she hoped they would again, and she'd be damned if their second kiss was going to start with stale garlic crouton breath.

Five, four, three, two, and—

The scream ripped through the dream exactly as it had that night.

Sloan had thought nothing of it at first until others joined in. Until the screaming turned to crying, to begging. Until a heavy thunk—followed by the sticky wet sound of what she had at first thought was a watermelon being split, but later turned out to be the sternum of one of the other counselors—had made her bones rattle and her teeth ache.

Something was wrong.

Very, very wrong.

Sloan set the toothbrush down and crept over to the tiny, frosted bathroom window, just as she had that night. The rough, unfinished pine logs that made up the cabin walls scratched her cheek as she tried to pry the window back. She couldn't see anything through the cloudy glass, but maybe if she could get it open, she could make something out through the screen, even though it was pitch-black outside.

The solar-powered motion lights on the other cabins began to flick on, and then off, as if someone—or something—was moving from place to place. A shiver ran down her spine as the light two cabins down clicked on. Whatever it was, it was heading in her direction, getting closer.

And she supposed that made sense.

Most of the other cabins were empty, after all.

Next week the summer camp would be bustling full of little kids, mostly middle schoolers—but also the occasional elementary kid whose parents needed them out of the way, or high schooler working as a "junior counselor."

But that was next week.

This week, the week Sloan learned that chopping watermelons doesn't sound all that different from chopping bodies, there was only a small group of counselors and workers. Ten, to be exact. Spread out all over the camp.

And somehow, even then, still trying to unjam the bathroom window and get a better look, Sloan knew that number wouldn't last the night.

She gave up on the window, blurry and stuck shut, even though it had worked every time before that. Sloan paused for a second to try to remember if it really had been stuck that night; she had a sneaking suspicion that was a new detail, only for the dream, her mind trying to take away even more, to hide it away where it couldn't hurt her . . . but she couldn't be sure.

And if she started thinking too much, if she pressed too hard, if she started taking control instead of running on time-loop autopilot, she knew she would be flung back into the waking world before she even got to the doorknob. Would wake up sweaty and hot even in the cold autumn night, her sheets tangled around her like a straitjacket.

Sloan was determined not to let that happen.

Not tonight. Not again. She had to stay. She had to stay.

Sloan dropped to her knees when the second scream hit, followed shortly thereafter by a deep rustling sound near the edge of the cabin. She crawled to the main room, the sound of her breathing too loud and scratchy in the stillness, bordering on hysterical. The room was small, barely room enough for a bed and a table and a woodstove. Barely any room to hide.

Splinters bit into her skin as she crawled across the floor and up onto her bed to peer through the dusty screen of another stuck-shut window. At least this one wasn't frosted. She wedged her shoulder against the little lip of the window and got it to open just a crack, just enough to let the air from outside slip in, cocooning her in the scent it carried.

The breeze had transformed from something earthy and crisp to something metallic that made her stomach clench. Sloan couldn't place it, but somewhere deep inside her, every single cell in her body was screaming at her to run. Now. Go. Leave. Danger. Danger! Her primal instincts taking over as if she was more feral beast than house cat. Every muscle tensed to bolt. To save her. To escape whatever it was that smelled like that.

But that's when she saw the man.

At least she thought it was a man. She was pretty sure. He was tall, lumbering, a body in stark relief, an inky shadow beside the bright yellow of the motion light on the cabin next to hers. But the shape of his head was distorted into something odd, something pointy.

It wasn't until he stepped under the light, the machete in his hand stained red—god, so much red—that Sloan realized it was a mask. A crudely made monstrosity, carved out of wood and affixed to where the face of a person should have been.

Sloan thought it was supposed to be a fox, but it had been thoroughly distorted by the slices and gouges in the wood. This man wasn't a fox; he was an approximation of a fox, a sloppy kid's drawing come to life. An insult to arts and crafts everywhere.

And it made Sloan mad. If she was going to be murdered, if this was going to be her last night on this dying earth, she at least deserved a quality, clever, talented killer.

But no, that wasn't right. That hadn't been what she was thinking then at all. That was Real Sloan leaking in—frustrated and furious from the future—and no, no, no, no, the real her needed to pull back before she got ejected.

Autopilot. Time loop. "Be a casual observer," Beth had once said. "Let your memories lead the way."

So she did.

Sloan blinked, observing the man—The Fox, as she would come to call him—as he turned and started walking, walking slowly toward the cabin she was in, his head tilted to the very window she looked out of, and all that fear, all that lizard-brain survival instinct came flooding back. Could he see her?

Her stomach roiled as her eyes fell on the slumped shadow left abandoned on the porch in the man's wake. At first, she thought it was a pile of clothes. But it wasn't. It wasn't someone taking a nap or passed-out drunk; it wasn't any of the good things that the first days had brought. It was sweet Beckett, a college sophomore from Virginia. She could tell *it was him from those expensive hiking boots he never took off. A dark puddle slowly spread beneath him and surrounded him like a halo.*

Sloan clamped her hand over her mouth to stifle a scream and then rushed to the exit, tripping over her comforter as she clawed her way past. Panic sent her careening toward the door on hands and knees. If she could get the door open, if she could just get out, she would run, far and fast. Never stopping. Never looking back.

She hoped Cherry would be waiting on the other side of the door, like she supposedly had been in real life, with a kiss and an outreached hand and running feet that had ultimately led them to the old canoes stacked up next to Kevin's office. They had hidden under them, had lain as still and quiet as mice while the director's blood soaked into Sloan's hair.

But when Sloan turned the knob, it was locked. Locked hard, as it had been in every single dream before. Sloan clawed and cried and screamed, pounding against it even as the motion light flicked on over the door.

Then there it was, like every time, the sight of Cherry's face in the small window, at first relieved and then confused, as his blade pushed through her, pulling up, and Sloan was hit with the realization of exactly what that wet thwack she'd heard earlier was.

She would never eat watermelon again.

And Cherry? Cherry slid down, her blood slipping underneath the still-locked door, wet and warm beneath Sloan. The Fox stood at the window, tilting his head left and right, exactly where Cherry had been a second before, and then he—

"Shhh, shhh, I got you. I'm here. It's not real. We're okay."

Sloan struggled against the body holding her down, kicking

and screaming until the words wove into her brain and dragged her from the dream. Her eyes opened, wide and painful. Every light in the room was on, and there were so many—she had added them after her parents brought her back home, stained inside and out and still wrapped in the shock blanket she had refused to let go of during her long days in the hospital.

She clenched her fingers around Cherry's T-shirt and buried her face against her girlfriend's belly. Cherry was here. Alive. It hadn't been real. She had never been stabbed. It was okay.

It was okay.

Cherry gave Sloan a moment to pull herself together, letting her take big, gulping breaths through the open window that Cherry had slipped through.

"You were dead. You were dead."

"It was a dream, baby," Cherry, real and alive, said over and over again until Sloan stopped crying.

"You came," Sloan said eventually, when she could finally find her voice through the sobs.

One side of Cherry's mouth slipped up into a smile. "Well, it's family night, right?" she teased. "I couldn't miss that."

Sloan tried and failed to push out a smile. She melted into Cherry instead, let herself go limp in the other girl's arms, let Cherry hold her up . . . until her door swung open and tore them from the little peace they had found.

Sloan's parents took in the sight of the girls—wrapped tight around each other like two halves of a lock—and then the opened window, the tattered blankets, the tears, and they scowled. Well, Sloan's mom, Allison, did. Her father, Brad, simply shook his head and walked away.

"I told you to use the door, Cherry. My insurance won't cover you breaking your neck climbing the side of my goddamn house," Allison said before she slammed the door shut behind her.

Cherry giggled. She dragged Sloan down onto the bed with her and carefully arranged the blankets over them both. "Your mother loves me."

"I'm the only one who needs to love you," Sloan answered and drifted off to the sensation of Cherry tracing slow circles on her skin.

She was here.

She was real.

She was safe.

FOUR

THE FIRST TIME Sloan saw Cherry, she was all long-legged and smirky, standing next to a tall Indian boy named Rahul and a white kid named Beckett, who looked like hiking was his whole personality. Sloan had barely noticed the boys, as she was thoroughly lost in the freckles dotting Cherry's peachy sun-kissed skin. She had almost forgotten her own name, forgotten words completely, and was left blinking when Rahul introduced himself.

Sloan had arrived a day later than all the other counselors, the product of her mother insisting that Sloan stay home an extra day for her little brother Simon's birthday party. She had missed whatever icebreakers and team bonding that had happened the day before, and as she watched the ease with which Beckett draped himself around Cherry, she was annoyed about it all over again.

"Family emergency" was what Sloan had told her boss, because that seemed more mature than saying, *My mom won't let me leave until I ooh and aah over an eight-year-old cutting into his LEGO cake.*

She supposed it was an emergency of sorts because if she hadn't stayed for it, Sloan knew she would have heard about it for the rest of her life. *No thank you,* she thought as she sent the email to her boss.

Kevin, the camp director, had been cool about it. He'd even personally shown her to her cabin the afternoon she arrived. It was a small, ten-by-twelve wooden rectangle embedded in the middle of the woods with several others just like it. It was constructed from rough pine logs, patched together with some sort of mud or cement or something, but she could still see hints of light shining between them. The roof was tin, which she supposed would bake her alive that summer, but she didn't care. It was hers, and it was private, and she could escape from her mother's prying eyes for once in her life.

The fact that she had her own bathroom was the cherry on top of the sundae. It was something she'd never experienced in her own modest two-bathroom house—her mother had declared one a "guest bath" that was basically off-limits unless you were a distant relative visiting from out of town. Which meant that the four of them—her mom, dad, brother, and Sloan—were left fighting over the other one.

Mornings during the school year were especially fun.

When the opportunity arose to spend her entire summer in the woods three hours away—in the form of a little flyer tacked up on her school's bulletin board—she had jumped at it. Sure, the camp's website was outdated and the photos looked shoddy, but Sloan didn't care.

She'd padded her résumé and cover letter with a slightly (extremely) exaggerated list of experiences that included working at the day care and summer program at the YMCA—she had attended the after-school program there until she was twelve, and that counted for something in her opinion—and community service work. (She had to get a certain number of hours in for the National Honor Society, and if it was more "writing letters to senior citizens in retirement homes" and less "taking any kind of leadership role in the community," well, Camp Money Springs didn't have to know.)

The interview had taken place over Zoom, a conference call between her, Kevin, and a woman named Charla. Sloan still wasn't sure how she was tied to the camp.

Sloan had sucked up, made sure she pasted on her best smile as she said all the right things, made them laugh, and molded and shaped her personality into exactly what she knew they were looking for, based on their reactions to anything and everything she said.

Sloan was good at reading grown-ups. She was a pro at analyzing every facial expression, every twitch up or down in the corner of a lip, the difference between a furrowed brow and a raised one. She'd brought it up to a teacher once, as if it was a special talent, and the woman's smile had fallen. The teacher had sent Sloan to the school counselor, said so many words that Sloan didn't understand. Sloan had to google "trauma response"—it wasn't a part of her vernacular yet—and was relieved to read it was something that could fade. She desperately wished it would, wished that it weren't as automatic as breathing.

Just another thing marking her as different from the other children, like the spot on her wrist or her heavily redacted birth certificate.

But the habit never left her. No matter how many years she lived with her utterly bland and even-keeled adoptive father and her overprotective, overbearing adoptive mother, it lingered. A part of her forever. Another parting gift from her birth parents, one that couldn't be stored in the tiny box on her dresser where she kept the other mementos from that blurry, forgotten time before Allison and Brad.

As she grew, Sloan learned to again appreciate this constant cataloging of how she was being perceived and how other people were feeling. It meant she interviewed well—she conned them well—and so within minutes she was sure that she had gotten the camp counselor job.

Still, when Sloan received the offer email that listed what to bring (so much bug spray and sunblock) and when to be there (earlier than she thought, which made Connor and Rachel upset that they didn't have time to plan a better going-away party for her), her hands shook. For as much as Sloan trusted herself, adults could be unpredictable. Her mother could change her mind about letting her go. Kevin could find someone else.

Nothing was set in stone, nothing, until she was there.

The delay, even by a day for the birthday party, had felt like torture. But when Sloan set her bag down in her little pine cabin and smiled at Kevin's ruddy, sunburned face, she felt at peace, finally. She had arrived.

Sloan had no idea that when she ripped the camp flyer off her school's bulletin board, she also pushed down that first domino that would lead her straight to the most important person she would ever meet.

Cherry Barnes.

Charlene Addison Barnes, if we're being technical. Although Cherry warned Sloan once—their bodies pressed together under starlight, their lungs empty from confessing everything about themselves and who they were outside of that perfect place soon to be overrun by children—that if she ever dared to call Cherry by her full name, she would cut Sloan's tongue out herself. It sounded romantic at the time somehow, a secret shared in the darkest of nights. A truth kept from everyone else. It was small, tiny, minuscule even, but knowing Cherry straight down to her full legal name felt powerful. Vulnerable. No one knew Cherry like Sloan did. Probably no one ever would.

It was hot the day they met, scorching already by morning, and the sweat beaded up along Sloan's hairline and trailed in small splashes down the bumps in her spine before getting sucked up by her moisture-wicking tank top and the elastic band of her Nike shorts. Sloan had packed carefully, deliberately. Just because she was going to be in the middle of the woods didn't mean she couldn't also look cute.

"The rest of the counselors are down by the water," Kevin called. "Unpack and then get down there to help. We want to get the canoes patched and painted before the little campers get here. If there are any too far gone, drag them up to my place, and I'll see about replacing them. We open in five days whether we're ready or not," he said gruffly and then headed back toward his office, the only air-conditioned place in the whole camp. The only place with real piped-in electricity instead of tiny solar panels just big enough to power a single light in each cabin.

He had barely gotten inside before Sloan heard the first notes of "Smells Like Teen Spirit" hit the speakers. It was one of her dad's favorites, and she had been subjected to it on several long road trips, both her and her mom groaning while he relived his glory days. Sloan turned to unpack. She hoped she wouldn't be able to hear it as well by the water.

Sloan hadn't brought much with her. There was no point. A journal, a sketch pad, a battery backup for her phone, which she was hoping she could at least keep charged enough to look at pictures of her friends when she got homesick for them, or play stupid games that didn't need Wi-Fi.

Each cabin was outfitted with an LED solar-powered lamp—which they were instructed to put outside to recharge every day before they went to work—and a sink, a stand-up shower that only ran cold, and a toilet in a bathroom about the size of a closet. She could wash her hands sitting on the toilet if she really wanted to, her knees knocking the sink and her thighs getting pinched between the seat and the shower stall.

Sloan hoped the lamp was the kind that had a little plug on it so she could charge her phone. Even if it took all the power, every day. Who needed a light bulb when she could be bathed in the glow of her iPhone at night?

Sloan set her journal, notepads, and assorted pencils on the table, shoved her mostly Nike wardrobe beneath the bed, and placed her toothbrush beside the sink, along with her tube of toothpaste and Secret aluminum-free deodorant.

She had thought about bringing her makeup but then decided to forgo it. Her mom expected the makeup, required it, honestly. So worried about appearances. But this summer was about freedom. This summer, she didn't want to deal with any of Mom's expectations.

Next, she lined up her various serums and sunblocks. Just

because she was forgoing makeup didn't mean her mom's other lessons on skincare—Mom was a dermatologist, to be fair—hadn't sunk in. Her white skin was prone to burning, and her mother loved to terrify her with pictures of what sun damage in their teens did to people later in life.

Sloan slathered on extra sunblock, changed out of her sneakers and into her Nike slides—painting didn't seem like something that required heavy footwear—and then followed the winding dirt path labeled LAKE, which disappeared between pine trees as tall as skyscrapers. The sky was overwhelmingly blue through the thick branches, and she smiled to herself despite the heat. She wasn't exactly a fan of nature, but she was a fan of being *somewhere else,* and this, she thought, was the *somewhere elsiest* of all.

Sloan stopped short at the clearing at the end of the path, or rather at the sight of Cherry grinning with Rahul and Beckett. The boys had barely introduced themselves before they started running around, spattering each other with the white paint they were supposed to be using on the boats. A little hit Sloan, cold and thick, and she laughed.

But when Sloan remembered it later, the paint wasn't white; it was red.

And it was warm.

THERE HAD BEEN ten of them altogether, tasked with opening the camp. Most of the counselors were in their early years of college or about to be. Sloan, Cherry, Rahul, and Beckett were joined by Dahlia, a white college sophomore from downstate with the longest, prettiest brown hair that Sloan had ever seen; Hannah, a

Korean American who considered not keeping up with the latest celebrity gossip a moral failing; Anise, who once boasted without a hint of irony that she could trace her ancestors back to the *Mayflower*; and Shane, a quiet Black boy with an unusual obsession with cryptids, who upon meeting Sloan had launched into a speech about the Mothman's continued relevance in American history, and had barely uttered another word after. Then there were the actual tried-and-true adults: Ronnie, the camp cook, a thirty-four-year-old Black man obsessed with perfecting his own snow cone syrup recipe, and Kevin, the middle-aged camp director, who had turned his white skin various shades of red and brown due to his aversion to sunscreen, and had a penchant for listening to Nirvana and Soundgarden on repeat all day.

Literally. All. Day.

In fact, much to Cherry's delight and Sloan's distress, he had announced that afternoon that this was the only music he would authorize to be played over the camp's speakers.

Sloan had originally mistaken him for a fake hipster trying to cash in on the grunge resurgence, until she realized with a start that he was probably actually *alive* the first go-around—he mentioned being born in the late '70s.

Jesus, she thought, that was old.

Music had been on all their minds the following night around the fire as the counselors argued the merits of cottagecore versus pop versus grunge versus punk, while slurping down Ronnie's snow cones and old Gatorade that Kevin had dug up from somewhere. Cherry, in her paisley tank top with flowers in her hair, held court among all of them. Sloan, off to the side like the rest, watched, transfixed.

A lull in the conversation led to Sloan daring to suggest that clearly pop was the superior genre. She was swiftly met with groans from everyone except Hannah, the debate quickly picking up steam again. Sloan just listened after that, lost in the conversation and reveling in the fact that she had spent a full twenty-four hours *and then some* away from home.

She was thriving, content, happy. Free.

The conversation moved on, the mood light, almost giddy, until Beckett called Cherry "environmentally irresponsible" for decrying straw bans, and Cherry called him "ableist as fuck and a good little capitalist." Dahlia tried to break it up, but they just shouted over her.

"What about you, Sloan? What do you think?" Cherry demanded. Dahlia shifted beside her—probably trying to avoid Cherry's ire.

Sloan shrugged. "I don't—"

"Think Beckett knows what he's talking about on this one? Good." Cherry crossed her arms. "Nothing we do is going to make a difference anyway. Not with billionaires and corporations accounting for, like, alllllllll this mess."

"That's so fatalistic," Beckett snapped. "But what did I expect from your bleached cottagecore ass?"

Cherry laughed at that. "Bleached," she giggled, barely able to catch her breath. "Beckett's got insults."

Beckett smirked, clearly pleased. Despite his annoyance, he seemed to be as enamored with Cherry as everyone else at the camp.

"Besides, none of it matters anyway," Cherry said. She dropped in front of Beckett and leaned back. "The earth is going to course correct, just like it did with the dinosaurs."

He made room for her between his legs, his arms circling hers to pull her back against his chest. Sloan wondered at first if they were dating. But no. That was just Cherry. She made you feel a certain kind of way, right off the bat.

Anise flicked ice at Cherry with her very unbiodegradable straw. "Are you implying that dinosaurs polluted the oceans and stuff so much that the earth created an asteroid and then directed it at *itself*? I don't know what's scarier, to be honest: us destroying the world, the world being sentient enough to enact revenge, or the earth being such a piss baby that it would cut off its nose to spite its face."

"Fine." Cherry shrugged. "The universe, then."

"God?" Hannah asked, tugging at the gold cross that she wore around her neck. "You mean God?" Sloan hoped that Hannah wasn't here in some kind of missionary capacity. Save the heathens in the woods from the demonic campfire stories or whatever. But no, Sloan found out at her funeral—number six of eight that she and Cherry attended—that Hannah had actually taken the camp counselor job as part of a community service plea deal after getting caught shoplifting expensive perfume for the third time. Cute.

Cherry just waved them all off. So confident in her position that Sloan wanted to swallow it whole and make it a part of her beliefs too.

"I mean balance," Cherry finally said. "The universe will re-balance itself, somehow. It'll course correct. We'll all tip into global warming and get fried up until, someday, thousands of years from now, dinosaur babies will be digging up our bones and telling stories about what assholes *we* were."

"Wait." Ronnie snorted, walking up to the fire with a fresh round of snacks. "Dinosaurs are coming back?"

"And they can talk?" Hannah laughed.

"It depends. Is Beckett taking away our straws?" Cherry tilted her head to look up at him, her hand skimming his now-smiling face.

Sloan was jealous, even then, but Cherry never belonged to Beckett the way she would belong to her. And somehow, Sloan sensed that, right from the start.

But still.

Beckett's was funeral four.

The only one Sloan didn't cry at.

"EARTH TO SLOAN." Cherry's voice snapped her out of her memory and left her wincing against the sunlight reflecting off the windows of Cherry's pickup. They were at Cherry's new apartment, ready to unpack.

"Sorry," Sloan said, noting the slight frown tugging at the corners of Cherry's mouth, and no, no, Sloan couldn't stand for that. She had already ruined last night with another stupid nightmare. She wasn't going to ruin another day, especially not a happy day like this, when the girls would finally have enough time to finish setting up Cherry's new room.

"Where'd you go?" Cherry teased, tracing a little circle on Sloan's thigh with her finger. "Thinking about all the pretty girls that came before me?"

Sloan smiled; she couldn't help it. Cherry was like that, could diffuse tension with a single sentence. Could pull smiles out of Sloan like she had a magnet.

"No, just you," Sloan answered.

Cherry raised an eyebrow. "Oh yeah? And what exactly was I doing?" She said the last part low and flirty, and it tugged at Sloan's belly in a very welcome way.

"Meeting me," Sloan said, blush creeping to her face. "Painting boats, arguing about dinosaurs around the campfire. The usual."

This time, Cherry's frown was unmistakable. Shit.

"Hmm." Cherry hopped into the bed of her truck and grabbed some of the boxes. She pushed them to the end, hard, before hopping back down. She grabbed one and shoved it into Sloan's arms with a terse "Give me a hand?"

Before Sloan could reply, Cherry walked off with a box of her own, leading the way into the building.

Cherry didn't like talking about camp, and Sloan supposed that made sense. What was the use of reliving the eleven days they had spent together with the others—when there were others, that is? What was the use of remembering how good it *could* have been if they had gotten to spend an entire lazy summer together instead of just under two hundred and sixty-four hours (and that was only if she counted the time in the ambulance)?

Sloan shoved the memories away and followed Cherry inside.

Today would be good. Today had to be good, even if it killed them.

FIVE

SLOAN PUSHED A tack into the wall and stepped back to admire her work. It was the last of Cherry's posters, this one advertising an all-girl grunge group called the Hissing Kitties, which Cherry had become obsessed with these last few weeks. Sloan didn't even know how her girlfriend had gotten the poster, to be honest, since from what Sloan could tell, they were just a small local bar band out in South Dakota. The wonders of the modern internet, she supposed. Which reminded her . . .

"Did you google today?" Sloan asked.

"Nah," Cherry said as she surveyed some papers sprawled out on the bed in front of her. "There hasn't been a good headline in days." She shifted the clippings around, her eyes narrowed in concentration, before she selected one and held it up. "This one?"

Sloan studied the headline written in giant block letters— EIGHT DEAD, TWO INJURED IN ATTACK AT LOCAL SUMMER CAMP—then nodded with a small smile. "That one's definitely going back up."

Seemingly satisfied with the answer, Cherry stepped over the cardboard box separating the two girls—it was the last one to un-pack, the words *funeral clothes* scribbled across the top in messy Sharpie. Cherry seemed to be avoiding it. To be fair, Sloan had donated all of her funeral clothes the moment she stepped out of the eighth service in as many days.

Cherry took a moment to give her a kiss on the nose before she reached toward the desk and snatched up the tape beside the pile of tacks. Sloan watched her carefully put up the paper beside the others. It fit perfectly, as she knew it would, a missing puzzle piece finally found. Cherry was good at this.

While Sloan had been busy hanging garage band posters and framed selfies of them from the last few months, Cherry had been busy building a fresh mosaic to replace the one that she'd had to tear down when she moved a few days ago. Just layer upon layer of newsprint and computer paper, headline after headline and article after article of what they had been through—no, what they had *survived*—together.

It started in the upper right-hand corner of Cherry's bedroom wall and spiderwebbed out, like it would swallow the rest of the room whole if given half the chance. Like it would swallow *them* if they let it.

It was smaller than it had been at the old place. Many of the clip-pings hadn't survived the move and would have to be reprinted, but Cherry had worked hard to protect her favorites, laminating them with packing tape that caught the sunlight in weird ways, making them look shiny and preserved—frozen even, the way Sloan and Cherry were frozen every night in Sloan's dreams, tangled up in her memories.

Like bugs pinned to a mat for inspection.

Cherry dropped back onto her bed and studied the rest of the clippings lying around her. "These are all boring." She frowned.

Sloan crawled up behind her. Cherry was taller by several inches, which Sloan loved, but it was all legs. When they were sitting like this—Sloan's hands tucked through Cherry's arms, her legs wrapped around Cherry's torso—it felt like they were the same.

"We could try Reddit again," Sloan said.

"No one's desperate enough for that yet." Cherry huffed out a quiet laugh. "Besides, don't you still have it blocked?"

"True." Sloan untangled herself and leaned over to see what was left. With a smirk, she held up a newspaper clipping. "What's wrong with this one?"

Cherry gave her an exaggerated pout. "They call me Charlene."

"You are Charlene."

"Only very technically," she said. "It makes me want to take a machete to my own eyeballs every time I see it in print. Maybe Dahlia had the right idea all along."

"I doubt very much that taking a blade to the face was Dahlia's idea at all," Sloan said with a snort, thinking a little too hard about the girl who had stayed only three cabins down from her. She had been the first to die, according to the investigators.

It was a bad joke, a cruel joke. Dahlia was kind and gentle and didn't deserve the ending she got. Hers was funeral seven, and for that one Sloan had cried a lot.

But whenever it got too hard, too overwhelmingly sad, Sloan just drifted back to the *60 Minutes* interview.

Both of Dahlia's parents came from old money, which meant she came from old money too. Her parents had both wept through their interview, her mother wailing that Dahlia wasn't supposed to be there. That she didn't *need* to be there. They said it so many times.

She didn't need to be there. She had plans for her life.

As if the tragedy of death increases with the economic privilege of the victim. *What a waste,* their faces seemed to be saying. She could have been home playing polo or whatever else it was that rich kids did during the summer, instead of reliving *Friday the 13th* in real time with a bunch of poors.

Dahlia should have been the one to live, not those other girls. Sloan had seen it in their eyes. Had paused the TV and rewound twice to make sure she wasn't wrong.

She wasn't. They were sad about their daughter, sure, but more than that, they were bitter. Jealous. Positive that their daughter had deserved to live most of—

"Well, still," Cherry said and tossed the printout into the trash. "There are worse things than a blade to the head. Like being named after your great-aunt who nobody in your family even talks to."

"Yeah, true devastation," Sloan deadpanned with a little smile.

She liked that they could laugh about it. She thought it was healthy.

Her previous therapist had been very anti–dark humor. She said it wasn't appropriate to snark about other counselors getting stabbed or make jokes about Jason Voorhees all the time. She said it was an "unhealthy" coping mechanism. That it was deflection.

That was when Sloan stopped talking to shrinks. Well, most of them.

She frequently met with Beth at her mother's insistence. It was one of the only times the girls were separated, and Sloan hated it.

But Beth wasn't *really* a shrink. She just wanted to hypnotize Sloan and talk about energies, not save her, not tell her how to feel. Beth wanted to get the door in Sloan's mind open and let her walk through it, and Sloan . . . well, as much as she pretended otherwise, she'd be lying if she said she wasn't at least a little curious to see what was on the other side. So much of that night was a blur, a haze of fear and blood and hiding, and sometimes she wanted the details back.

Cherry grabbed her laptop off the desk and did a quick search for "Money Springs Massacre." Nothing new. The news cycle had died down over the last few months, especially since the people responsible had been captured. Well, one of them anyway: The Fox, who haunted her dreams every night. The rest of them—The Stag, The Bear, and a few others she hadn't gotten a good look at—had seen fit to off themselves right as the raid had started. Cyanide pills, the whole lot of them.

But it was okay.

Sloan picked up her phone and joined in on the fun. What had started as a compulsion—at one point she had checked for headlines every hour—had eventually dulled into a quieter sort of tradition. They even had their search terms down, neatly divided to efficiently share the work.

Cherry would search "Money Springs Massacre." Sloan would search "Money Springs Sleepaway." Cherry would search "upstate machete murder." Sloan would search "sleepaway killers." If she was in a particularly good mood, Sloan might also search "Charlene Addison Barnes," printing out the photos of Cherry walking out of the hospital with her full name listed in the captions. Those were her favorite.

The newspapers hadn't identified the girls at first; victims are given protection from the media sometimes if they're pretty enough and white enough. But Cherry's mom had done a press conference. Well, sort of. More like staged a paparazzi event for when Cherry was being discharged. Cherry's mother had wanted her day. She said it was to show Cherry's strength, but Sloan suspected it had something to do with her newest performance-art installation—whatever that was—and plugging her OnlyFans, although most of the news stations had bleeped that out.

Sloan remembered her own mother staring out the second-floor window as the crowd gathered around the little run-down hospital, if you could call it that—it was more of an urgent care one town over from where the attack had taken place that allowed overnights. The nearest real hospital was over three hours away, and neither girl was injured enough to warrant a transfer.

Cherry had only been kept overnight, but Sloan had stayed longer on account of her injuries—a moderate concussion and a deep gash in her arm that required sixteen stitches and an IV antibiotic. Sloan wished she could remember how she got them.

She remembered going to open the door, and she *thought* she remembered Cherry taking her hand, but then she didn't remember anything at all until she woke up beneath the canoe with her arm bleeding and a splitting headache blurring her vision. Cherry's hands had been over Sloan's mouth to keep her from screaming. There had been blood, so much blood, but most of it wasn't theirs. And then there had been lights flashing, red and blue.

Cherry had smiled and kissed her.

If Sloan could just remember what happened in the space between—

"Nothing new on my end. You?" Cherry's words slipped through Sloan's brain, jarring her back to the present.

"Just this incredible picture." Sloan smiled and turned her phone toward Cherry. She had done an image search, which had led her down an internet hole, and found some random person had photoshopped Cherry's hospital exit to make it look like she was running from Jason Voorhees instead of running from the paparazzi.

"Cute." Cherry smirked. "Print it."

Sloan hit a few buttons on her phone and waited to hear the soft whirring sound of the printer coming to life before she hopped up and grabbed the scissors. The whole setup—Cherry's laptop, the printer—it all came from a "violence victim fund," which was supposed to go toward paying off any medical bills that Cherry had, but she and her mother, Magda, had siphoned some off the top.

They told their victims' advocate that Cherry needed them both for virtual college, that Cherry was so anxious she couldn't go to class on campus and had to go online. The organization was even covering the internet bill.

Except Cherry wasn't taking online classes. She wasn't even registered for college *before* everything went down, and she wasn't about to start now. But they had wanted a MacBook. *The universe owes us a MacBook* were Magda's exact words, and maybe it did. A laptop seemed like a fair enough consolation prize for narrowly escaping maniacs with machetes and axes.

Magda always boasted, "You don't survive in this world as an artist without a little grift now and then."

If this grift happened to come in the form of a laptop and a printer that Cherry could use to print articles and Magda could use to post the YouTube clips and OnlyFans videos that paid the rent, well, what was the real harm in that?

Besides, it wasn't like it was their first grift.

Cherry and her mother had been on their own for a long time, and they were no strangers to relying on the kindness of others to get what they needed. If that meant the occasional fake GoFundMe—the one for their imaginary dog's dental surgery had even gone viral—or skimming off the top of the latest PTA fund-raiser at the high school, then so be it.

"You're just resilient," Sloan had told Cherry that third night at camp as they lay down by the fire. Cherry had whispered stories of her childhood to her, shame keeping her voice low and sad. Until Sloan had smiled softly and said, "You're not scammers; you're resilient."

The light that broke across Cherry's face then was brighter than any fire could be, and Sloan had promised she would do whatever she could to keep it there. She was keeping that promise, wasn't she? Even now, sitting beside Cherry, trimming headlines, in the quietest part of the after.

"Oh, holy shit," Cherry yelped, and Sloan nearly cut off Jason's head when her hand slipped in surprise. That would have been a travesty.

"What?"

"They just released The Fox's picture. Look!" Cherry spun the computer toward Sloan, and a red breaking-news banner was now splashed across the CNN website. Minutes ago, it had just been the latest presidential scandal, but apparently a bunch of people in masks attacking teenagers took priority. Sloan swallowed hard and stepped forward.

For all her bravado, she wasn't sure if she was ready to see the man behind the crude animal mask. The mask let her keep things separate, like a hypothetical, like a bad horror movie she had watched once and hoped to never see again. It was just Charlene Addison Barnes running from Jason in the movie of their lives.

The man behind the mask wasn't a real human doing horrible things to sweet boys and funny girls and an adorable line cook, who Sloan now realized had tried very hard to look and act like Lafayette Reynolds from *True Blood*. (A show that Sloan was only aware of because her mother had an embarrassing crush on Alexander Skarsgård and had insisted they watch it together during forced family bonding last month.)

Sloan crept closer as Cherry clicked through, and before she could even ask her to wait, there he was.

The Fox.

Or at least, the man beneath The Fox. The lone surviving member of the group.

His cyanide capsule had been a dud, and now here was his face, staring blankly out from the screen in one of his many mug shots.

Edward Cunningham, the caption read.

"Girls?" Magda said, startling them both so much that they almost dropped the computer. Cherry recovered quickly and clicked it shut before turning toward her mother with a smile.

Googling for headlines, making mosaics, these were strictly *no mothers allowed*. No anyone allowed. Just them.

"Can you give me a hand? Some of those boxes you brought up to my room earlier are gonna have to go in the closet downstairs. This shithole's got smaller rooms than our last place."

"Sure, Mom," Cherry said and instantly hopped up. For all her bravery and bluster, she was fully wrapped around her mother's finger.

Stepping into Magda's room felt like stepping into another world, one full of lush blankets and brightly colored scarves and veils. Cherry's mom was, to put it politely, eccentric. She called herself a mixed-media performance artist, although she spent most of her time lying around complaining bitterly about her muse, rather than really working. She was popular among a subset of patrons who liked to watch her punch paint onto a giant canvas by way of a paint-covered speed bag. In a bikini. She called it "the violence of beauty." Cherry called it embarrassing, but Sloan was mesmerized. Obsessed. She had never seen anything like it.

And if Magda occasionally lost the bikini for her OnlyFans subscribers, who could say.

"Those over there," Magda said before she dropped onto her bed dramatically and pulled a heavy silken scarf over her eyes. "I need to rest."

Cherry looked at her mother worriedly and then scooped up the first box. Sloan quickly followed suit. "She's not sleeping well," Cherry said as they carried the boxes down the stairs.

"Isn't that normal for her?"

"It's getting worse. Since everything."

"I don't think any of us have been sleeping well since then, to be fair," Sloan said, trying to lighten the mood. She hated when Cherry worried. Wanted to kiss away the divot between Cherry's eyebrows and make her feel safe, the way Cherry did for her.

"I guess." Cherry shrugged. "Did I tell you she wants to include an homage to it in her next performance? I swear to god, if she even tries to get me to join her . . . Like, not everything is about her and her art, you know?"

Ah yes, Sloan had accurately predicted something for once. She had hoped Magda wouldn't try to capitalize on the tragedy they had lived through, were still living through. But . . . this was Magda.

"At least she's not pretending it didn't happen?" Sloan said, desperate to find a bright side. "My mom refuses to acknowledge it at all, unless it's to ground me or send me to therapy. Otherwise, we can't even talk about it."

Cherry kicked open the closet door and dropped her box inside before reaching for the one in Sloan's arms. "Grass is always greener." She snorted. "But I bet you'd feel different if it was your mom chanting poems about the worst night of your life in nothing but body paint."

"Touché." Sloan laughed. "I'll tell you what—I'll go grab that last box upstairs. Why don't you make us some tea, and we'll go for a ride? I think you just need a break."

Cherry smiled. "Deal. Just toss it on top of these. I'll get the travel mugs ready."

If being in Magda's room with Cherry was weird, being in it without her felt downright invasive. Magda lay as still as the dead with the long silk scarf wrapped three times around her head, her lips pursed lightly. Sloan had intended to pick up the box and go, truly she had. It wasn't her fault that her foot snagged on one of the many delicate nightgowns Magda had draped over everything, which made the lid on the box slip ajar.

Magda sighed and rolled over on the bed. Guilt careened down Sloan's spine for disturbing her, and she quickly rushed out of the room and into the hall. That would have been that, honestly . . . it should have been. It was just that there was a *rabbit* in the box.

Not a real one, although that might have been less weird, to be honest, but a crude carving made of wood. Pine maybe?

Sloan set the box on the hall table and pushed the lid all the way off, coming face-to-face with its little rabbit head. A shudder ran lightly through her as she took in its details. Its dead, wooden eyes stared up at her, and Sloan squeezed her own eyes shut.

Relax, she thought. *You're safe. You're fine. The men aren't here. This isn't theirs. This isn't The Fox's. They can't lay claim to every piece of wood transformed, even if it does look a little like—*

No, she wasn't willing to go there.

But she did want to see what else was in this box.

Sloan carefully lifted the rabbit sculpture out and found it was sitting on a pile of photographs—old Polaroids, some of their edges turning yellow, causing a fading effect that Insta only wishes it could replicate.

Most of them were of Magda looking barely older than Sloan and Cherry were now. She was pregnant in some of the photos, holding a baby Sloan assumed was Cherry in the others. Sloan reached into the box and pulled out two pictures that were stuck together. The top one was of a robust toddler running across a yard with the very same carved rabbit sculpture in her hand. Was that baby Cherry? Suddenly the rabbit didn't seem so scary.

Sloan pulled the pictures apart and winced as some of the paper backing tore, leaving little scraps of white on the one beneath. The photo was of two men, their arms slung around each other, smiling. There was something familiar about them—even if the torn paper covered half of each of their faces—something that tugged at her.

That sensation when you know that you know, but you can't quite place them. No context, just vibes.

"What are you doing?" Cherry asked, coming up the steps with two mugs.

Sloan dropped the photos back into the box and reached for the rabbit. "Uh, nothing."

"Stop going through her things!" Cherry rushed toward Sloan, practically throwing the mugs on the table as she yanked the rabbit out of Sloan's hands and shoved it back in the box, hard.

"The lid fell off," Sloan said when she finally found her voice again.

"And you took that as an invitation to go through her shit?" Cherry asked and slammed the lid back on the box. "What the fuck?"

"I wasn't going through her stuff," Sloan said, her stomach in her throat. Cherry's defensiveness caught her off guard. It was hard and cold, and Sloan had never been on the receiving end of it. This kind of attitude was typically reserved only for Allison.

Cherry stared at her for a beat and then scooped up the box herself and walked away. "Whatever."

Sloan rushed to follow her—she couldn't leave it like this—their nice tea forgotten on the table, their good day out the window. "Okay, I'm sorry. Genuinely. You're right. I was going through her stuff, I guess, but the lid fell off when I tripped, and there was a rabbit staring at me. I was just . . . surprised."

Cherry gave her an unimpressed look and then trudged down the steps.

"What's the big deal?" Sloan asked, hating every second of this.

"The big deal is that it's not yours to look through."

"I—"

"You could have—you could have broken it!" Cherry cut her off. She set the box on top of the others in the closet and then gently slid them all back against the wall. "That wasn't for you to touch. It wasn't *for* you."

"Whoa, whoa." Sloan held up her hands. Cherry had never pushed her away like this before. She didn't like it. It made her feel sweaty-sick from the tips of her hair down to her toes. "I wasn't trying to hurt anything. I was just looking. I'm sorry."

Cherry shut the closet door, sighing, as if she had locked up something precious. She set her forehead against the cold wood, her back stiff and hard as she took one deep breath, and then another.

"Cherry?" Sloan stepped forward and rested her hand on her shoulder. "Cherry, what's wrong?"

"I shouldn't have snapped at you," Cherry said, still not moving after thirteen long seconds—each one counted painfully inside Sloan's head.

She was shaking then, not just a little tremble or a shiver. Sloan could feel it easily through the fabric of Cherry's flannel shirt, and pinched her eyebrows in confusion. Cherry was the strong one. Cherry was *always* the strong one. What in the world was going on? And how could she make it stop?

"It's okay," Sloan lied, as if her very soul hadn't flinched from Cherry's raised voice. As if the idea of Cherry having things that she didn't want Sloan to see, things that were *not for her*, didn't make her ache down to her core. Didn't make her want to slip off into a puddle of red, sticky things.

Cherry lifted her head and shrugged off Sloan with an almost convincing smile as she turned. "It was just weird to see that stuff. Sorry." She leaned down and gave her girlfriend a kiss on the cheek. "I shouldn't have yelled," she added, and let her lips drift lower to Sloan's neck.

Sloan couldn't help but feel like Cherry was trying to distract her. That she was going to brush her off. At first, she let her, ecstatic that their fight was over as Cherry's hands pulled her close and danced along her hips.

But Sloan felt a tiny niggling in her chest that something was very, very off about all of this.

Cherry's lips be damned, just this once.

"What was it?" Sloan asked. "The box, I mean?"

"Nothing. Just old stuff. Brought back memories."

Sloan narrowed her eyes. "What happened to *no secrets, no lies?*" she asked. That had become their mantra. They'd sworn that if one found out something, she would share it with the other. No secrets, no lies. They were, as far as the world was concerned, as far as any future trial was concerned, one single entity. "Two halves of a whole," Cherry had said, and Sloan had liked that very much.

Cherry sighed and looked at Sloan like she had just been punched in the stomach. "Fine. No secrets, no lies. It was my dad's, alright? Now do you get why I didn't want you going through it?"

Her dad's.

Right, that made sense. Cherry's father was the one subject that the girls never spoke of. Because while Sloan's biological father was essentially a question mark, and her adoptive father not much better these days, Cherry's father had been a looming presence before he passed.

A larger-than-life character who loved big and fierce. Who loved Cherry most of all.

Who had been dead since his daughter was fourteen, which Cherry had shared between aching breaths, forcing herself not to cry because tears were a sign of weakness. And Daddy didn't allow for weakness. Daddy had raised Cherry to be strong, to be brave, to even out her mother's bad ideas and keep the ship steered straight.

It was probably Cherry's father the girls had to thank for their surviving that night.

After all, if she hadn't been taught to stay calm, conditioned to be brave and clearheaded—logical and critical, unemotional and rigid—Cherry probably would have fallen apart just like Sloan had.

"He used to . . ." Cherry trailed off, taking another deep breath and then lifting her chin, almost as if she could shake off her human emotions entirely. "He used to make these little carvings for Mom and me. He said it relaxed him."

Sloan studied Cherry's face, wanting to believe that was all it was. Still, the idea wriggled in her brain, like an unwanted parasite, that there was more to the story. No lies, but maybe secrets? But Cherry's closed-off face meant that this was going to be the end of it. At least for now.

"Let's get that tea and head out," Sloan said and smiled wide enough for the both of them, even though she didn't feel it.

She would choose to believe this. To quiet the rude theories in her head about the girl standing in front of her. She would choose to believe that the men in the photograph only looked familiar because they bore some resemblance to Cherry. That Sloan's eyes simply reacted to their shared DNA with her soulmate.

That the rabbit carving looked nothing like the fox mask she had seen that night.

"Let's," Cherry agreed and reached for Sloan.

A warm, easy feeling spread through Sloan the moment they touched, shoving the thought that something was very wrong down deep in her bones, where they could never find it.

SIX

SLOAN SHIFTED IN her chair and eyed Beth warily, even though her decision to come today had been her own. She had wanted to come, actually, after a long night obsessing over what she had seen in the box from Magda's room.

It wasn't that she didn't believe Cherry. It was just that . . . she didn't trust her all the way now. No, that was wrong. She trusted Cherry; she just didn't trust herself. Because with every minute that passed, the urge to know, to see, to understand everything that was in that box was growing. Sloan was scared it would overwhelm her.

It was hard to explain.

If Beth had been a real therapist, and not some kind of hippie quack, maybe she would have been able to help Sloan sort through this. Instead, they both just stared at each other, utterly confused. Sloan didn't want to do any energy work around it. She wanted to sort her feelings properly for once.

"Maybe we could try opening the door," Beth suggested after a long stretch of silence.

Sloan's fingers curled around the fake leather of the chair. The door never opened, would never open. She was becoming more and more sure of it in every dream and failed attempt with Beth.

But also . . . she didn't have a better idea.

"How will that put away my feelings about Cherry snapping at me because of the box?" Sloan glanced out the window to where Cherry sat in her truck. Cherry was looking at her phone, no doubt scrolling through TikTok or checking her Insta. Sloan wondered if Cherry was checking for headlines. Had there been any new developments since the release of his name and photo? What was she reading? What was she thinking about? Sloan's thoughts swirled angrily around her head.

Beth hesitated. "Maybe it's not the box that's bothering you. It's the fact that it's being kept from you. It's bringing up your feelings about the blank space between opening the door and becoming aware again underneath the canoe. Perhaps you feel like there are other things Cherry is keeping from you, things from that night."

Sloan bit her lip. It was true that still bothered her. But was this all really just some kind of mental metaphor for what she was really worried about—that missing piece of time that had been neatly sliced right out of her memory? The one Cherry had, but Sloan did not?

Except that wasn't true, was it? Cherry hadn't kept things from her about what happened that night, at least not for long.

When everyone first realized that Sloan had pretty much No Idea—capital *N*, capital *I*—what had happened, there had been panic. Well, at least on her parents' side. The doctors had reassured her it would all come back, and Sloan had been just fine waiting. She had been too scared to ask Cherry back then, hadn't wanted to know, hadn't wanted to relive it, hadn't wanted to fill in those fuzzy spaces between reaching for her cabin door and waking up with blood in her hair. She knew it was bad, whatever it was, and if her mind didn't think she could handle it, then who was she to argue?

As time passed and it became clear those memories weren't just taking a break, that they had been locked up, imprisoned, buried as deep in the soil of her brain as her friends had been buried in the cemetery . . . her curiosity had nearly killed her.

"Maybe it's a good thing," Mom had said once, casually over supper, like her brain locking up memories was just something small and insignificant that happened sometimes, like forgetting a password or locking your keys in the car. "You know what they say," she added when Sloan didn't reply. "Curiosity killed the cat."

But satisfaction brought him back, Sloan thought.

So she had asked Cherry. She had asked even though she really didn't want to know and knew Cherry really didn't want to tell her. But still, they had to. No secrets, no lies.

Cherry had been very matter-of-fact, as if it was a book report that bored her and not the story of the worst night of their lives. Sloan appreciated that. It made it easier.

"First we went to Kevin's office because he had a landline that actually worked," Cherry had said. "He was awake still, blasting Nirvana, so he hadn't heard the screams. It was the acoustic version of 'Come As You Are.' We screamed at him to call 911, but the men broke in before he figured out that we weren't joking. It was The Fox and The Stag.

"Kevin tried to shove you at them and get away, but I pulled you back. The Fox grabbed him instead and held him while The Stag . . . you know. I dragged you out the window while they did that. We ran to the woods. The Stag followed, but he was slow. I'm not sure what The Fox was doing, but based on Kevin's screams, it was nothing good.

"We came across a giant old pine with branches low enough to grab, and I made you climb up the tree first. We got covered in sap, but The Stag walked right under us without noticing. You had stopped responding altogether by then, and I got really scared. I held you in the dark until it was safe to get down. I promised I would keep you safe.

"Once I was sure they had given up and gone back to the camp, I helped you climb down, but you slipped—that's when you hit your head and cut your arm. You were woozy but could still sort of run. I took you back to Kevin's office—I thought we could get to the landline now—but you were too dazed to keep going. I hid you under the broken canoe and told you not to move, then I crawled in through the window and managed to call 911.

"I didn't want to leave you alone for too long, so I just said, 'Help,' and whispered the address. I hung up and bolted back under the canoe with you. That's when I realized I fucked up. You were lying on the ground, and some of Kevin's blood had pooled around you. They had thrown his body into the grass beside the canoes, and you two were face-to-face. I'm so sorry about that. I'm sorry forever about that. I shoulda left you in the tree or someplace else—someplace far away from all the blood. But what was done was done. I pulled your face toward me and kissed you, but you just kept crying those silent tears with those blank eyes, and I wanted to die for leaving you even for a second.

"Then the phone started ringing—the police calling back, I think. I started to crawl out to get it, but you grabbed my hand. The men in the masks came running by a second later and smashed the phone, but they didn't look under the boat. You didn't say a word, but you saved my life just the same.

"We hid there, silent. I had to keep turning your head toward me because you kept trying to look at Kevin, and I knew that wasn't good. I tried to rub the blood out of your hair, but I just got more sap into it. Pretty soon the police showed up, and it was over. You and I lived. Everybody else died. The end."

Cherry presented it just like that, all unemotional and straight-forward. She saved Sloan. Then Sloan saved her. And now they were completely even.

But sometimes, in the worst moments, when everything was too quiet, Sloan wondered if maybe that wasn't all. If she was missing something. Because when she remembered the cut, when she remembered the sixteen stitches that held her together, it wasn't because of a fall.

It was because of a knife.

Satisfaction brought him back, her brain echoed again, twisting itself up with the memories of before and after, and the things Cherry had said.

"Maybe you're right," Sloan said finally, glancing up to see Beth already sliding her chair closer. "Maybe trying the cabin again is a good idea."

IT WAS NOT a good idea.

At least that's what Beth would say after Sloan screamed herself out of whatever spell she had been under.

Because this time it was different.

It took Sloan a minute to realize, as she put down her toothbrush and stepped out of the cabin bathroom, that she had been transported, like magic.

There were no lights flickering on and off from the other cabins. No jammed windows. There hadn't even been a scream.

She had expected to feel harsh wood prickling her feet when she stepped out of her bathroom, but instead she felt carpet. The cheap kind. The kind you find in even cheaper apartments.

Apartments like Cherry's.

Sloan wriggled her toes, reveling in the unexpected softness for exactly as long as it took for that thought to make its way from the soles of her feet to her head.

I'm at Cherry's, she thought. Well, that's new.

She turned around slowly in a circle and took it all in. She could hear someone, Cherry's mother maybe, in another room. The woman's voice sounded far away and underwater. Sloan couldn't make out what was being said.

Sloan blinked and she was on top of the carpeted steps, the very same ones that led straight to the closet.

How would this work? she wondered. It wasn't like she could unlock a memory she'd never had in the first place. Still, curiosity dragged her down to the closet that held the box with the small wooden bunny that was the source of all this angst. If she could just see it again, hold it, maybe it could reverse whatever the hell was going on.

Maybe she would see it was different.

Sloan found herself in front of the closet door faster than she expected. No sooner had she stepped down a single stair than she was on the ground floor, precisely where she had wanted to go. She smiled. She could get used to this dream logic . . . hypnotism logic? Whatever. Either way, she was in.

The voice in the other room got louder. It was closer now that she was downstairs.

Sloan thought it was coming from the living room. That made sense. Cherry's mother often sat in a rocking chair there on nights she couldn't sleep. Cherry had complained about it just the other day, that the creaking of the old chair—a salvage from Goodwill—along with her mother talking on the phone all night had kept her up.

But now there was another sound. A scraping. As if Magda was carving something made of wood. As if she was carving a mask to—

Stop it, Sloan told herself. Focus.

The closet door loomed large in front of Sloan, had somehow grown larger while she had been standing there. Twisted paint drops collected along the edges of the panels. The old metal handle dared her to try it. Sloan ran her fingers along the bumps as she trailed them down to grip the doorknob. It was thick and cold in her hand as she turned it. Waiting. Hoping.

It was locked. Of course it was locked, just like the door of the cabin, just like everything. She couldn't remember a memory that hadn't happened. Sloan felt stupid for even trying.

Still, she tugged on it a few more times, and even shoved herself against it. Maybe she couldn't make a new memory, but maybe it could lead to something new. Maybe a fresh look at the pictures when they spilled out. Surely that existed somewhere inside of her. That had happened, after all, no matter how quickly.

Or maybe the door would open to somewhere else, like the cabin porch. There were no rules here, none at all.

She kicked the door, hard and loud, and it echoed across the apartment as if it was a cave. The voice in the other room—Magda's voice—stopped. There was a shuffling sound, followed by more silence.

"Someone's here," Magda said.

And then another voice, a new one. A man's voice, more of a grunt really as he came around the corner of the living room, dragging a heavy blade behind him. The Fox.

Magda trailed after him. Even though she was wearing a rabbit mask, Sloan recognized her, recognized the nightgown, silky and floral, the same one that Sloan had tripped over just the day before.

No. That wasn't right. That. Wasn't. Right.

Sloan turned to run up the stairs, but they were gone.

Everything was gone.

She was in the cabin again, but the killers weren't on the outside. They were in her room. With her. The scrape of the blade against the pine floor, the swish of the silk nightgown behind it.

No, that was wrong. Cherry's mother wasn't a part of anything. Cherry's mother shouldn't have been there. Sloan might not remember everything, but she was sure she would have remembered that.

Cherry had told her. Cherry had told her what happened! Cherry had filled in the gaps!

But as The Fox and The Rabbit reached her, held out their clawed hands, swung their blades, she wasn't so sure anymore. She wasn't sure.

She woke up screaming, with one single thought.

What if Cherry was hiding something?

SEVEN

IT WASN'T THAT Sloan wanted to remain fixated on the box even while holding Cherry's hand. Even while they were curled around each other, their legs as tangled as their hair. Even while their lips were pressed together and promises of "I'll love you forever" were whispered breathlessly into the night air.

What it meant, what it was, what it had to do with her nightmare of a session with Beth—Sloan had wanted to forget it. All of it.

It meant nothing, she decided. It had just been a mishmash collection of missing things—missing memories, missing information—all of it just swirled up together like those chocolate-and-vanilla twists Sloan used to inhale every summer, before her stomach hurt all the time from nerves.

As much as she told herself to forget it, she couldn't. The memory of it haunted her.

It reminded her of a movie she had watched at a sleepover once—a cat-and-mouse-type thing that they were definitely too young to have been watching. Sloan had missed almost all of it, as she had been distracted, painting Mia Scallion's nails blue. She had just wanted to hold Mia's hand, and that was the perfect excuse. It wasn't until the man came on the screen—Brad Pitt, she thought, but she couldn't be sure; she tended to mix him up with the other old white actors her mother crushed on—and started yelling "What's in the box?" that she paid attention. Every single one of the girls stopped talking. Their little twelve-year-old heads swiveled toward the TV, watching him melt down this way and that. It was, spoiler alert, a head in the box.

The somber, respectful interest had quickly dissolved, leading to a chorus of faux anguished shouts of "What's in the box?" well into the night. Sloan remembered a particularly funny instance when Mia's mother carried in some Cheez-Its and Ritz Crackers and every girl shouted "What's in the box?" at her. Confused, she had backed out slowly, probably wondering what this gang of feral girls was talking about. It was printed right on the packages.

Lying in bed beside a sleeping Cherry, Sloan's mind snagged on the memory of that box again and again.

What's in the box? it teased, over and over. It would have been better if there *had* been a head in it, instead of a rabbit, Sloan decided. She could have made peace with that. Another head, another murder—it was just more of the same. Unsurprising. Add it to the list.

But a secret, a mystery? Something solid and unshared between them? The idea that there was a piece of Cherry that Sloan wasn't a part of? It wriggled inside of her, chewing holes in her head. It coursed through her bloodstream, poisoning her with doubt.

What's in the box?

Sloan looked over at Cherry, who still slept soundly beside her.

It was three in the afternoon, "the perfect time for sleep," Magda always said. In fact, Magda had gone to bed first that afternoon.

Then, Sloan got a horrible idea. The worst idea. Or maybe the best idea. She slowly pulled her legs back and out, freezing each time Cherry sighed and snuffled. Inch by inch, Sloan extracted herself from underneath the weight of Cherry's delicious sleep-warmed skin, until she found herself standing on the stiff brown carpet on the floor of Cherry's room.

She tiptoed as quietly as possible to the closed bedroom door and flipped the lock to open it. She glanced back at Cherry and held her breath for a reaction. Seeing none, she grasped the doorknob firmly, and then was hit with a sudden wave of fear.

What if it didn't open?

What if Sloan was still asleep? She couldn't be sure. What if this was like before, when Beth had sent her nightmares spiraling into each other's paths, creating one supernightmare prepared to take her out? What if she was still at Beth's?

She looked over at Cherry, asleep in bed, her lips parted ever so slightly, and noticed a hint of a smile. A smile! It wasn't often she saw that. It wasn't something her traitor brain would have even thought to make up.

This was real. She was sure now.

She was at the house. At the apartment, rather. With the box. And only she was awake. Now, that was something to smile about.

Sloan turned the handle. It twisted fully, disengaging from the doorframe with a gentle click. The soft whoosh of the door ruffling against the carpet felt like a secret between her and the universe.

Sloan might not be sure what other secrets were held in all those quiet pockets of things not remembered, but this box, this place, was real. The answers were within her reach. Her fingers practically itched in anticipation. If she could just see the box, if she could just put her concerns to rest, then maybe her singular focus, her absolute obsession, would end.

She would see it was nothing. She would be done.

Sloan walked down each step carefully, already mindful of the ones that creaked more than others, even in the short time that Cherry had been living there.

That was something she was used to noticing by now: floors creaking, steps with a slant, tiny things that could give her position away. Now it was automatic, her body and brain cataloging everything, memorizing everything, doing their best to keep her safe and hidden and alive.

Survival was an instinct, her first therapist had told her. She didn't need to make any apologies for how it happened or what it looked like that night.

Of course, Sloan couldn't remember what it looked like, even if she wanted to. (And she desperately wanted to these days.) But still, the guilt ate away at her, clawing and gnawing at her insides. Why me? she wondered. Why not the others, why not the sweet—

No, she thought, skipping a particularly creaky step entirely. She was not going there, not now. Sloan was on a different sort of mission today, with a different sort of door to open. The tangible kind, in the real world, holding real-world answers behind it. Why did those men in the picture look familiar? Why did the rabbit carving look exactly like the masks the killers wore?

Satisfaction brought him back, her brain chanted, louder and louder, until she found herself in front of the door.

It was a regular door, unassuming. The kind of cheap closet door found in every apartment from here to California. But the secrets this one kept? Those were special, maddening, delicious even.

"Sloan?" Cherry's voice tore through the quiet of the house, crisp and questioning, without a hint of sleep in it.

Sloan jumped. "Oh, hey," she said, spinning around quickly to face the stairs behind her. She hoped she didn't look too guilty, but she was pretty sure she did. "I couldn't sleep."

Cherry's face remained still, the gentle smile long gone. Instead, her expression was blank, passive . . . waiting. "I didn't hear you have a nightmare," she said finally as she stepped off the bottom stair.

"I didn't," Sloan said. "I just couldn't fall asleep. I didn't want to bother you."

"So you came down here? For what?"

Sloan searched for an answer and, finding none that would be believable, simply said again, "I didn't want to bother you."

Cherry smiled, but it looked strained, fake, a mask over something beautiful, as she gently tucked a stray strand of Sloan's hair behind her ear. "You're never bothering me," she said. "You couldn't."

Sloan smiled too, resisting the urge to glance back at the closet that was right behind her but might as well have been a million miles away.

"Should we get you a glass of water while we're down here?" Cherry asked.

Sloan nodded.

Cherry took Sloan's hand in hers and gently tugged her toward the kitchen. She moved around the room with ease, finding a tall glass behind a bunch of chipped coffee mugs, and then pouring crystal-clear water from a Brita. Sloan hopped up on the kitchen counter and observed the action from her little perch of laminate and stick-on tiles.

She didn't know how to feel or what to think.

Cherry finished up and set the glass beside her, saying nothing. Sloan said nothing either. Instead, she watched the condensation bead up on the glass and slide down in tiny drips. It reminded her of the heat of summer, of snow cones by the fire. She reached back into her memories and thought she could almost feel that night, an echo of its heat.

"Were you trying to sneak into the closet?" Cherry finally asked.

"What?" Sloan asked, trying to sound believable. She was going for offended but landed somewhere closer to caught, and both girls knew it.

"It's just . . . you were gone, and when I found you, you were . . ."

"I was just wandering around. I couldn't sleep."

"Usually when you can't sleep, you wake me up." Cherry walked her fingers up Sloan's thigh, freezing when Sloan shifted. "Historically, we've found much better ways to pass the time than pacing a half-unpacked apartment."

Sloan parted her legs, just a little, just enough to make Cherry's eyebrow pop up. Yes, they had much better ways to pass the time indeed. Better distractions too.

Sloan leaned forward and pressed a gentle kiss to Cherry's lips. Cherry responded eagerly, hungrily, as if she was the one doing the taking.

This was Cherry. Sloan's sweet Cherry. What had she been thinking?

Cherry dug her fingers into Sloan's hips and pulled her forward roughly, never breaking the kiss.

"I love you," Cherry panted when she finally rested her forehead on Sloan's shoulder.

"I love you too," Sloan said, her whispered words feeling loud and painful in the face of her deceit. Cherry might have a secret, but now Sloan had a lie, and that thought twisted her stomach, made bile crawl up her throat. She hugged Cherry tighter and wondered what was wrong with her.

If Cherry had something she wasn't ready to share, it had to be for a good reason. It was either too painful or too bright or too much. Cherry's dad's death had hit her hard. Sloan was aware of that, knew that was where Cherry's unwillingness to show her the box was born from. Nothing else. Nothing sinister.

What was Sloan doing? She was trying to force, trying to push, trying to take from someone who already had proven she was willing to give everything. Cherry had already saved Sloan's life, had already kept her safe. Shouldn't that be enough?

Sloan tightened her grip on the other girl. "I love you," she said again, louder this time.

"But do you trust me?" Cherry asked, leaning back to show her red-rimmed eyes. And no, Sloan thought, Cherry wasn't supposed to cry. She was the strong one, had always been, and now Sloan's sneaking around had hurt her girlfriend in ways she hadn't even considered.

"Yes, of course," Sloan said, peppering Cherry's face with fresh kisses, her lips lingering on Cherry's eyelids, her cheeks, her nose. Sloan would let Cherry feel the love that was bursting out of her. Sloan would let their love swallow the guilt of her lies, let their love be enough.

"Okay," Cherry said quietly, as if she was only speaking to herself. "Okay."

Sloan slid off the counter and into Cherry's arms.

"Promise?" Cherry asked, a slight hitch in her voice. Where was this coming from?

Sloan stepped back. "I promise," she said, the almost-betrayal like iron in her belly. She would melt it down; she would get rid of it. She should never have doubted this girl in front of her. This person sent to save her.

Cherry looked at her then, right in the eyes. "Then stay out of that closet, Sloan. That's not for you. Trust me when I say that. I can't open that door for you right now. I can't talk about my father, not when I'm still trying to hold us both together from this summer, okay? I can't take on any more grief than I have already. I need that to stay in its box until I can. I know you think I'm brave and hard, and . . ." She paused, her eyes tearing up. "I want to be that for you. I *am* that for you. But if you pile dead-dad stuff on top of everything else, it'll break me."

"I'm sorry," Sloan said as she reached up to wipe at Cherry's eyes. "I get it. I'm sorry. I'm sorry." She would apologize a hundred times if she had to, even if her apologies were also an admission.

Suddenly, a thought hit Sloan: What if she was the monster?

Not the men at the camp, not whatever was in the box, not whatever Cherry was keeping from her. No, it was Sloan, and her pushing, and her pushing, and her pushing.

She leaned back and tilted her head to see Cherry's face better. It was sad and somber, her eyes a little glassy and too tired for Sloan's comfort, but beyond all that she looked . . . nervous? Worried? And that wasn't right. That wasn't fair.

"I love you," Sloan said again, and she hoped Cherry knew what she really meant was *I'm sorry, and I trust you.*

Cherry's entire body slumped, as if she had been holding her breath, tense and ready for a fight.

Later, after the sun had set and Cherry was in a better mood, Sloan wondered if it would always be like that between them. If the line between love and war, fear and joy, right and wrong would always be so thin, so slippery—if they would always get glimpses of both sides whether they wanted to or not.

Sloan blinked and nuzzled closer to Cherry. It didn't matter, she decided. She could be content, with their hands in the softest places, their tiny gasps pressed like prayers into skin. It could be enough.

It would be enough.

EIGHT

"I JUST THINK you should get out more, see your old friends again!"

The argument was pointless. They'd had it hundreds of times since Sloan had returned to her parents "less than she was before."

Those were Allison's words, not hers, and they weren't quite right. She wasn't *less than*; she was *more than*. Because now she wasn't just their daughter who had once loved tennis and romance movies and sneaking off behind the bleachers with her friends and some warm cans of spiked seltzer. Sloan was also a survivor and a certified adult . . . even if her parents still paid the bills, and the pictures on her walls were exactly the same as they were last year.

It amazed Sloan how much a person could change in the span of only a couple of weeks. She had left for camp excited and nervous, a recent high school graduate ready to take some safe, parent-sanctioned steps out of the nest: first a summer camp job, and then college—adulthood lite—where she would be on her own, sort of, but all her expenses would be tied up neatly in a tuition bill, and she'd have a meal plan to ensure that she never wanted for anything, except maybe her mom's home cooking.

The universe had apparently seen her on the cusp of adulthood and decided she didn't need a nudge; she needed a shove, a push off a cliff that had her diving face-first into a jagged ravine full of ravenous alligators.

At least that was how it felt.

And her mother just didn't get it.

"Sloan, pay attention to what I'm saying!" Allison said, her voice loud and annoyed. "I ran into Rachel and Connor at the coffee shop yesterday. Did you know they're both working there now?"

Sloan nodded in affirmation. She seemed to remember something like that from a past life, back when it mattered that her friends were excited about working together, back when friends mattered at all. But that was *before*; there was a clear delineation now.

It had been weeks since she'd responded to either of their texts. Rachel had stopped texting altogether. Her insistent messages that Sloan "move on" proved to be the last dying gasp of their friendship. But Connor, to his credit, still occasionally popped up in her chat log.

"Then how come you haven't stopped by to see them? They were asking about you. They miss you."

"Did they say that?" Sloan snorted. She seemed to recall them not visiting her either, not when she got home from the hospital, not when she was scared and having waking nightmares. No, they had opted for the bare minimum: occasional texts and prying for info.

"Not in so many words," her mother said as she pulled out a

chair and sat down in that way only parents can, a subtle hint of disappointment bleeding into their every move. "But you need to stop shutting them out or they'll stop trying."

"It's fine if they stop trying." Sloan sighed, not bothering to clarify that at least one of them already had. "I don't need them."

"Right, you don't need anyone except *Cherry*."

"Don't say her name like that," Sloan said with a frown. "And it's not that."

"Then what is it?" Her mother rubbed tiny circles around her temples, as if she was trying to will away a headache—or struggling to hold her tongue.

The action caused Sloan to pause, to notice not for the first time (but every time it still struck her as new, a fresh little knife twist inside her tenderest parts) how this was affecting her mother. Allison Thomas had only recently been a vibrant, cheerful forty-six-year-old. Her eldest, Sloan, had just graduated high school and was on her way to a prestigious university to study social work. Her much younger son was shaping up to be a baseball whiz. The future had been bright . . . until it wasn't.

Sloan stared at the dark circles under her mother's eyes, the gaunt look that came with not sleeping or eating well, and only then did Sloan wonder how this was affecting the rest of the family, because it was clearly hurting her mother.

"What is it?" her mother asked again. "It's like you're not even here anymore, Sloan. You spend all day stuck inside your own head until Cherry comes around, and then you get stuck inside hers. It isn't healthy. It isn't! I can't sit here and watch you—"

"Do you want coffee?" Sloan asked suddenly.

Her mother's mouth first hung open and then snapped shut, a look of confusion pinched across her face. "Do I what?"

"I do want to hang out with them, Mom," Sloan said, but she could tell her mother was having trouble keeping up. "Well, no, that's an exaggeration. I mean, I don't *not* want to hang out with them. It's just . . ."

Unfortunately, this statement didn't do anything to help quell her mother's confusion either.

"Sloan—"

But Sloan held up her hand before her mother could continue. "I'm not the same person, and I know that you're trying to understand that. Connor and Rachel aren't. Connor actually texted me a couple weeks ago asking me if I wanted to go see *Scream* with him because it was playing at the drive-in."

Even her mother had to wince at that one.

"Yeah." Sloan sighed. "He said he wanted to understand what I'd been through, and he thought seeing that movie would help us both. I just . . . nobody knows what to do with me but Cherry, and I don't know what to do with anybody but Cherry. But if you want me to get you coffee and smile politely at people and pretend, I will. Because there's no sense in us both being miserable."

"I don't want you to pretend; I want you to try."

Sloan didn't register that her mother was crying until Allison's arms wrapped around her and she felt the warm, wet sting of her mother's tears against her neck.

"Please just try," her mother said, before pulling back to study Sloan's face. "I may not have given you the gift of life, but life gave me the gift of you." The familiar refrain that used to bring comfort to Sloan now landed softly inside her chest, prying at the heart she was trying to keep locked up. "And I'm sorry that someone saw that gift and tried to break it. But I'm going to be right here, helping you put it all back together for as long as you need. So no, I don't want you to pretend. Please don't pretend, but please try. Sloan, please try."

As she stared into Allison's eyes—no, *her mother's* eyes—as she took in the exhaustion, the desperation, the pleading, Sloan realized that she wanted to be okay, not for any real reason beyond not wanting everyone around her to cry and be sad, but still, that counted.

Maybe she could do this, a fresh start. A healthy start, and it would all begin with a cup of coffee at Professor Java's Coffee Emporium. She should call Cherry. No. She should do this alone, then *surprise* Cherry. She would get her a coffee too.

This felt big.

So okay, maybe she couldn't take a slasher movie. Maybe she couldn't take any extended period of time with her two best friends—former best friends—but she could (hopefully) go and order coffee like a normal person. Like a *before* person. Like someone who hadn't lived through trauma and tragedy and had it splashed all over the national newspapers, someone who hadn't had random strangers speculate about them on the internet—like why did Sloan and Cherry deserve to live? And were they in on it, and did it hurt, and why didn't they cry, or why did they cry too much?

It was the speculation that hurt the most, the constant speculation, all happening in real time without a shutoff button or the ability to turn the page.

But maybe she could go to Professor Java's.

A fresh start in the form of an old favorite. She could say hi and bye and see you soon, and then race home with her emotional-support iced coffee and hide in her room until Cherry came over to pick up her caramel latte.

Maybe she could baby-step herself back out of the ravine. Ravenous alligators be damned.

"I'll try," Sloan said softly.

Allison's eyebrows raised. "I don't want to make you. Beth said not to—"

"You're not." Sloan forced out a smile. It probably came out as more of a wince. "I'll go get us coffee."

A fresh start. A fresh start in the form of an ice-cold coffee with a splash of oat milk.

NINE

THE COFFEE SHOP was warm and inviting—the hustle and bustle of college kids studying, hopeful authors huddled in corners, and customers coming and going a nice change of pace. It was loud and overwhelming, sure—Sloan had spent the better part of the last few months tucked away in her quiet bedroom or Cherry's, and this was . . . not that.

But this place was familiar, with its sticky floors and chairs that had been painted in brilliant yellows and oranges and greens, making everything seem so simple and happy. If Sloan was going to walk in anywhere, go anywhere, do anything truly on her own for the first time in months, this was probably the safest destination possible.

Her mother had dropped her off outside. She was parking in the lot across the street and had a quick errand to run—just a simple visit to the post office to drop off a package and pick up some stamps.

The trip to the post office had been Sloan's idea.

Sloan didn't want her debut back into the real world to happen while holding her mother's hand. Her first time holding a coffee she had ordered by herself. Her first time seeing her old friends.

Part of her hoped they weren't working, but part of her hoped they were, or at least that Connor was. And as the comforting smell of grinding coffee beans and baked goods swirled inside her head, she could almost imagine, for a second, that it was last spring again.

"Oh my god, Sloan, hi!" Connor said excitedly. He set down the rag that he had been using to wipe the glass of the display case—the one full of muffins that had looked mouthwatering only a moment before, but now might as well have been made of sand—and took a step toward Sloan with a smile.

Sloan stood up a little straighter, as if she was readying herself for a fight and not greeting one of her oldest and closest friends. She tried to force out a smile, but when that failed, let out a small shrug instead.

He looked exactly the same. The same golden brown skin and dark curly hair that had always felt like home to her. The same warm, welcoming eyes that saw her better than she could ever see herself. The familiarity was overwhelming, like she had traveled back in time and now had whiplash.

"Hey," Sloan said quietly, taking him in.

The grin on Connor's face broke somehow impossibly wider as he came to a stop in front of her. "Can I?" he asked and gestured for a hug.

Sloan nodded automatically but regretted it almost the instant his arms surrounded her. This was Connor, she reminded herself. Her first best friend ever. The boy whose hand she'd held when he told his father he was bi. Whose hand had held hers when Laura Maxon told the entire elementary school that Sloan had been adopted because her real mom didn't want her. Hugging Connor used to be as simple as breathing, a near-constant greeting between them.

But while he was the same, and his hugs were the same, Sloan wasn't. She reluctantly patted her former friend's back and then stepped away to give herself some much-needed space.

Disappointment flashed on Connor's face, but only for a second before he brightened considerably, the perfect best-friend smile pasted back in place. "I missed you!"

"I missed you too," Sloan lied, searching for the easy rhythm they had once shared.

"But you never text back." He immediately scrunched up his nose like he smelled something bad. "I shouldn't have said that. It's just, you said you missed me but—oh man, Rachel *just* left. She's gonna be so pissed she wasn't here for this," he said, switching gears to a safer conversation, one that felt a little less like blaming to Sloan.

"Yeah, I bet," Sloan said, hoping he couldn't tell how relieved she was to find only him.

"Do you want to sit?" Connor asked, his hand already on the back of a bright orange chair. "It's slow right now. I could take a fifteen."

Sloan looked skeptically at all the people filtering in and out of the coffee shop. "It is?"

"Okay, it's not, but I can still take a break for my best friend coming back from the dead." Connor covered his mouth with his hand. "I didn't . . ." He trailed off, sighing before he pulled out the chair and dropped into it. He ran his hand through his hair and then buried his face in his palms. "Fuck."

Sloan stood awkwardly for a moment before slowly sitting down across from him. This, *this* was why she hadn't wanted to come, why she hadn't returned his texts.

Connor peeked at her through his fingers. "I don't know what I'm doing."

"I don't know what I'm doing either," Sloan admitted as she fiddled with an abandoned straw wrapper. The table was sticky and damp in the way only tables that have been painted over and over again can feel sticky and damp. She pressed her hands against it, letting the coolness of it ground her. She regretted coming. No, she regretted sending her mother to do errands. No, scratch that. She didn't regret ditching her mother; she regretted ditching Cherry, who was probably sitting in her bedroom, wondering where Sloan was.

It was supposed to be a happy surprise, Sloan getting them coffee for once. But it was turning into a hurricane of awkwardness and anxiety.

"This is weird, huh?" Connor asked.

"I guess," Sloan said. Because what else could she say?

"It doesn't have to be," Connor said. He grabbed Sloan's hand and squeezed.

She was sure it was meant to feel reassuring, but instead she felt trapped, panicked. It was too loud, too bright. There were too many people, and now someone—*not Cherry*—was holding her hand. Connor's hands were rough and calloused, too big by a mile. Sloan shut her eyes and tried to breathe.

"I'm still me," Connor said reassuringly. "I'm here for you."

Sloan didn't know how to tell him that was the problem.

Sloan had changed, entirely and irrevocably, from the events of this past summer. And Connor was still the same person he had been after crossing that stage in a graduation cap last June. It was unfair how the world kept spinning, kept moving, even when she wanted it to stop.

Connor shouldn't be the same.

Professor Java's shouldn't be the same.

The entire world shouldn't be the same, not now that people were dead. Not now that Sloan knew how many washes it took to remove the scent of Kevin's blood from her hair. She pulled her hands back and tucked them into her lap.

"Thank you." She pushed the words out, let them scrape up her throat like they belonged there. Like she felt them or something.

"I mean it," Connor said. "I want to be there for you. Text me anytime, day or night. I want to know it all. All the gory details. You can tell me."

Sloan tilted her head. "The details?" she asked. "Like what? How I watched people die in front of me? Or like the speed and consistency of blood as it flows from a head that's been nearly split in two? Or what it felt like to listen to my new friends beg before their deaths? Those kinds of details?"

Connor shifted in his seat. "No, not . . . Sloan, not literally. I want to be there for you, for the good and the bad, the way we used to be there for each other before. If you need to vent or complain— that's all I meant."

"This isn't the same thing as fucking up at a dance competition or getting cut from varsity." Sloan swallowed hard. "And *the good*? What good is there to this? Please tell me, because I'm dying to know."

Connor stared at her.

"No pun intended."

Connor sat up a little straighter. "That's just what people say, Sloan. I have no fucking clue. All I know is you survived something awful, and you stopped replying to my texts. I haven't seen or heard from you in months until you suddenly walk in here out of the blue. I don't know what to do with that. So, yeah, I keep saying all the wrong things. But being pissed at you for ghosting me after what you went through doesn't seem like the right thing either." He rubbed his face. "I'm just trying to say whatever bullshit pleasantry that will keep you coming back. Because I meant it when I said I missed you, and I hope someday you're enough yourself to miss me too."

"Connor—"

He held up his hand to stop her. "Let's just get you an iced coffee, okay? I might not know what to say, but I promise you, I've gotten really good at being a barista. And I still remember your order. So let me do that. We'll figure out everything else later."

Sloan smiled, relieved. She couldn't help herself. "An iced coffee sounds good."

"Great," Connor said as he stood up and pushed in his chair. "I'll be right back."

Sloan watched as her best friend, her former best friend, whatever the hell he had become, walked back behind the counter. He held up two different cups—one large, one supersize—and although Sloan wasn't sure that she could finish either, she pointed to the larger of the two. Maybe the ice would ground her. Maybe the sensation of holding the cup like she had one million times before would pull her back into herself in a way that sitting in her bedroom or in Beth's office or in the bleachers at Simon's baseball field never could.

Her phone buzzed with a text from Cherry: Where are you?

Shit, Sloan really had left, hadn't she? Just walked out her own front door like that was something she did now. Like she was in the before, or could be. It was supposed to be a surprise, but instead it felt selfish. Cherry was probably at her window. Cherry was probably worried sick. She should have told her where she was going.

I'm—Sloan started to reply, but she didn't know what else to say. *I'm getting us coffee?* That seemed anticlimactic considering all the inner turmoil that had gone along with it. *I'm visiting a friend?* That seemed like a lie. *I'm working on a fresh start, but don't worry, it still includes you?*

"Hi, sweetie," Sloan's mom said and pulled a chair out beside her. She tucked her post office receipt into her purse and then looked over Sloan's shoulder at the chalkboard menu. "Did you order?"

"Hey, yeah," Sloan said and slid her phone back into her pocket. Her mom had explicitly said no Cherry on this adventure. It was a family afternoon, only this time, instead of being strangled with board games or bombarded with baseball . . . it was coffee. "Yeah, I did. I didn't know what you wanted, though."

"Oh," her mother said, eyebrows furrowed. "Just the usual. We can order it when the waitress comes."

Sloan racked her brain trying to figure out what *the usual* was. She had known this once, but it had somehow slipped out of reach, buried, she supposed, with all the other missing memories. She wondered why.

Allison glanced around and suddenly looked very concerned. "Don't worry," she said as she stood back up in a rush. "I'll go order it. Stay here."

Something had just happened; Sloan was sure of it. Even as her body and brain cataloged everything in the background—fight-or-flight to the extreme, even in this corner seat in the quietest part of the café—she had missed something. Something that had made her mother jump up and run to the front, urgently gesturing to Connor, who incidentally had just set the most glorious iced coffee that Sloan had ever seen onto the counter.

There, that would be her excuse. She wasn't ignoring a direction to stay put. She wasn't spying. She wasn't panicking for no reason (even though she definitely was). Sloan was simply getting her coffee.

Her feet carried her over on autopilot. One hand wrapped around the coffee, and the other pulled the paper off the top of her straw—plastic, of course; Cherry would love that. Sloan took a sip and turned toward her mother with a puzzled smile.

Keep it low-key, she thought. *Act normal and all that.*

Connor frantically reached for something, and Sloan had to tell herself over and over that it wasn't a knife. But it was hard not to let the terror wash over her as her mother's face fell and Connor struggled to free something from a drawer.

"I don't need a coffee," her mom said, her smile looking forced and nervous. "Let's go home."

"But it was your idea," Sloan said. She truly didn't care if her mother got coffee or not, but she wanted to know what was going on. If she gave in to her mother, let her grab Sloan's arm and pull her through the coffee shop like she was trying to do, Sloan worried she would never figure it out.

"I don't need any. It's too late in the day," her mother said. "It's already after one! I'll be up all night if I have caffeine now. What was I thinking?" But Sloan couldn't resist looking back to see what Connor was doing. He had finally gotten the drawer open and was pulling out something long and black.

Sloan planted her feet, fight-or-flight giving way to the stubborn need to see. If it was a gun or a knife—and why would it be, honestly? But if it was—she wanted to see it. Face it head-on this time, instead of hiding.

Except it wasn't either of those things.

It was . . . a remote?

Her mother switched from holding the door open for Sloan to actively trying to drag her through it, but Sloan yanked herself back, as confused as everyone else who was watching them wrestle by the entrance.

Connor pointed the remote at the TV in the corner. It had been muted, a news channel with bad captions that didn't keep up. Sloan had roundly ignored it until now, had missed it when she first walked in. It was a new addition, proof that Sloan wasn't the only thing that had changed. She kinda liked it. What was everyone's problem?

"What are you doing?" Sloan asked, but she wasn't sure if she was talking to Connor, whose eyes had gone wide with panic, or if she was talking to her mother, who still yanked at her arm.

The screen pulsed off and then on again as Connor hit every button on the remote. After more panicked button-pushing, the mute setting turned off too, and sound flooded the now-silent room.

"In a statement earlier today, Police Chief Dunbar promised to release new information regarding this summer's attack on an up-state summer camp dubbed 'the Money Springs Massacre.' Sources close to the investigation say a resolution could be at hand. We bring you live to the press conference."

The screen switched from the standard cityscape-behind-a-studio-desk shot to a close-up of a podium covered with microphones. Sloan's fingers tightened around her cup. She hadn't seen Chief Dunbar since that night. He had come to her hospital room to apologize, as if it was somehow his responsibility since it was his town. Except his apologies had quickly turned to questions—until her parents asked him politely, yet forcefully, to get out of her room.

It was his deputy who came by two days later to take Sloan's statement. The deputy said it was because the chief was running the manhunt and couldn't get away, but Sloan always thought it was because her mother had threatened to call a lawyer and file a complaint about his badgering a victim with head trauma.

But there he was, up on the screen. Exactly as Sloan remembered him.

"Good afternoon," Chief Dunbar began, adjusting the dozens of microphones on the podium in front of him. "First, I would like to thank the Money Springs Police Department and the State Bureau of Investigations for their assistance in handling this case and helping us get to the bottom of this sordid story. As we discussed at the last presser, we do have one perpetrator in custody. Today, we were able to reach a plea agreement the satisfies all parties involved, and we're looking forward to transferring him into a maximum-security facility in the near future.

"We thank ADA Sheridan for her hard work and for fast-tracking this case to get the victims the closure they so desperately deserve. I'll let her get into the details of the agreement a little more in a moment. We handle the investigative side and leave the rest up to the courts. Speaking on that," he continued, red-faced as he messed with the collar of his uniform, "while there are still leads to be followed, we feel confident that this attack was the work of a group that called themselves Morte Hominus. They were a fringe group—I would personally call it a terrorist cult, but I was advised not to say that—based out of Vermont." He shook his head. "We believe that we have everyone we need either in custody or in the morgue at this point. A raid on their caravan compound resulted in the discovery of the deceased bodies of over two dozen suspected Morte Hominus members. At this time, it appears that they took their own lives in a . . ."

Sloan didn't know when the coffee had fallen to the floor, only that it had. Only that she was using both hands to try to rip her phone out of her pocket.

She needed Cherry. She needed Cherry, and she had ignored Cherry's text. She had put her phone in her pocket. She had—

Cherry's truck screeched up to the front of the café, the tires up on the sidewalk, causing bystanders to jump out of the way and curse at her.

Sloan shoved her mother's arm off her as Connor rushed toward them.

"I didn't mean to unmute it," he said. "I was trying to turn it off, but I hit the power button twice, and . . ."

Everyone was staring now. Everyone.

Cherry pushed open her truck door and waited for Sloan to crawl safely inside.

TEN

CHERRY DROVE FOR hours.

And while Cherry drove, Sloan alternated between crying and dozing, curled up in a little ball across the long seat. She wasn't buckled, and yes, that was bad, but it allowed her to rest her head on Cherry's right thigh, and that was good.

She could feel the muscles in Cherry's leg flex and tense beneath her cheek as the truck accelerated and braked. Sloan let herself get lost in the rhythm of it, and in the sensation of Cherry's fingers as they slowly combed through her hair.

Cherry hadn't said anything for a long while, and Sloan was worried Cherry was mad, but she was too scared to ask. She was too scared of everything again. She couldn't focus on the fact that an honest-to-god fucking cult had tried to murder her—a cult with so many more members than they had even realized—when she was preoccupied with whether or not she had pissed off her girlfriend.

Which was probably another reason Sloan wasn't asking, if she was being honest.

For now, she could stay inside this little bubble they had made, with cheeks on thighs and fingers in hair, but she knew the second she moved, whether to sit up or ask a question, the bubble would pop. And then Sloan would be back in the real world, with plea agreements and pain and iced coffee spattering on rainbow-colored tiles like blood from a body.

And Sloan didn't want that. Not at all.

In the end, it was Cherry who popped the bubble, in a slippery kind of way.

"Morte Hominus," she said softly. "Death of man? Death of mankind? Whatever they were trying to get at, I'm not sure they were obvious enough." Cherry huffed out a little laugh.

Sloan exhaled a breath that could maybe have been a laugh if you squinted. From a hundred miles away. And had never heard a laugh before.

But still, it was something. That particular kind of relief that only Cherry could draw out of her.

"How did you know where I was?" Sloan croaked out. Her throat was thick from all the tears she had tried not to cry.

"Find My Friends app." Cherry shrugged and pulled into a Walmart parking lot. She circled the lot slowly before taking a spot beneath the biggest, brightest light. The sun had set at some point while they drove. Sloan had never even noticed until now, lulled by the feel of the wheels on the pavement, soft songs and softer fingers. "When the DA called my mom to warn her about the press conference, I rushed over to your house, but you weren't there. I didn't—I wasn't stalking you or anything."

"No, I'm glad. I'm glad you found me. I needed you. I need you." Sloan pushed herself up to look into Cherry's eyes. "Wait, they called you? Why didn't they call us?"

Cherry arched an eyebrow.

"Oh," Sloan said as the realization hit her. That's why her mom had tried to drag her out of the shop, why her mom had tried to keep her from seeing the news. "I'm glad you came."

"Good," Cherry said, and slumped a bit to rest her head against Sloan's.

Sloan wondered for the first time if maybe Cherry had been just as worried as she had been about having an upset girlfriend.

It was a ridiculous thought, like Cherry hadn't just saved the day again and again and again. Sloan couldn't be upset with her if she tried. Not really.

"I just went to get coffee with my mom," Sloan said. "I was going to surprise you with one too. I wanted . . . I don't know. I just wanted to do something *normal*."

"That'll teach you," Cherry said, but Sloan could hear the smile in her voice, the teasing lilt that Sloan had come to love.

"That poor iced coffee," Sloan snorted. If Cherry was willing to dance around the real situation, then so was she. But just as all good things must come to an end—

"Which phrases are you googling, and which ones am I?" Cherry asked, sitting up rigid in her seat. "We should get this over with."

Sloan took a deep breath. Part of her had known this was coming, had known they could only outrun it for so long. The curiosity worming its way into the backs of their brains.

She was sure most of the world would be googling tonight as well, and maybe there was a power in that. The more people pulling stuff up, the more things would be found and brought to light. There was Reddit and Web Sleuths and a million others just like them.

Sloan had mostly stopped checking those sites when they started heavily implying that perhaps she or Cherry had been in on it, and then she blocked them entirely so she wouldn't be tempted to look, tempted to watch people dissect her life in real time.

Beth had said it was a healthy decision, and Sloan had almost unblocked them just to be contrary, but maybe it was. The problem was, now she needed them. She scrolled through her phone settings.

"Sloan?" Cherry said, her jaw clenched like a soldier readying herself for battle.

"I don't know," Sloan said and stared up at the bright parking lot light shining in her face.

She had no doubt that Cherry had brought them to this particular parking lot on purpose. It was the brightest place at night in their whole area, even if they did have to drive twenty minutes to get to it. It had dozens and dozens of LED lamps flooding the asphalt below with light, and cameras everywhere recording and keeping them safe. And it was open twenty-four hours in case someone needed a Diet Coke or a witness.

The girls had come here a lot in the beginning. Back before Cherry had lived nearby, back when the nights were too long and the drive too far and they just needed to be somewhere that was nowhere at the same time. Was there anywhere that was more of a nowhere than a Walmart parking lot in the middle of the night? Sloan didn't think so.

"I don't want to be scared of them anymore," Cherry said, her eyes fixed on the store looming in front of them. "Knowing helps. No secrets, no lies, right?"

Sloan's mind, for just a second, snapped back to the box in Cherry's closet. Some secrets, she thought, and maybe a lie. They had come up with that phrase in the beginning, back before the collage spiderwebbed across an entire wall. Back when things had seemed so much simpler. You lived, I lived, and now we love. Why couldn't it have stayed like that?

"Knowing helps," Cherry said again, mostly to herself.

And she was right—it did. They had unmasked the boogeyman, and all that was left was a hulking, doughy white man with a head full of bad ideas. Edward Cunningham. When Sloan had seen his real name, she had almost laughed at the simplicity of it. She had never laughed at The Fox, though.

"Knowing helps," Sloan whispered and stared down at her phone. "I unblocked everything."

Cherry nodded once, and then together they lifted their phones and googled.

ELEVEN

SLOAN WOKE UP early the next morning, twisted in Cherry's bedsheets with a sleepy smile. They had sat in the Walmart parking lot for hours last night—googling whatever they could, falling down every rabbit hole—but it still wasn't enough, would never be enough, could never be enough. Not until they found everything. And disappointingly, everything seemed to elude them.

"I made coffee," Cherry said from beside the printer. A pile of papers had been spit out from it, and Sloan wondered how long Cherry had been up, or if she had even slept. "It's on the bedside table."

Sloan pushed herself up and grabbed the mug beside her. Magda said it was still too early in the season to turn on the heat, but the early autumn mornings were brisk. Sloan welcomed the warmth of the ceramic cup, even if she did usually prefer her coffee to be stale and full of ice.

"Working on the wall?" Sloan asked, arching an eyebrow at her girlfriend. She glanced up but didn't see any new additions.

Maybe Cherry hadn't been awake for quite as long as she had thought.

"Mmmm," Cherry hummed, not looking up as she frantically scrolled through websites on her laptop. "Getting ready to."

"Which means . . ." Sloan knew what was coming next. It was her favorite part.

"Which means." Cherry smiled. "It's time to compare notes."

Comparing notes: the step after they had googled things to death and before they collaged it all on the wall. The part where they actually took a step back and discussed everything they had learned. When they combined forces to tease out as much of the truth as they could.

Last night, they had both been too busy to talk much, their only communications their gasps, squeezed hands, and raised eyebrows as they sat side by side in that parking lot with their heads in their phones. When they were done, or as done as they could be, they had been too tired to compare notes.

Instead, Cherry had backed out of her spot and turned her truck toward home. Sloan had sat up for that ride, safely buckled, not because she was worried about self-preservation, but rather because she had needed something to tether her to the earth. Something to hold her down when her head was spinning out with thoughts of Foxes and Stags and alligators. Something to keep her present until she could tuck herself safely into Cherry's bed, their bodies coiling around each other. Until Cherry could make the world seem solid and real in a way that very little else could.

But there was no use delaying the inevitable any longer. Sloan had learned things; Cherry had learned things. Now it was time to spread them out in front of each other like shiny little treasures.

Sloan reached for her phone and pulled up her notes. Cherry scooped up the papers and tapped them against her desk, corralling them into one neat pile.

"Me first? Or you?" Cherry asked. She pulled long gleaming scissors out of her desk drawer and placed them beside the pile—a threat and a promise. Some of the articles would end up in the trash, sure, but others would be clipped and added to the collage, keeping the girls safe under a blanket of facts and information on the wall above their heads.

Knowing helps.

"You," Sloan said and cleared her throat.

Cherry nodded, spinning slightly in her chair to better face Sloan as she held up the first page. "Okay, so this one is from CNN, but it says AP, so I think it's the 'official' story," she said, making air quotes with her free hand. "Do you want me to read it or just summarize?"

"Summarize," Sloan said, because she was fairly certain she had come across the same AP report herself last night. She wouldn't admit it, though, because real news sites were Cherry's. Sloan was supposed to stay in the armpits of the internet—the Reddit boards and Facebook groups and Twitter hashtags.

"Okay, so Chief Dunbar held a press conference yesterday, a joint one with ADA Sheridan, which you saw some of, but basically the dude in custody—Edward Cunningham, the one in the fox mask—took responsibility. He said he was a part of what they're calling a 'collective,' aka a cult—I don't know why they aren't calling it that, especially after Dunbar did, but whatever. They called themselves Morte Hominus. Details about the organization are still emerging, but the belief is that everyone affiliated with it died in a mass suicide after the attack on Camp Money Springs. Everybody except old foxy, I guess. Poor buddy, shoulda checked his cyanide pill. Although I guess a cyanide quality assurance department wouldn't last long. But still. Oof." She giggled.

Sloan forced out a smile. She knew that Cherry was probably just trying to inject some levity into these batshit reveals, but Sloan wasn't in the mood for levity. She wanted to get through this. She wanted to pick the best articles and posts and pin them on the wall and then sleep for the next ten years.

Cherry seemed to catch on. She studied Sloan's face with a slight frown pulling at the corners of her lips, all the laughter gone. "Hey, are you good?"

"I'm great," Sloan snarked. "Murderous cults, coffee shop panic attacks, Walmart fact-finding—just another day in paradise, right?"

"Do you need a break? We could take a break."

Sloan thought she needed a total life reset, not just a break, but she couldn't say that. Not without people worrying. Not without Mom starting to talk about doctors and rehabilitation retreats, which Sloan was definitely not up for, even if the brochures did boast horses and skate parks.

Fuck that.

"Never," Sloan said, and forced herself to get into the spirit of things. "Especially not when I'm going to win."

Cherry grinned. "You always do."

It was true. She did. That was the other part of comparing notes. Whoever got the best material, the most interesting stuff to pin on the wall, won. The prize changed every time, winner's choice.

Sometimes it was a decadent mini cake from the bakery on the nice side of town. Sometimes it was making out and a back rub.

Sometimes it was the latest Isabel Sterling book. Everything was on the table—provided it was legal. (God knows neither of their parents needed to spend any more on lawyers than they already had.)

"What else did it say?" Sloan asked when she realized Cherry was still watching her.

"Oh, yeah, okay." Cherry looked down at her paper. "It really doesn't get into the beliefs much, except to say it was an offshoot of ecoterrorism, which I don't think means what this reporter thinks it means, because I'm pretty sure that ecoterrorism is like when you murder a bulldozer for taking out the rain forest or something."

Sloan didn't bother to point out that you didn't murder the bulldozer; you murdered the person driving it.

She knew Cherry was compartmentalizing. They both were. It was easier to say that "camp counselors were murdered" than it was to remember that the camp counselors had names and birthdays—like Shane, who was only a week away from turning nineteen, or Dahlia, who had definitely spent two hours the day before her death braiding Sloan's hair.

"Man, this is going to make the wildest *Dateline*," Cherry said with a smirk. "I hope we get Keith Morrison."

"Same," Sloan agreed, only half listening as she searched for the right page on her phone. "Do we want to put yours on the wall?"

"I don't know. You really think it's wall-worthy?"

Sloan considered this. "Well, it's the Associated Press, so I guess we should have it as a base? It's kind of official."

"Ooooh." Cherry smiled as she trimmed the paper as close as she could to the words. "An early lead, that hasn't happened to me in a while."

"It's only because I haven't gone yet," Sloan teased. "Don't let your head get too big."

Cherry grabbed the tape and marched across the room. She climbed up on the bed to stick up the article and then slid down until the girls were face-to-face.

"I wouldn't dare," Cherry said, and she leaned forward to kiss Sloan. "Now, what did you find?"

"Oh, I don't know," Sloan said. "Just somebody on Reddit claiming to be The Fox's sister, saying he tried to get her in the cult once. She had some inside information from her time there. But you probably don't want to know about that, right? You want to stick to the AP?"

Cherry sat back on her knees and smacked Sloan's leg. "Shut up! I can't believe you sat on that all night without saying a word."

Sloan shrugged. They both knew they had been too wrung out to compare notes last night. The idea of speaking at all, let alone about this, had seemed an insurmountable feat.

"Do you think it's real?" Cherry craned her head to see Sloan's phone.

"I have no idea; it's Reddit. But it didn't seem . . . unreal."

"Hmm," Cherry hummed.

Both girls had made a hobby of calling out fakes on the internet when things first went down. There were a lot of people who claimed to be Cherry or Sloan. Or their siblings, parents, cousins, best friends, etc.—anyone who could have firsthand knowledge. But they never did. Sloan thought one maybe could have been Rachel, not that Sloan would ever admit it. (She wasn't sure she'd ever want to face the idea that Rachel would sell her out for five seconds of internet fame, but cutting her off seemed like an effective enough way to deal with it either way.)

"I know we can't prove it's real. But we can't prove it's not either. It does shed some light on the whole ecoterrorist angle that your beloved AP seems to be taking."

"Okay." Cherry shrugged. "Whatcha got, then?"

Sloan slid her thumb across the screen to wake it back up. "Okay, so Sissy23 posted this last night, not long after the press conference. It was in defense of The Fox—"

"Edward Cunningham," Cherry corrected. She had been big on calling him by his real name since yesterday.

"Fine." Sloan rolled her eyes. "It was in defense of *Edward Cunningham*, so it's a little . . . aggressive."

"I can vibe with that," Cherry said. "These people make me feel aggressive too."

Sloan smirked. "Alright, this lady starts off by saying that her brother had a difficult childhood."

Cherry scoffed. "So did I, but you don't see me slaughtering people."

"Then there's the obligatory 'he's not a bad guy, just got caught up with the wrong crowd' stuff."

Cherry dropped down onto the bed and rolled over. Her head dangled off the side next to Sloan. "Uh-huh. Sure. Because totally normal, reasonable people join cults and dress up like little bunnies and foxes."

"Bunnies?" Sloan asked, all her muscles gone tense. There had been other animals that night besides The Fox—The Stag, of course, and then The Bear, and what she thought was supposed to be a lion . . . but there hadn't been a rabbit.

Sloan was positive.

The police had even asked Cherry to help identify which masks had done which killings. They'd brought Sloan along too in case her memories came back. There hadn't been a rabbit among them. No, the only rabbit Sloan had seen was in the box in Cherry's closet.

"I don't know," Cherry said with a laugh. "Horses? Chipmunks? Whatever. Animals! In general." She rolled over and nudged Sloan. "Why? Do you think rabbits are saner than foxes? Did I besmirch the good bunny name?" she teased, a smile dancing across her face.

Cherry's smile—Sloan's favorite smile—triggered something inside of Sloan. It made her muscles unclench and her mind stop spinning, if only for a moment.

This was Cherry. Her Cherry. She hadn't meant to say *bunnies* at all.

Let it go, Sloan thought.

"I think you could make a case against both of them," Sloan said. "In terms of animal sanity, I wouldn't exactly trust either one of them to hold my drink."

"I don't think I would trust any animal to hold my drink." Cherry laughed. "Maybe a dog?"

Sloan shook her head. "Too close to foxes."

"Fair enough." Cherry winked and glanced at Sloan's phone. "So, what *does* the fox say?"

"His sister, technically," Sloan snorted and prayed that horrible song from her childhood didn't come rushing back into her head. She could already hear the chorus now.

Cherry shrugged, not eager to have her joke dismantled for the sake of accuracy.

"Anywayyy," Sloan continued, "Sissy23 said that her brother

was basically this huge hippie, and that he got involved with the group when it first started. It was like this peaceful commune—no spooky name, no cyanide pills or murder plots. It was some kind of 'sustainable living community,' I think she called it. They were all living in vans, traveling to concerts and festivals and stuff. She said it was like a 'frog-boiling-water situation.'"

"Not that the idea of a little frog in his kitchen prepping pasta isn't cute . . . but don't you mean boiling a frog in water?"

Sloan tapped her chin. "It's a direct quote, but yeah. That's what she was getting at. Nobody realized what was going on until it was too late. It started off all innocent vegan hippie crafter hashtag van life or whatever and—"

"Ended up turning into a summer camp slasher?" Cherry laughed. "That doesn't even make sense."

Sloan tucked some hair behind her ear and sat up, crossing her legs next to a still-lying-down Cherry. "I guess? It gets all confusing. She said they wanted to stop global warming, and then they met a guy who, like—I don't know—convinced them the earth needed a hard reset."

"The earth does need to reset," Cherry said. "But what does that have to do with murdering people?"

"Your guess is as good as mine. She only knows what she does because he took her to a couple group meetings when she went out to see him. But she said it didn't use to ever be anything like that. They were just a bunch of like-minded weirdos trying to figure out how to save the world. The last time she visited, it got dark, I guess. Her brother cut her off after that. She said she doesn't know where things all went wrong, but she's going to get to the bottom of it."

Cherry huffed. "How? She going to waltz in and just ask her brother, 'Oh, hey, gee, why'd you kill all those people?'"

"I mean, that's what I'd ask him if I got the chance," Sloan said. "It's better knowing, right?"

Cherry dropped her head back and ignored the question. "So is Sissy23 wall-worthy or not?" she asked. "Because if I have to get up to get the scissors, I need to know before I start making out with you in earnest."

"Wall-worthy," Sloan said. She tried not to be disturbed by the fact that Cherry hadn't asked any more questions. It was like she didn't care. Or—a deeper, quieter part of Sloan thought—like maybe she already knew.

Sloan herself was champing at the bit to get to the bottom of things. She was dying to see if maybe there was a way to get ahold of Sissy23. She had hoped the post would turn into a thread, that would turn into a book, that would turn into everything Sloan needed to make this all make sense (and maybe also to move on). But as far as she could tell, Sissy23 never replied again.

She couldn't worry about that now. Not when Cherry slid the phone from her hand and replaced it with her fingers. Not when Cherry laid Sloan back onto the bed and waited for Sloan to nod her consent before leaning forward and tracing kisses along her neck with her lips and tongue.

"Delicious," Cherry murmured, flexing her hand around Sloan's. "You sure you want me to get those scissors?"

"No," Sloan whispered. "It can wait."

Cherry captured her mouth in a long, lazy kiss, both girls rolling to their sides with a smile.

"Positive? Because I can go." Cherry started to get up, smirking like she knew it all along, when Sloan grabbed her arm and pulled her back down.

"It is wall-worthy," Sloan said, smoothing some of the hair on the side of Cherry's face. "But it can wait."

The whole world could wait.

TWELVE

BETH'S OFFICE WAS cold, as it usually was during early appointments. The landlord was cheap, Beth had explained, and turned the heat off in the evenings. This time of year, it made for uncomfortable mornings. Later in the year, it got brutal. Beth tried to comfort her by saying she brought in blankets and a space heater, but none of that sounded particularly good to Sloan.

It had been three days since the press conference, since the Reddit thread, since Sissy23 had come onto her radar, and Sloan was no closer to finding more answers or finding Sissy23 herself than she was before. The post was wall-worthy, and they had hung it later that afternoon, but now that page, resting on the edge of the collage, glistening with fresh, shiny tape, no longer held the same allure. It wasn't enough.

Instead of feeling the proud buzz that came from "winning," from having her entry be the chosen one, the most interesting, the best . . . it taunted her from where it hung. It had gotten so bad that Sloan actually *chose* to stay home last night—alone even. Her mother had taken that for a sign of growth—that for once they wouldn't have to argue over curfews and whether Sloan did or did not have permission to sleep over Cherry's that night—but really it was just a sign that Sloan needed to figure her shit out, and fast. She had become obsessed with the idea that someone out there—Sissy23 to be precise—knew more than she did. It bothered her that Cherry had distracted her from it, days ago, when it was all still fresh.

It bothered her that Cherry had mentioned the bunny and then took it back. It bothered her enough to brave last night's nightmares alone.

When Sloan's mother woke her up this morning with the offer of an extra session with Beth, she had jumped at the chance. It wasn't that she wanted to meet with Beth per se, but with so much of the rest of Sloan's life currently a question mark—everything from her birth parents to what she was going to do with her life now, in the *after*—she wanted to take another stab at the one door she *knew* she held the key to unlock . . . if she could just find it.

The memories of what happened that night might be locked up, but they were there. She had been awake and conscious, able to run and hide. She had the answers she needed—well, some of them, somewhere. And it was time for them to come out and play.

These were the things she tried to focus on as Beth moved around the room to get her supplies—calming music, the space heater, a metronome, the lavender diffuser that made Sloan's nose itch.

"Shall we?" Beth asked at last, and dropped into her seat.

"Ready, as always." Sloan wavered between the chair and couch before ultimately deciding on the couch. She didn't care if it was cliché or not; it was a *nice* couch. The one good thing about this whole experience was getting to lie on it.

Sloan's couch at home was stiff and unforgiving. The kind you use for company only. She tried not to think too deeply about what it meant to be using her hypnotherapist for a comfortable seating arrangement.

"Alright, Sloan. I want you to lie back and follow the sound of my voice. Follow it down into . . ."

Sloan didn't know when she stopped feeling the couch beneath her and when she started feeling the rough wood of the cabin floor. Only that one second, she was there, and then she was here, in the past, living it all over again.

But no, that wasn't quite right.

Remembering it all over again. It was, as they said on her favorite sci-fi show, a fixed point in time. She could observe, but she couldn't manipulate. She couldn't change anything. But that was fine, better even, she thought, to exist without the added responsibility of survival. Spoiler alert, she already had. Now she just needed to remember how she had done it.

Sloan smiled and ran her hand over the rough pine.

Let the show begin.

She cracked her neck and then her knuckles, and then rushed to the bedroom window in time for the first scream to break out.

She was early, she realized. The first scream had taken place at the sink in every previous iteration. She wondered if you could rush memories, or if she had she simply been wrong before. Had she been at the sink or the window the first time, the real time? The sink was where it had always started, yes, but the window felt right somehow, correct.

Like the picture and audio didn't line up, and then suddenly it buffered and synced.

It was as if—Sloan realized with a start—she herself had been buffering and was suddenly course correcting. The scream was at the window. Always. She was positive.

But then what came after the scream? She rushed to push the window up, surprised this time that it budged.

This memory was different.

Sloan crouched down and peeked out. There was only darkness . . . and then another scream. Yes, it had been the bathroom window that had been stuck, not the bedroom, Sloan remembered. She hadn't even tried for the bedroom. She had seen the lights clicking on and off, the slumped forms through the crack, and she had fallen to her knees. No. She had run. She had run straight to the door.

But what came next?

A shadow.

She'd seen a shadow through the glass beside the door and dropped to the floor. A splinter had jammed in her knee, and she'd had to clamp her own hand firmly over her mouth to keep from crying out.

Whatever was happening, whatever monster was making her friends scream, he had been there, on the other side of the wall.

He had come for her.

Sloan dropped to her knees and waited. Her eyes stung as the rough wood floor tore into her knee. She watched it bleed in tiny trickles as she waited, trying to calm her breathing, trying not to breathe at all. Someone climbed the steps in front of her cabin, made them squeak and groan as he inched closer.

"Edward!" a voice called out from the side of her cabin. A man's voice? She wasn't sure. Sloan jumped and shrank back, her breath coming in quiet, stuttering exhales. Now there were two monsters at her door. "Not this one. This one's mine."

It sounded like they were both right on top of her. In there with her. In her head. She was going to die.

Wait.

No.

That wasn't right. This wasn't real. It was all a dream, a hallucination, a hypnotist's wet dream. It had to be. Because the alternative—that she was back there, that this was happening now—was too much to bear.

Sloan told herself that she was safe. That everything that had happened was already past. The worst wasn't yet to come; it already sat there, three months back, with the blood in her hair and the sound of '90s grunge.

This, now, here? It was an echo.

Sloan pushed herself up, the floor rough and steady beneath her feet. Look again, she urged her mind. Rewind.

"Not this one. This one's mine."

Again. Go back.

"Not this one. This one's mine."

Again and again, the voice repeated as Sloan took step after step to the window.

It wasn't a man's voice. It wasn't anything like that. She knew this voice as well as her own now. This voice was as familiar as her mother's perfume, and if she could just get to the window, if she could just look out to see for herself . . . because this voice shouldn't have been there.

Shouldn't have been talking to the monster in the mask.

None of this made sense.

"*Not this one. This one's mine,*" *the voice said again, each syllable a knife through Sloan's skull that sent the room spinning.*

"Sloan!" Beth's hands shook her, gently and then harder.

Sloan blinked herself back into the world with a shout. Her throat burned as she stared up at the scared face of her hypnotherapist.

"You were screaming," Beth said, her voice shaken. "I had to end the session. What happened? Where did you go this time? We need to debrief before you forget."

"What do you mean?" Sloan croaked and reached for the cold glass of water on the stand beside her.

Beth leaned back, clearly relieved now that Sloan was talking. "The reprocessing was going well. You were being so brave and using all the tools we've been working on. It was a breakthrough." Beth sighed. "Until it wasn't. Do you remember?"

Sloan nodded, even though she wished she couldn't. She wished she had kept it buried.

"Good, good, it will help us for next time. We just need to figure out where you went."

"Why do you keep saying that?" Sloan said through gritted teeth, everything irritating her. The sound of Beth's voice, the scratchy fabric of her own shirt, the coolness of the air, the whir of the space heater in the corner—it was all too much. Sloan wanted to go. She wanted to climb inside that old pickup truck that was surely waiting outside and curl up until she was safe and warm and content and had forgotten everything she had just remembered.

"Sloan," Beth said softly, and the girl snapped her eyes back to her. "We had just reached what I like to call the breakthrough moment—when the patient has carried enough of their consciousness into the darkness that they can safely experience the memories without fear. You were able to fully distance yourself; that's how we'll get your real healing. But..."

"But what?"

"But then your face went blank. You stopped responding to my cues. It was like you weren't even in there. I've never experienced someone being totally unreachable in the history of my practice. And then you started screaming."

Oh, Sloan thought, *that explains the sore throat.*

"You can't do that," Beth said, as if Sloan had somehow done it on purpose. "You can't go off exploring things without taking me with you. It isn't safe."

Sloan bristled at the idea that she wasn't safe inside her own head, her own memories, but given what she had just experienced, maybe Beth was right. "Sorry," she mumbled, even though she wasn't sure how she had done it in the first place. "I didn't go anywhere, though. I just looked out a window and..."

"It's okay," Beth said and gave her a soft smile. "It's fine. I just need you to tell me what you experienced after you stopped talking. You stood up and said 'wait' and 'again,' and then you were gone until the screams started. Anything that you remember could help us to get back in there and do some more work around it—safely this time. So walk me through it. You scraped your knee on the floor. Your hand was over your mouth. You realized it was a memory. You stood up, and then what happened? What do you remember next?"

Not this one. This one's mine.

Sloan's hands clenched tightly around her glass as the words ripped through her mind. "I have to go."

"Sloan, wait," Beth said as Sloan jumped up from her seat. "We have to—"

"I don't remember anything," Sloan lied. She grabbed her coat from beside the door and rushed outside. She nearly tripped twice as she ran down the steps in front of the building. She took big greedy gulps of air in the weak autumn sunshine as she raced to the truck, and to Cherry, who was standing beside it.

"There she is." Cherry smiled and held open the door as usual. "Now that that's done, this one's mine."

"What?" Sloan's eyes went wide, and she shoved Cherry away from her. "What did you just say?"

"Jesus." Cherry's smile dropped as she closed the gap between them again. "Are you okay? What did that woman do to you in there?"

"What did you just say?" Sloan shouted.

Cherry narrowed her eyes. "I said, 'Now that that's done, you're all mine.' We're still on for lunch, right? That's all I was talking about. If you aren't up for it, we can—"

"No," Sloan said. She shook her head as if she could shake out the sound of that voice from her memory. "No, I am. Of course. Red Front?"

Cherry pulled her into a hug and kissed the top of her head. "Best waffle fries in town, right?"

"Right," Sloan said, and then moved to climb into her seat. Her hands trembled as she buckled.

This one's mine.

It wasn't Cherry's voice she'd heard outside the cabin in her memories, she told herself. It couldn't have been. Cherry came later, after the screaming stopped. Didn't she? Didn't she?!

"Ready?" Cherry shot Sloan one last puzzled look before putting the truck into drive.

"Yeah," Sloan said, and oh, her throat burned.

THIRTEEN

I AM A horrible girlfriend. That was the first thought that ripped across Sloan's mind when she opened her eyes the next morning, followed quickly by, *But what if I'm right?*

No, this was crazy. Legit crazy.

There was no way that she had heard Cherry talking to The Fox that night, and there was double no way that she would have forgotten it if she had. She needed to get a grip. She needed to stop.

Unless.

Ugh, it was too early for this. She flung back her blankets and shoved her feet into her slippers. It was one of the rare occasions she'd slept at home, made even rarer by the fact that Cherry had left early. Magda had needed her help setting up a "new installation," so Cherry had slid out Sloan's window with a lingering kiss sometime around 6:00 a.m. Sloan's own parents had left for work, and Simon was no doubt off to school like the perfect kid that he was.

Sloan glanced at her acceptance letter from NYU—printed out and proudly hung on the fridge beneath a magnet she had made in preschool—and pulled it down. *That* Sloan, the one who had been so excited to get into her first choice (her super-ultra wish list school, if she was being honest), the *before* Sloan who had felt like her dreams were right on the tip of her tongue, waiting for her teeth to grab them, seemed so far away.

She pulled out the orange juice and drank straight from the bottle as she walked over to the kitchen junk drawer. There, beneath the random batteries of dubious charge and the tape measure and a few stray tacks, rested the folder full of takeout menus—largely obsolete with the creation of smartphones, but her father still saved them compulsively, muscle memory from when he was younger probably. Nobody ever touched them, which was exactly how Sloan wanted it.

Because it was there, pressed between a greasy Golden Wok menu and a crinkled Domino's ad—its coupons expired in the early 2010s—that she shoved her letter from NYU. Officially obsolete.

Sure, she had only deferred a year, but that girl—the one who had wanted to study social work and save the world—was gone. Off in an alternate timeline getting drunk in the dorms her freshman year. But this one, this one here, was too busy wondering if her girl-friend was a secret axe murderer—*and if that was a dealbreaker*—to have time for something as meaningless as college.

Sloan had something better to do today. Something that she hoped would put this "was it or was it not Cherry's voice she heard outside her cabin door that night" thing to rest.

She carried the jug of orange juice back upstairs and took a deep breath. Everything was quiet for once. Just the sound of her breathing and the hum of the heat kicking on. She soaked up the stillness of the house as she flipped open her laptop. The website autofilled before she could even finish the first word, and she scrolled down to the post from Sissy23.

Except it was different this time. The contact information was highlighted. Sissy23 had linked it sometime between Sloan first finding it and now. That was surprising. Sloan figured the woman, if she really was who she said she was, would have wanted some privacy. Surely the reporters were having as much of a field day with her as they were with Sloan. But still, everyone had a little luck sometimes—even if it did come in the form of an email hyperlink to the inbox of the sister of the man who murdered her friends and then tried to kill her.

The bar? It was low.

Sloan clicked the link and then stared down at the blank page for approximately two eternities. She wasn't sure how to start. "Dear Sissy23" felt weird. "Dear The Fox's sister"? "Dear Edward Cunningham's sister." Or she could just cross her fingers Sissy23 had never changed her name by marriage or otherwise and risk a "Ms. Cunningham."

In the end, she settled on . . . hello. Just hello.

Hello,

My name is Sloan Thomas. You probably know who I am, but just in case: I was one of the survivors of that night. I shouldn't be writing to you, probably. I'm sure neither my lawyer nor your brother's lawyer (or yours if you have one) would like this. But I saw this post, and if you really are his sister, I want to know more. I want to know whatever I can. Especially whatever you know about that night and how everybody got there.

I also want to know: Why me? Why did it have to be where I was? But also, why didn't I die? Do you know? Because god knows the therapists and doctors and my parents don't. It's funny how parents warn you about the dangers of the internet, but not the dangers of a cabin in the woods, ha ha.

That night is a void in my life, and I'm hoping you can help me fill it in. If you are willing to meet, please bring proof that you are who you say you are, and I will bring proof that I am who I say I am.

And if you aren't who you say you are, then please disregard. If you bring this to any news outlets or try to sell it, I will march out to the reporters on my lawn and deny all of this, embarrassing you in front of the world. I have fans now. Weird, right? Mass murder victims and survivors—and hell, even your brother—get fans. And they can be more rabid than those Swifties were that time some random guy no one has ever heard of said Taylor didn't write her own songs. So basically, if you don't fuck with me, I won't fuck with you. I can meet you any day or time.

Please write back.

Thank you,
Sloan A. Thomas

When Sloan hit send on the email, she was expecting to feel anxious at worst, excited at best. But instead, she felt nothing.

She felt nothing for five whole minutes, which worried her considerably.

She felt nothing right up until her computer pinged with a new email. Sure, it could have been spam. An ad for Nike or for the sushi place she used to love—she had signed up for their mailing list to save a permanent 5 percent on all takeout orders. Its card still sat at the bottom of her purse even though she hadn't been there since June and probably wouldn't ever go again. (The knives were too big, the raw meat too unsettling.)

But she knew, somehow, without even checking, that when she clicked over to her inbox it would say Sissy23. She could feel it as surely as she had felt the splinter digging into her knee that night.

Sloan slid her finger across the touch pad and squinted as the screen lit up. There it was, right on top in big black letters.

From: Sissy23
Re: is this you?

Sloan took several deep breaths and big swallows, followed by a few minutes of a panic-prevention exercise, courtesy of the hospital therapist: "something you see" (the email), "hear" (her own blood rushing through her ears), "feel" (her nails digging into her palms), "and smell." (Is fear a thing? Otherwise, carpet cleaner, she guessed.)

Sloan waited until she felt sufficiently grounded to open it. She couldn't afford to spiral off into uselessness. Not with clearing Cherry on the line—that's how Sloan had found herself thinking of it this morning. *Clearing Cherry*, like her girlfriend was some kind of suspect or defendant, rather than her partner. Rather than the love of her life. Her soulmate.

The email from Sissy23 was brief and to the point.

Sloan,

I can meet you tmrw. Where?

Sloan stared down the screen. She didn't even know where this woman was. Sissy23 could have been on the other side of the country for all Sloan knew. She was tempted to agree to meet her anywhere, whether that meant down the road or two states over or on the moon . . . but the reality was that she had no car and a limited amount of time to travel, thanks to the curfew.

She could maybe borrow her mother's car. *Maybe.* But then Allison would want to know what Sloan was doing and where she was going and with whom, so that wouldn't work at all. Cherry would definitely drive her anywhere, but that would also defeat the purpose.

Sloan needed this to be a secret, the way the box in Cherry's closet was a secret. She would happily share everything she learned with Cherry, just as soon as she was positive Cherry wasn't in on it first.

Her stomach twisted at that thought.

She had to be sure, though. And that meant she would need a ride.

Sloan clicked over to her text messages with a heavy sigh and scrolled down to her conversation with Connor. She hadn't replied to him in weeks and hadn't talked to him once since the day at the coffee shop, but his name was still there, third down, right under Cherry and Mom.

She shook the metaphorical cobwebs from her chat and fired off a text asking Connor if he was down to run an errand with her tomorrow—just her—and if so, it had to be a secret.

Connor responded immediately, first with a string of eyeball emojis, followed by: Of course. I'll switch shifts with Rachel. Is 1pm okay? I have a class in the morning.

Sloan smiled and then clicked back over to the email where Sissy's question stood waiting.

Yes, she thought, 1:00 p.m. was perfect.

FOURTEEN

TO SAY THAT Sloan's mother was relieved to see Connor's car pull up in front of their house instead of Cherry's would be, quite possibly, the understatement of the century. To say that Cherry wasn't extremely confused and maybe also a little suspicious would also be an understatement.

But as Sloan dropped into Connor's car and pulled the door shut beside her, the comforting smell of coffee and his Yankee Candle seafoam air freshener forcing ten thousand memories of other days just like this one across her mind, she knew she'd made the right choice.

"So," Connor said, "what's the plan?"

Sloan hadn't gone into details with him, just said that it was important and she would tell him in the morning. It wasn't that Sloan was worried about someone overhearing or finding out, but more that she was worried Connor would have backed out if he had known the full situation. *I want you to take me to see the sister of the guy who tried to murder me* seemed like a big ask. But a ride to visit a "friend"? Less so.

"We need to meet someone in Jacobsville," Sloan said, watching Connor's mouth for any sign of annoyance. It was an almost ninety-minute drive.

Connor just nodded as if he had expected something like that.

"I've got gas money for you—don't worry," she added hastily and tried not to think about how she had nicked it earlier from her baby brother's rather robust piggy bank. She would replace it, she told herself, but from where she wasn't sure.

"I don't need money," Connor said as he backed out of Sloan's driveway. "It'll be nice to go on a road trip with you like old times. Here." He tossed his phone into Sloan's lap. "Punch wherever you want us to go in the GPS. I think I've even got some of your play-lists still in there from last summer, before . . ." He trailed off. "You know."

Sloan studied her friend's face. "You can say it."

"I wouldn't even know what to say," he said. "I'm sorry, for what-ever it's worth. I wish you didn't have to go through what you did."

Why are you sorry? You didn't do it. You don't mean it. Maybe you feel sorry for me, but it isn't the same thing.

"It's okay," she answered, because it seemed like the right thing to say during these kinds of circumstances. She'd said similar things a hundred times before to other people about their trage-dies, no matter how big or small. If she had a way back to the past, Sloan would swallow *I'm sorry* every single time.

"It's really not okay," Connor said. He glanced at her as he sipped his coffee, but Sloan pretended not to notice. She didn't know what to say to that.

Instead, she punched in the address for the little diner she had found on Yelp. It had terrible reviews, and she hoped that meant it would be mostly empty when she got there. The last thing she needed was anyone recognizing her while she was talking to whoever was behind the Sissy23 account. The press would have a field day with that. And Cherry? Well, she didn't think Cherry would be too happy to find out about it that way either.

"Thanks," Sloan said when the silence hung too long between them.

"Come on, you know I can't drive without music," Connor said, the perfect subject change.

Sloan couldn't remember the last time she picked the music. Cherry kept them on a steady diet of folk rock and retro riot grrrl–sounding shit, and she had nearly forgotten that she used to listen to anything else. As Sloan clicked through the playlists on Connor's Apple Music account, she found an old one she had made just barely a week before she left for summer camp. It was weird to find her own picks there, lined up neatly where she had left them. It was the closest she had come to seeing her old self in a very long time.

Pushing play felt like slipping into her favorite pajamas after a long day. It felt like home. It felt . . . terrifying.

"What do you think of her new song?" Connor asked, nodding toward the car stereo, where Doja Cat blared out of the speakers.

"It's . . . great," Sloan said, too embarrassed to admit just how much of her world had stopped the day she got on that bus to Money Springs. With less than zero reception and a boss obsessed with commandeering the camp speakers to only play Nirvana and Soundgarden all day . . .

The divot between Connor's eyebrows deepened, concern etching elevens into his forehead exactly as Sloan's mother always warned her about. "You'll get wrinkles," Sloan almost said, parroting the refrain she had heard from her mother practically since birth.

He didn't seem to care. His grip tightened almost imperceptibly on the steering wheel, his lips curved down. New music had been their thing, especially new pop, and now it was just . . . gone. Deleted. Unimportant to her.

She wondered how he would react.

"Hey, Siri," he said, and his voice caught Sloan totally off guard. "Play the new Doja Cat." He flashed her a smile and went back to watching the road. "Sorry, I know it was overplayed pre-release, but I'm not sick of this song yet. I just really wanted to hear it again. I don't listen to the radio enough to get bored of it. You know?"

Sloan grinned, grateful for the out he was giving her. He could probably tell she hadn't heard it yet, but rather than making it a thing, he simply played it for her. Connor was always easy like that.

"Yeah," she said, sinking into the beat. She had missed this. "It's so good."

"So DO YOU want to tell me what we're doing here?" Connor asked as he parallel parked his Jeep—well, technically it was his dad's Jeep—on Main Street in Jacobsville.

They had done a good job dancing around it the whole way down, Connor not wanting to push her too much, and Sloan not wanting to volunteer anything she didn't have to. They had stuck to safer topics, like how his dog was doing, and did she know Rachel got a new kitten, and how great it was that their little brothers were in the same class this year. Sloan answered as best she could: "I'm glad he's good" (she forgot he had a dog); "how cute" (after the masked men, Sloan had had her fill of animals); and "oh, that's so sweet" (half the time she forgot she even had a brother). Connor carried most of the conversation. Sloan couldn't. And neither held it against the other.

The farther they drove, the guiltier Sloan felt. She had forgotten how much he meant to her. How much he mattered. That he was a real person and not just some abstract concept from her past that became obsolete the second that first machete found flesh on that dark summer night.

Now that she remembered, she didn't want to pull him down with her . . . but if he was going to outright ask like this, then she didn't seem to have much choice.

Maybe *no secrets, no lies* didn't just apply to her relationship with Cherry.

Connor turned in his seat, one knee against the shifter, and studied her face. He frowned at whatever he saw there. "Okay, real talk, Sloan," he said, licking his lips. "I'm here for you."

When anyone else said that, Sloan rolled her eyes. (And so many had: countless doctors and therapists and well-meaning friends, up to and including the boy in front of her.) But there was something so goddamn believable when Connor said it, so earnest it almost hurt.

"Connor—" she started, but he held up his hand to stop her.

"I'm not going to ask you anything you don't want to tell me. I asked if you *wanted to tell me.* If you don't, that's okay too. I know it's something important, something that's really big and probably really private, or else your girlfriend or mother would be here with you."

"Yeah," Sloan said softly.

"We didn't use to have any secrets between us. Pony bros for life," he said with a sad little smile. God, Sloan remembered how they used to be so obnoxious about My Little Pony in middle school. Connor rubbed the back of his neck. "But I've had a lot of time to think about all that, what with you not responding and all."

"Connor, I didn't—"

"No, I'm not trying to make you feel bad or anything. I'm saying that I get that I'll never really understand what you've been through and that our friendship was changed because *you've* changed. And that's okay. I still love you. That's all I mean. If I have to choose between none of our old friendship or just tiny bits of it whenever you need to get away from everyone else, I'm choosing tiny bits all day long. No questions asked, no apologies needed. If you tell me that you want to walk into whatever is waiting for you in there alone"— he nodded his head toward the run-down building—"that's fine. Me and Doja Cat will wait out here with bells on."

Sloan smiled despite the nagging feeling that she didn't deserve this level of kindness. Especially not after she blew him off for so long.

"But," he said and flicked her hand with his pointer finger. "If you tell me that you want me to go in there with you—for moral support or just to eat cheese fries in silence—I'm also there for that. You are not alone. It's not you against the world, even if all your instincts are still telling you that."

Sloan opened and shut her mouth, her words escaping her, but Connor just waited, a warm expression on his face. She finally settled on "You're too good to me."

"No," he said. "Well, maybe. I am amazing, and selfless, not to mention adorable and charming and well-mann—"

Sloan's laughter cut him off. "Naturally."

"Naturally," he agreed, fanning himself. "So are you good?"

"No," Sloan said.

"Is there anything I can do?"

Sloan shook her head. "I don't think so."

"We could just sit here for a while, if you're not in a rush."

"Okay." Sloan let her head fall back against her seat. She was forty minutes early anyway, had made sure of that before they left. What was the harm in sitting here a little longer?

Connor followed suit. He pushed his sunglasses way up on his head and shut his eyes. She would have thought he was asleep if his fingers hadn't still been tapping the beat of some song out on the bottom of the steering wheel.

Sloan watched him openly, now that it was safe. She soaked up the sight of him like she was the ground and he was the rain. Or the blood. She'd seen an awful lot of that soaking into the earth too.

God, what was she doing?

She couldn't afford to be distracted, not even by her former best friend. She was a little over half an hour from meeting someone who might be able to finally give her answers about what happened, and here she was worried about playlists and Pony bros.

"I can tell you're freaking out," Connor said, without opening his eyes.

Sloan snapped to attention. "I wasn't," she lied.

"If you say so," he said, and that made her mad.

Here was this perfect golden boy, fake dozing beside her with his nice Jeep and his perfect life, and he had no idea, *no idea!* the fight it took Sloan to keep going after everything that happened. Maybe she was freaking out, just a little, but didn't she deserve to?

Wouldn't anyone?

"I'm meeting The Fox's sister here," she spat out, because she wanted to see him freak out for once. Because he would—she was sure of it. He would think this was a mistake. Hell, with every mile that ticked through the odometer, Sloan had wondered if this was a mistake herself.

An evil that should have been left in its box, that could've been, easily. If only she could bring herself to stop pulling on all these threads, maybe she could find some peace too. Maybe she too could be content to fake doze in the autumn sun.

"Whose sister? A fox?" Connor asked in confusion. And oh, right, Sloan realized. That detail hadn't been released to the press. At least not yet.

"Edward Cunningham," she said, and his eyes widened.

And yep, there it was: the panic, the stress, the worry. At least she didn't have to feel it all alone anymore.

"I'm meeting Edward Cunningham's sister here. She posted on Reddit, and I reached out to her. She had already flown in from Alabama and was at the jail just outside of Money Springs trying to see her brother when she got my message. This diner is the exact midpoint between Money Springs and my house."

"Jesus, Sloan," Connor said. He rubbed his hands over his eyes. "No wonder you didn't bring your mother."

"Yeah, that was definitely going to be a no go."

Connor tilted his head then, his eyes already narrowed before the words pushed out. "But why didn't you bring Cherry?"

That? That's what he wanted to know? Out of all the things in the world, that was what he chose to focus on? Not *for the love of god, why are you meeting the murderer's sister?*

"It doesn't matter." Sloan bristled.

"Fair enough." He shrugged and dropped his head back to the seat. He even flipped his sunglasses back down so that she couldn't see his eyes at all.

"You aren't going to ask me why I'm meeting her?"

Connor pushed his glasses back up just long enough to make eye contact, his piercing brown eyes locked on hers, and then dropped them again. "I told you I wasn't going to pry. I shouldn't have even asked about Cherry. Sorry," he said. "Besides, I already know why you want to talk to that guy's sister. I would probably do the same thing."

"You would?"

"Yeah, you want to see what's behind the monster you've built up in your head, right? It makes sense."

Was that what she was doing? Did she want to humanize him somehow, defang the man in her nightmares? No, this was about Cherry. *Cherry.*

"I didn't bring Cherry because I'm worried that she had something to do with it."

Connor's jaw clenched hard on that reveal, and Sloan smirked. He definitely hadn't seen that one coming, and now that it was here, it was obvious he was fighting not to react. To stay steady and calm, with no follow-up questions. She decided to throw him a bone.

"I don't know for sure. I actually can't remember most of that night. I'm working with someone to regain my memories, but they're all jumbled. So there's this box, right? And . . . Cherry said it was her dad's stuff, but I don't know. There were things in there that reminded me of that night. I was hoping his sister might know if there was any connection between Cherry and the men at the camp. Like if she could have been somehow involved. That's why I didn't want her here."

"Oh," Connor said, and then clamped his mouth. Sloan supposed his promise not to pry was becoming harder to keep by the moment.

"Yeah, so on a scale from one to ten, how much do you regret driving now?"

Connor tapped his chin in mock contemplation. "Negative five?"

"Oh, no," Sloan clarified. "Ten is the worst. One is the best."

"Yeah, negative five." He shrugged. "If your girlfriend is a psycho killer, then we should probably find out sooner rather than later, right?" His voice was strong and steady, a smirk on his face showing off his dimple like usual, but the slight tremble in his hands betrayed how he really felt.

"I shouldn't have said anything," Sloan said, because this was too much. It was too much to thrust on another person. It sounded ridiculous, even to her.

"I meant it when I said I was here for you," Connor said. "Even if your life is batshit right now. I do have one question, though. If you don't mind me asking?"

"Yeah, go for it," she said. It was kind of the least she could do.

"*Am* I getting cheese fries out of this, or nah?"

FIFTEEN

CONNOR SLURPED DOWN his cheese fries beside Sloan while she watched the clock over the door. It was an old-school one, the kind that ticked away like the metronome in Beth's office, a steady sound no matter how busy the place got. Which is to say, the place never got very busy at all.

Sissy23 was late.

Twenty minutes and counting, and Sloan had a sinking feeling she wasn't going to show at all. That she had lost her nerve or, worse yet, that it hadn't been his sister at all, just some random internet catfish looking for a few seconds of fame.

"We'll wait ten more minutes," Sloan said, Connor's leg pressed warm and firm against hers. It was keeping her from a full-on freak-out whether he knew it or not. Sloan suspected that he did.

"No rush," he said. "I have nowhere else to be. Dad doesn't need the car until tomorrow."

"I have curfew."

"Still?" Connor asked. "Well, that's not till midnight anyway. We have plenty of—"

"Ten p.m. now, actually." Sloan shredded her napkin, embarrassed.

"You have an earlier curfew now that you're a graduated, legal adult than you did when we were in eleventh grade?"

"Mom didn't want me to keep driving to Cherry's house."

"Understandably, if she's an axe murderer," he teased. "But didn't she, like, move here anyway? Anytime I see you around town, you're together. Except now, and the other day at the coffee shop, but she picked you up, so half credit, I guess."

"I'm a horrible person for even suspecting her, aren't I? I shouldn't have ever said it out loud. Oh god, why am I like this?"

"I don't know? Maybe because you went through some major fucking trauma? Like to the point where your brain deleted its own memories so you could deal."

"Sloan?" an unfamiliar voice said, and both teens' eyes flicked to the woman who'd just walked in the door. "You are Sloan, right?" she asked and came toward their booth. She was older than Edward looked, by decades maybe. Her hair was white, and her skin was wrinkled and thin, nearly translucent, aside from the pinkness of the heavily applied rouge on her cheeks. She was dressed in a long winter trench coat with a fur-trimmed hood—heavy for this time of year. In her arms, she carried a folder and a book.

Sloan cleared her throat and stood up beside the booth. "Sissy23?"

"Sasha, please," the woman said, holding out the top of her hand. Sloan wasn't sure if she was expecting her to kiss it or clutch it or what, so she just shook it weakly and awkwardly at a weird angle until Sasha pulled it back. They sat down, neither of them saying a word until Sasha broke the silence with a "And who is this gentleman joining us?"

"Connor Young," he said. "And I'd say nice to meet you, but I guess we'll see how this conversation goes first." Sloan nudged him under the table, and he went back to eating his fries with a shrug. A silent observer, he had promised her. Backup in case this lady was as batty as The Fox.

Sloan was glad he was there.

Sasha pulled her license and two photographs out of the folder—Polaroids, just like the ones she had found in Cherry's box. Sloan couldn't help but notice there were others tucked below them. They would get to those in time, she hoped. Right now she focused on the items Sasha slid toward her.

"Here's my license, with my first and last name on it. I never did change it when I married. Good thing too, because that relationship lasted about as long as an overripe banana. And here is a picture of Edward and me when we were children, and another of us about fifteen years ago, before he joined up with what would later become Morte Hominus." Sloan looked up at her, puzzled. "You said to bring proof."

"Right, thanks," Sloan said, and she needed to be sharper than this. She needed to remember.

"I would ask you for proof, except I've seen your face splashed on the news enough times to know it's you. Where's the other one, though? There were two of you."

"Cherry couldn't make it," Sloan said.

Sasha frowned and tucked her pictures away. "You have questions about my brother and Morte Hominus, I suppose. Waitress."

She waved the girl over and looked her up and down. "Coffee, black. What do you have here that's not fried?"

"T-toast?" the young waitress answered, clearly intimidated by the woman in front of her.

"Toast," Sasha said dully. "I see. Black coffee, then, and... toast."

"Right away, ma'am," the waitress said before scuttling off to the back.

Connor pressed his leg firmer against Sloan's, not looking up from his fries, his steady warmth like a beacon guiding her back to the present whenever she got lost in her head.

"As I was saying, you have questions. Hopefully I have some answers."

"I . . . what do you know?" Sloan asked. "I want to know everything. Why us, why there, why anyone at all? Why is he still alive? Why wasn't anyone tracking the cult?"

"Not a cult," Sasha said and held up a single finger. "Edward always called it a 'pod.'"

"A pod?"

"Yes, you know, like whales traveling together. They liked to use animal terms since they considered themselves to be no more important than any other creatures on earth. Do you find it odd how disconnected we are from nature? Because he did. He used to always complain that 'no one calls it a herd of people, even though mankind has less sense than a herd of wildebeests or a pack of jackals.'"

Sloan swallowed hard, which Sasha apparently took as a cue to keep going.

"Anyway, I doubt you care about all that. You're here to vilify him, right? You don't want to hear that he was a kind, gentle boy who grew up to be an easily confused man—most of them do, unfortunately."

Connor scoffed at her, but Sasha raised her eyebrow as if in challenge. Connor, to his credit, was not the first to look away. Perhaps they were more like animals than any of them realized.

"I don't know what I want," Sloan said, "beyond the truth. If I have to listen to you talk about how great the man who put on a fox mask and murdered my friends was to find out, then I'll do it."

"They wore their masks?" Sasha asked.

Sloan winced. She wasn't supposed to be telling people about that, yet she somehow seemed to keep doing it.

"They carved those themselves, you know. It was supposed to be their favorite animal or the one they most related to—something along those lines. Edward fancied himself a fox, clever in his opinion, but shy. He was right about the second part. If he was right about the first, I suspect that he wouldn't be in jail right now."

Sloan noticed that she didn't say "he wouldn't have killed anyone" or "he wouldn't have joined a cult." No, Sasha only seemed concerned that he had been caught.

"So it was like an arts-and-crafts thing?" Sloan almost laughed.

"You tease, but that's how it was at first. Edward was so excited when he found them online. I checked out his chat rooms. I had always felt responsible for him—our parents died when we were very young. Being eighteen to his six, I suppose I took on a mothering role for him, for whatever it's worth. They say kids just need one role model to get them through, but that wasn't the case with Edward. Edward needed the whole world to love him, and as you've no doubt realized, the world can be a cruel, awful place. When he told me that he was joining up with this pod, I was skeptical. But he was an adult, and who was I to stop him? When he got there, he began to change."

"Into a murderer?" Connor snorted.

"No, into someone happy and fulfilled. It was like the piece of him that disappeared when our parents died had come back to life. Edward and his friends would make their little crafts and sell them, traveling around to music festivals and farmers markets in their converted vans. I was very jealous."

"Of a cult?" Sloan said. She couldn't help it. If she had to listen to one more second of this utopian spin, then she was going to vomit up that cheese fry she had stolen from Connor earlier.

"It wasn't like that, like I said," Sasha warned. "They were good people. Yes, they had strayed off the beaten path, but they weren't harmful. They dedicated their lives to reducing their environmental impact. They made a living upcycling anything they found and living off the land. They would keep their vans parked for months at a time, riding bicycles to get wherever they needed. They wanted to save the world and spread the happiness they felt."

Sloan was incredulous. "They sure spread the happiness, didn't they? I bet it was a super-joyful experience for them to put their upcycled axes into my friends' heads." Beside her, Connor nearly choked on his fry.

"Things went on like that for years," Sasha said, seemingly intent on ignoring that quip. "And then Marco came."

"Marco?"

"Yes, he was a beautiful Italian man, very attractive and very charismatic. That's a dangerous combination around an audience so desperate to be loved. Things started changing almost immediately."

"How so?"

"The pod became more isolated. Before, Edward would come and visit me several times a year. We talked on the phone at least once a week. Sometimes I would even get a hotel near wherever they were staying. I couldn't stomach sleeping in the van, but it was fun to be around them. Once Marco took over—if that even was his real name; if you ask me, his accent always seemed a little put-on—the calls from Edward stopped.

"I got a single letter from him stating that he was no longer interested in a relationship with a 'capitalist who valued consumption over happiness and sought to destroy the world in her wake.' He begged me to change my ways and join the pod. He left an address where I could find him if I did so in the next three weeks. After that, they would move on, *he* would move on, without me. I gave up my entire future to raise that boy—you can't exactly bring a first grader to college with you—and Marco turned him on me in a matter of months."

The waitress chose that moment to come back and set the coffee down, along with a plate of toast. Sasha took a long, hard pull from the mug, as if she needed to let the remainder of the story rest for a moment.

"What did you do?"

"I went to the address in the letter, of course," she said as she picked up her toast. "Everything had changed. They weren't worried about painting old dressers or finding the next music festival. It was about recruiting more people to protect the earth."

"How, though, and what does that have to do with committing mass murder in the forest?"

"Like any good leader, Marco had instilled fear in them. He

prepared them for an extinction-level event. It would bring 'the darkness,' whatever that meant, which would somehow cleanse and restore balance to the world. Apparently, we're overpopulated and overpolluted, and Marco was here to usher in a global reset."

"Like the asteroid and the dinosaurs?" Sloan asked.

"Something like that. Just the usual end-of-times bullshit that charlatans seem to thrive on."

"Okay?"

"I tried to get Edward to leave with me. It—it wasn't right what they were doing. Marco had them all so isolated and confused. He had changed things slowly and deliberately. By the time he started talking about ritual killing and restoring balance, they had already, you know, committed to the process, let's say.

"Edward refused to leave. I spent the next two weeks there with the pod trying to convince him and a few others to get out, while they tried to convince me to join. Eventually Marco labeled me 'a hostile' and said I wasn't welcome to visit the pod. The day after they kicked me out, I came back to try to reason with Edward one last time, but they had moved on in the night, and that was that."

"You never saw him again?"

"Not for nearly six years. Not until I was hiring him a lawyer this summer after the *incident*. Occasionally, I would get a letter in the mail. Not a letter, really, just some photographs. Some were of us when we were little; some were of his life there. It was like he couldn't bear to sever our connection completely. I had hoped he would come back someday."

Sloan tilted her head. "So what about Money Springs?"

"I think it was a ritual of sorts."

"A ritual?" Sloan asked in disbelief. "What does that even mean? What do you know about it?"

"Not enough to stop it, clearly. If I'm being honest, I didn't think anything would really happen. It was so outlandish." Sasha slid a worn book across the table. "Before I left, I took this."

"What is it?" Sloan was scared to touch it.

"It's . . . I guess they'd probably consider it their version of the Bible. It has some information in it I thought you might find useful."

"And they didn't notice you stole it?"

"I'm sure Edward did, but for whatever reason he must have protected me. I have no doubt now that I would have met the same fate as your friends had Marco found out I had a copy."

"Did you read it?"

Sasha shook her head. "I skimmed it, but it was disturbing stuff. Rituals and the like. I didn't want that in my head." She flipped open the folder and spread the pictures out. "I wanted to remember him like this. Not like whatever was in that book."

"You just sat on it?" Connor leaned forward. "You just sat on a plan to murder a bunch of people?"

"Hardly. I took it to the police. I filed a missing person report on my brother and used this as proof that he was in danger. I even tried to declare him incompetent, but when the officers eventually made contact with him, they felt he was fine. No one cared then, and now it's too late. What's the use in giving it to them at all anymore? So they can gawk at Edward's beliefs? Leak it to the media? No. What's done is done, and this book belongs to you now.

"I don't have the answers about what happened that night. I

can't explain 'why you' or 'why there' or any of the other things that you asked in your email. But maybe," she said and rapped her knuckles on the cover, "maybe this book does."

Sloan ran her hand over the faded blue cover. It was plain, not even a label on the front, but its well-worn leather was soft under her fingers. Edward, or whoever had it before him, must have read it a thousand times.

Sloan didn't realize that she was shaking until Connor set a heavy hand over hers. "I think we should go," he said gently.

"Can I have these pictures? The ones from his time there at least."

"It's all I have left of him," Sasha said, but then seemed to reconsider. "Here." She ripped one out from the bottom of the pile. "Take this one. It's Marco and another member of the pod with Edward. I don't want that kind of bad energy around me anymore."

Connor took the picture and slipped it into the book, which he carefully tucked under his arm. He scooted closer so that Sloan would stand up. She did, numb and confused and trying to process what she had learned—and the possibilities of what she would learn when she cracked open Edward's book.

"Thank you," Sloan mumbled and took a step toward the door.

"Oh, hey," Connor said. He tapped his hand on the table until Sasha met his eyes. "What was he? Marco, I mean."

"Excuse me?" Sasha's forehead crinkled.

"Edward was a fox, right? What did Marco think he was?"

"A rabbit," Sasha said. "Marco was a rabbit."

SIXTEEN

"YOU'RE SHAKING," CONNOR said once they were safely back on the highway.

He had tucked the book under his jacket in the back seat after telling Sloan that she should take a beat before looking at it. Sloan had been nauseous, dizzy even, as they walked to the car, and the worry had been plain on Connor's face. Later, when she was more herself, Sloan knew she would be sad about that. Sad about there being one more person who loved her—who loved the old her—upset and concerned over the shadow she'd become. But right now, she had to focus on calming down.

She pressed her hands against her thighs and willed them to go still. "I'm fine," she said, but Connor didn't look convinced.

"You're not fine, Sloan," he said. "I don't think anybody would be, in your shoes."

"It's just The Rabbit," Sloan said, as if that explained anything. "That box I told you about on the way up? The one Cherry doesn't want me to look in? It had a rabbit carving in it."

Connor's Adam's apple bobbed slowly as he chanced a glance at her, as if he needed to taste his words before he said them. "A lot of people have rabbit stuff in their house. My *mom* even has those two goofy ceramic rabbits on the TV stand, remember? I don't think that's the gotcha you think it is."

"Maybe not," Sloan said, her voice weak. "But there were also pictures in the box, Polaroids just like Sasha's. They looked familiar somehow too. I don't know. I just can't shake it."

"Familiar how? You've been through a lot, Sloan. I just—"

"You think I'm losing it, don't you?" She studied Connor's face. "Maybe I *am* losing it." Hot tears pricked her eyes.

"You're allowed to lose it. It's kinda fucking weird that you haven't," he said. He squeezed her knee, and then let go to pop open the center console. He fished around for a minute, his eyes never leaving the road, and then grunted happily as he tossed something her way. A soft travel pack of tissues landed in her lap, paisley flowers printed all over it.

She picked it up with shaking fingers. "Thanks?" she said, her voice lilting up like a question.

"I always keep a pack or two in there for when Rachel's allergies kick up."

"I'm fine," Sloan said again, even though his kindness brought on a fresh wave of tears. "Or I guess maybe I'm not."

"Hey," he said softly. "I'm not going to pretend to know what you're going through. And I'm not gonna tell you it's okay to not be okay or any of those other bullshit platitudes that people say when they can't think of anything else. But, right now, you *are* safe."

"Yeah," she said and let out a watery laugh.

"If you really think Cherry is up to something, just give me a second to grab my bat out of the trunk, because you have my sword or whatever. But if you think maybe you're just a little bit mixed up right now—I saw how hard that press conference hit you—then instead of my sword, you have my ear. Or a hug. Or anything you else you need."

Sloan wiped at her eyes and nodded. She wasn't sure she deserved his friendship after she'd blown him off for the last few months, but now that she had it, she hoped it stayed.

She pulled her phone out of her bag to let her mom know she would be home in about an hour. No sense being grounded for missing dinner on top of all of this, but Allison only replied with a cheerful: No rush! ☺

A far cry from what her reaction would be if Sloan was in danger of missing mandatory family time because of Cherry.

Cherry.

Sloan clicked over to her other messages. It had been oddly quiet today. Usually, Cherry texted her a hundred times when they weren't together. Panic sliced through Sloan when she realized she didn't have a single message from her.

She had been so caught up in this adventure, this "quest for truth"—as Connor had called it while they sat in their parking spot and worked up their courage—that she hadn't even noticed. The dull ache she had in her chest whenever she was away from Cherry had, for the first time since the incident, faded to background noise, but now it roared back to life with a vengeance.

Cherry knew that she was going to be spending the afternoon with Connor. Sloan had very deliberately told Cherry not to worry and that she'd call her when she got back. But *not to worry* didn't mean to disappear completely. Didn't mean to go away and leave Sloan all alone. Suddenly, Sloan didn't care if Cherry was in on the murder thing or not.

Everyone had bunnies, even Connor's mom.

She needed Cherry. Cherry kept her safe. Cherry hadn't murdered *her*, which had to at least count for something, right?

"Sloan?" Connor said, and he sounded very, very worried, which stressed Sloan out even more.

She needed Cherry right now. Everybody loved bunnies. Who didn't love bunnies? Coincidences were a thing. When you hear hoofbeats, you think horses, not zebras—isn't that what her dad loved to say? Sloan was just mixed up. She had to be. She—

"Take me to Cherry's," she said.

If Connor had looked worried before, he looked fully freaked out now. "The same girl you think was in on all this? That Cherry? You can't be serious right now."

"I'm wrong. I was wrong about her," Sloan said, not because she meant it, but because she needed it to be true. Everything was upside down and confusing. Cherry was steady, steady, steady. Sloan needed that. "You were right. I'm mixed up. I'm—"

"How about I bring you home, and then we call Cherry together? We can all hang out."

Sloan gritted her teeth, the anxiety roiling in her belly. "Take me to her house. It's on Birch, the apartments next to the liquor store just past the second set of train tracks."

"I don't want to leave you alone with her if—"

"Forget I said anything, please." Sloan grabbed his wrist. She would beg if she had to, but she hoped he wouldn't make her. Her breath was already coming in short, head-spinning pants. "I was wrong. I was confused. Right? Even you have bunnies—you said it yourself."

There was an earthquake in her head as all her thoughts crashed into one another and fell to the floor. Nothing made sense anymore; nothing mattered anymore, except for her need to get to Cherry.

"Okay," Connor said in a panic.

Sloan held his wrist, her fingers digging into his skin. She didn't want to hurt him. She didn't mean to hurt him. It was just, if she let go, she might float away.

Why did she think she could do this? Why did she think she could risk tipping her already unsteady world upside down? She didn't want the truth; she didn't care about the truth. She just wanted her safe bubble back. Kisses under collages and eccentric parents and, shit, she'd even take one of Simon's baseball games right now.

"I'm gonna call your mom," Connor said, and Sloan squeezed harder.

"You said . . ." she choked out. "You said whatever I needed. No questions asked."

"That was before you started going code blue in my car!" he shouted.

She didn't bother correcting him. She'd heard a code blue during her stay in the hospital. That first night, Anise had managed to hold on to life until the universe cut her strings one by one. She didn't even last till the med-flight. Sloan wasn't coding right now. If anything, she felt extra excruciatingly, painfully alive.

"I will never forgive you." Sloan seethed.

"You don't mean that," Connor said, and to his credit, he didn't pull back his hand. "You need to calm down. Sloan, *please.*"

Sloan couldn't calm down; that was the thing. If she could, she would have by now. What she needed was Cherry. Let them call her toxic and codependent, from their high horses and their perfect little lives. She didn't care anymore.

Sloan lifted her phone up to her face. "Call Cherry."

"Calling Cherry," Siri repeated in her little robot voice.

"Sloan?" Just hearing Cherry's voice pulled some of the razor wire out of Sloan's brain, and she sagged in relief. Connor rubbed his now-released wrist and looked over at his passenger with pursed lips.

"I need you," Sloan whispered into the phone.

"Where are you?" Cherry asked. Her voice was measured, calm. "You're not home."

Sloan didn't care how Cherry knew that. Didn't care if Cherry was checking in on her on one app or another. "I'm—" She looked at the GPS. "I'm still a half hour away."

"Okay," Cherry said. "I'll meet you at your house. I'll be there as soon as you are. Just stay on the phone with me, baby. We got this."

Connor's fingers tightened on the steering wheel, but Sloan ignored him. She had everything she needed now, almost. She had the voice but not the body, not the warmth or the scent or the soft, soft skin. But she would, soon.

Soon.

"WHAT THE HELL did you do to her?" Cherry's voice skittered across the darkness of Sloan's driveway. She had pulled up barely a minute behind them; her tires even squealed as she came to an abrupt stop. Sloan liked that. Liked that she was as desperate to get to Sloan as Sloan was to get to her. Liked that Cherry immediately got protective.

Connor got out of his car, his hands up as he came around to help Sloan out. "Nothing. Nothing!" he insisted as he pulled the door open.

"Get the fuck away from her," Cherry said.

Connor took a step back, and she crouched in front of Sloan. The porch lights flicked on. They were too bright.

"No, no, no," Sloan mumbled, because the last thing she needed was her mother to come out and get in the middle of this mess. Sloan felt stupid, wrong, like she had betrayed Cherry—and hadn't she just?

Pressing too hard had been a problem for Sloan even before everything happened, and it appeared to be the one part of her that unfortunately remained. If Cherry didn't want to share what was in the box, she didn't have to. It didn't mean Sloan needed to get carried away by her imagination.

"Shh, I've got you." Cherry wrapped her arms around Sloan. "Look at me." Sloan just curled in on herself, ashamed. "Look at me," Cherry said again, this time more firmly.

Reluctantly, Sloan did. She didn't deserve this comfort, she thought, not after breaking their pact of *no secrets, no lies*. Not after she actually let herself entertain the thought that Cherry could somehow be involved. Because of what? A box of her dad's old things?

"I'm sorry," Sloan said, even though it wasn't enough, would never be enough, could never be enough. "I'm sorry."

"Baby, no," Cherry said. She brushed some hair out of Sloan's face and flashed a worried smile. "You don't have anything to apologize for."

"I do," Sloan said weakly, but her mind raced too fast for her to catch any more words. To string them in the proper order. To get them out at all.

"We'll worry about that later," Cherry said and helped her from the car. They took a few steps toward the door. The curtains were already pulled back, and Allison's and Brad's disappointed faces glared at them from the window.

"Wait," Sloan said, turning back to Connor. "The book. It's in the back."

"I'll just hang on to it," he said and bit his lip. "You can come get it when you're feeling better."

Cherry narrowed her eyes as she marched up to the boy. "She wants it now."

"I don't really think that—" But Connor didn't get to finish that sentence because Cherry had already pulled open the back door and was shoving things around.

She emerged a minute later, the worn book in her hand. "This it?" Cherry asked as she held it up. Sloan nodded. "There anything else of yours in here?" Sloan shook her head. Seemingly satisfied, Cherry kicked the door shut. "Bye," she all but shouted as she walked past Connor.

"Wait, I'm coming in." Connor took a step forward, but Cherry held out an arm to block him.

"I think you've done enough."

Before he could answer, the front door pulled open, and a very annoyed-looking Allison stomped out. "Sloan? Get in the house."

Sloan started walking, but her legs felt shaky. Maybe she should sit. But before she could decide either way, Cherry appeared at her side, and her warm arm pulled her in close and steady.

"Are you sure that . . ." Connor trailed off, and Sloan lifted her hand in a weak wave goodbye. He shook his head and, with an upset kick to his tire, made his way back into his car and out of Sloan's driveway.

"I don't suppose I could get you to leave too," Allison said, her hands on her hips, as the girls made their way up the front steps.

Cherry didn't dignify that with a response. She walked right past Allison like she didn't even exist. Because right now, Sloan realized, she didn't.

The only real thing in this world was the hand in hers. The arm around her shoulder. The steady beat of the heart in the body beside her.

SEVENTEEN

SLOAN SLEPT.

It was restless and tenuous, as if sleep was just another promise to be broken instead of something she desperately needed. She thought she remembered waking up a few times. Once, she was screaming, and Cherry's comforting arms held her down until she stopped. Once, she thought she saw Cherry at her desk, the lamp arced real low over the pages of whatever was in her hand.

The rest was a blur of tangled blankets and things she couldn't quite remember, her dreams on the tip of her tongue, forever out of reach. Sloan awoke unrefreshed and irritable, the guilt burning her up inside like a brand.

She was a liar.

She racked her brain as she lay there, wondering how long she could get away with fake sleeping. Wondering how much Cherry knew about last night. What had Connor told her? Anything? Nothing? The entire conversation was a haze of porch lights and angry faces and Sloan stuck trying to remember how to breathe in the face of all that.

A mess. All of it.

Sloan slowly stretched her leg out behind her. She expected to nudge up against Cherry's sleeping body—she certainly wasn't ready to face Cherry's awake one—but was met with cold sheets on an empty bed.

Sloan jerked up then, and blinked hard against the light. Across the room, at the desk, Cherry let out a startled laugh.

"You scared me." Cherry set down her book and crossed the room. "I'm glad you woke up. I missed you."

Sloan shut her eyes against the soft kiss to her forehead. She expected Cherry to be irate, indignant, betrayed. Instead, she seemed . . . happy?

"You're not mad?"

"Mad at what? That you went out with your friend and had a panic attack?" Cherry asked softly. "What kind of a shitty girlfriend do you think I am?"

You're not, Sloan thought. *You're perfect. It's me. I'm the monster.*

"Do you know where I was?" Sloan asked, not quite trusting that this wasn't just another dream.

Cherry glanced over at the desk. "Probably somewhere awful for you to get your hands on that book."

So she didn't know yet.

Yes, she sat there happily kissing Sloan on the forehead, but only because she had no idea what kind of snake her girlfriend actually was—sneaking around behind her back, telling Connor that she thought Cherry could have something to do with it. This wasn't a dream. It was a nightmare.

"Hey." Cherry tipped Sloan's chin up so that their eyes met. "Whatever you're thinking right now? It's fine. Do I love that you went and did this *something* without me? No. But you called me, right? When things got hard and heavy, you called me?"

Sloan nodded.

"That's what matters."

"It's not, though. It's really not. I . . . I went and saw Sasha."

Cherry gave her a blank look. "Is that one of your friends from school?"

"No, it's . . . You know her as Sissy23 from Reddit. I went and met her at a diner about ninety minutes from here." Sloan forced herself to maintain eye contact even though she wanted to grab the blanket and yank it back over her head. To disappear entirely.

"Oh."

And Sloan didn't think it was possible for a person to fit that much emotion into a two-letter, one-syllable word. She could sense the confusion, the disappointment, the frown that tugged at the corners of Cherry's mouth.

No, no, go back to the forehead kisses, Sloan wanted to scream. *Even if I don't deserve them.* Because the hurt look Cherry gave her cut deeper than The Fox's knife ever could.

"I'm sorry," Sloan said.

"I said it was fine." Cherry didn't sound like she meant it. "Just . . ."

"Just what?" Sloan grabbed at Cherry's wrist as she started to stand, but Cherry easily shook her off.

"Just, why did you want to do that with Connor? I mean, it's my life too, right? If we're going to go talk to The Fox's nearest and dearest, shouldn't we have gone together? Shouldn't we have decided together? I mean, fuck, Sloan. Even if you wanted to go alone, you should have let me know." Her nostrils flared with an angry sigh. "So Sissy23 is the one who gave you that book? Sorry, I mean, *your buddy Sasha*?"

This, this had been the wake-up that Sloan had been expecting. Maybe she had stayed her own execution at first, but at last the firing squad had arrived.

"And why Connor? Do you like him? Have you been talking to him?" Cherry said, and oh. Oh? Is that the bigger issue? Not that she went but who she went with?

"God, no," Sloan said, just shy of laughing from relief. "No, of course not. He's practically my brother. Or he was. That's not what that was about at all."

"Then what was it about? Why didn't we go together?"

Sloan picked at the fabric of her comforter. It seemed silly now, in the light of day, in Cherry's presence, with lips that had kissed her and arms that had soothed her, to think that Cherry could have ever been involved. To think that there was anything to that old box in the closet except for a beloved dead man's affinity for rabbits.

"Fine. Don't tell me." Cherry slumped back into the desk chair. "I guess keeping secrets is something we do now."

She sounded miserable, and Sloan's heart ached. But then a tiny hint of anger blistered up instead. "You started it."

Cherry's head snapped up. "What?"

"You did!" Sloan insisted. "When I tried to ask you about that box."

"My father's stuff?" Cherry punctuated each word with a bitter tone. "Give me a fucking break. I didn't want to talk about my dead dad for one fucking second, and instead of accepting that, you run off with some random guy to talk to a murderer behind my back?"

"She's not the murderer," Sloan said, even though that wasn't the point at all.

"You don't know that, though. Do you? Just because she made her post sound like she was a casual cult observer doesn't mean she actually was."

And oh, that knocked Sloan back. She hadn't considered that. Had she just risked her life, and Connor's too?

"I didn't think about it like that," she said finally, shame making her belly iron-hot.

"Sloan, what's really going on?"

Sloan bit her lip. What could she say? That she had doubted Cherry so spectacularly that breaking bread with her ex–best friend and a murderer's sister seemed like the best course of action? That she had gotten so caught up in her quest for answers that she hadn't thought about anyone else? That a desperate curiosity was chewing her up from the inside out?

She settled on, "I just want to *know*," and Cherry's face softened.

"This is about your memories? Because I've told you what happened, and I'll tell you a thousand more times if you need me to."

Sloan looked away, the sincerity of Cherry's words twisting inside her, writhing around like snakes.

"I know you would," she said softly. "But it's not enough. I want my own memories back. I want to know what's real and what isn't. I want to stop being so paranoid and confused all the time just because I picked the wrong summer job."

Cherry sat on the bed beside her. "I wish you never came to Money Springs."

Sloan's eyes shot to Cherry's, hurt making her voice small and sad. "You do?"

"Yeah. If you hadn't come, you would be at college right now. You'd be so happy, I bet." Cherry tipped her head against Sloan's shoulder. "Instead you're stuck in this bedroom freaking out with me. If you hadn't come, you wouldn't have a schedule full of doctor's appointments and therapist's appointments. You'd have frat parties and new best friends and a whole new city at your feet." Cherry took Sloan's arm and traced a finger down its scar. "And you wouldn't have this."

"To be fair, I've always had that weird birthmark on my wrist. If anything, the slash is an improvement." Sloan tried to lighten the mood. Things had been too heavy for too long, and she was exhausted.

"I loved it, though." Cherry pressed her thumb into the small, round mark.

"Only because it matches the one on your hip!"

Cherry frowned. "Either way, it was perfect, and now it's ruined."

Sloan hadn't seen it like that. She had never viewed the mark as something someone might like. Something capable of being ruined. It had always just been the reason she preferred long sleeves and those hoodies that hooked around her thumbs. The new scar just added to it, another reason to hide.

Sloan smiled, determined to shift the mood. "And if you hadn't gone, you would be traveling around the country, having big, grand adventures like the hippie you secretly are." She accentuated her words with a press of her fingers into Cherry's side, right where she was most ticklish.

"I am not a hippie!" Cherry yelped and twisted away. She grabbed a pillow and playfully tossed it at Sloan.

Sloan, in turn, tackled her with a laugh. They froze, their faces inches apart, Cherry pinned beneath her with a sly little smile. Sloan narrowed her eyes. "What are you up to?"

Cherry flipped them so fast they both nearly slipped off the edge of the bed. Now Cherry was on top, in control, holding Sloan down just like she always did, keeping her on earth when her mind threatened to fly away.

"Sneaky." Sloan grinned as Cherry pressed a featherlight kiss to her neck.

"You love it."

"I do," Sloan agreed. "You know I do."

The relief in Cherry's face from hearing those words made Sloan's head spin in new and delicious ways. Cherry was safety, always. Warmth and safety. Sloan had just gotten confused. A temporary mistake. She had wandered too far to pull back in time. Her curiosity had gotten away from her—that was all.

And then she remembered something.

"Hey, what was in the book? That's what you were reading, right?"

Cherry's face fell as she sat back on her legs. "Can't a girl make out with her girlfriend without having to give a book report?"

Sloan pushed up to her elbows. "Yes, but I need to brush my teeth before we can have a proper make-out anyway, so you might as well just tell me."

"You're lucky you're cute."

"That's what they all say."

Cherry jumped up and darted to the desk. Before Sloan could even react, Cherry had thrown herself back on the bed, book in hand, with Sloan's legs trapped beneath her.

"Who's *they all*?" Cherry raised an eyebrow.

"You're the only one who matters," Sloan teased, which was met with a snort. "The book?" She held her hand out.

"It's weird." Cherry passed it over. "There are, like, these basic tenets. I'm trying to make sense of it. Basically, this guy Marco and his followers, they think mankind has caused an imbalance in not just the world but the whole universe. They want to bring on an extinction-level event to wipe out people so the earth can heal."

"Ha. You must have loved that part."

Cherry looked confused.

"You said stuff like that at camp. Remember? I'd be all 'Use a metal straw,' and you'd be all 'Why, when an asteroid will just wipe us all out when it gets to be time?'" Sloan almost laughed at the memory . . . until she saw Cherry's face.

"I wasn't trying to bring about the end of the world, Sloan."

Cherry's sharp change in mood, the bitter tone of her voice, gave Sloan whiplash.

"I know," she said, but a little voice inside her asked, *Do you really?* Sloan ignored it. "Sorry, where were we? Extinction-level event?"

Cherry sat still a moment longer, and then nodded. "Yeah, they wanted to reset things, and they thought they'd found a way. They believed there were these two soulmates they had to find, and they'd reunite to end the world." Cherry tapped her chin. "I suppose I've been on worse dates, honestly."

"Oh, now you have jokes."

"I've always had jokes." Cherry winked, her sour mood fading. "Unlike you, though, I know how to deploy them appropriately."

"Mm-hmm. So let me guess—Marco was one of the soulmates?"

"No, actually." Cherry flipped through the pages of the book. "It sounds like they were doing these rituals to find them. Each chapter is another ritual that seems to build on the ones before it. They thought they were getting close to bringing about The Great Reset, or whatever you want to call it. Marco was like this last bastion kind of thing, supposedly reincarnated from the old guard, here to set it all in motion."

"Creepy." Sloan flipped ahead a few pages and paused.

"Oh, don't read that one." Cherry tried to pull book away, but Sloan stopped her, running her fingers over the words.

The Culling, it read in fancy script at the top of the page.

Beneath that was an illustration. Animals attacking people, tearing them apart in the forest. There was a bear, a stag, a bobcat . . . but it was the last two that Sloan couldn't help but stare at: a rabbit and a fox. She counted the people in the picture. There were eight being eaten, the exact number of counselors that had been killed.

This wasn't an illustration; it was instructions.

Sloan set the book down. She stood up calmly. Walked to the bathroom.

And threw up.

"ARE YOU FEELING better?" Sloan's mother stood in the doorway with a steaming mug of tea. Sloan had just gotten out the shower, still raw and red from where she had tried to scrub the scent of blood out of her skin. It was no use on days like this; it always came back. Stuck to her. Tainted her.

"Of course," Sloan lied, because she knew it was the answer

everyone wanted. Or maybe not *everyone*, she realized, as Cherry frowned from her place at the desk.

"What's on the agenda today?" Mom took a sip from her mug. "I assume your friend will be going home soon?"

Sloan ignored the way her mother's eyes narrowed in annoyance whenever she looked at Cherry. It was frustrating, always, that the one thing that made her feel better was the one thing that pissed her mother off to no end.

"Yes, Allison," Cherry said, even though she knew that Sloan's mom preferred to be called Mrs. Thomas. "We'll be heading back to my house shortly."

"It's . . . a family bonding day," Allison said.

Sloan groaned. "Simon's at school. How would we have a family bonding day?"

"What about Connor? Didn't you guys have fun together? I didn't see him at the café today. Maybe he's off, and you two can—"

"Right, because he did such a good job of bringing her home in one piece last night?"

"Shush," Sloan said. She would fight her own battles on this front. "Connor isn't family either, so what's the difference?" She reached for her hairbrush and ran it through her wet hair with a glare. Her mom opened her mouth to speak, but Sloan knew it would just make everything worse. "What if I just make sure that I'm home by dinner again?" she offered, cutting off the inevitable rant.

"Fine." Her mother's eyebrows shot up. "But you'd better not be late."

"I won't. I'll go to Cherry's for a little while, but then I'll be back. Promise."

Her mom held the mug to her nose and took a deep, steadying breath. It was probably one of Beth's blends. Beth was always trying to get Sloan to take some herbal supplement or holistic healing crystal.

After two careful inhale-and-exhale combinations, her mother looked back up. "Yes, that works," she said slowly. "I'll have Dad make those flautas you love." And with that, she was gone.

The conversation had gone *much* better than Sloan had expected.

"You ready to go? We can add some of this to the collage." Cherry held up the book from Sasha. "I'll even type up the key points." She smiled like that was the most ridiculous thing ever, but Sloan nodded.

"I don't want to tear up the book, though. It could be useful or something."

Cherry frowned. "But it's already torn up."

"What?"

"Look—the whole back is ripped out. Sasha must have done it before she gave it to you."

Sloan took the book from Cherry's hands. She quickly flipped through it and discovered an entire chapter was missing. "It wasn't like that before."

"Yes, it was," Cherry said. She looked confused. "That's how it was last night when I took it out of Connor's car. If Sasha didn't do it, then maybe her brother did? Or for all we know, maybe Marco ripped it out himself. Maybe he got a ritual wrong," she teased. "I'm sure he corrected it in reprints."

Sloan knew that Cherry was trying to move them back into safer waters. Only, Sloan was sure the book hadn't been ripped last night. Maybe not even this morning. She would bet her life on it, if she had to. *Cherry did this,* her brain screamed at her. Cherry took something. She hid something. Or no, maybe it was already damaged, and somehow Sloan just hadn't noticed. She needed to get a grip.

"Sloan?"

Sloan startled, and the book slipped from her hand, falling open to The Culling. The Fox's hungry eyes stared up at them. Cherry kicked the book away and pulled Sloan into a hug.

"Don't look at that."

"I . . ."

"Are you sure you're doing okay?"

"Hmm?" Sloan asked, fully melted into the hug in spite of herself.

"The panic attack, getting sick—you're so jumpy." Cherry hesitated and then added with a little laugh, "Volunteering to be home for dinner?"

Sloan huffed a laugh into Cherry's hoodie and then pulled back. "Come on," she said. "Let's go. And grab the book. The last thing we need is my mom finding it."

Cherry leaned back, studying Sloan's face for a long second, a worried crease appearing between her eyebrows, and then she did as she was told.

EIGHTEEN

"THIS CAME FOR you," Magda said. She tossed an envelope onto Cherry's bed, where the girls were currently sticking tape onto articles for the collage. The wall was half filled already, and Cherry had only lived here for a few weeks.

The press coverage had expanded exponentially since the announcement of the Morte Hominus group and The Fox's plea deal, and it was taking most of the girls' time to keep up. Sloan thought she shouldn't be proud of their "collage of misery," as Cherry had started to call it, but she was. She liked the way the edges combined. The way things blurred together into abstract splashes of color and black and white if you relaxed your eyes. A Jackson Pollock of murder and disappointment.

"What is it?" Cherry nudged Sloan's knee. The envelope had practically landed on her, and she passed it to Cherry with an apologetic smile. She had been lost in her head again. She needed to get better about that.

"Kevin's celebration of life," Magda said softly. "It came the other day, but I forgot about it until just now." She wrapped her robe tighter around her. Magda was trying to do her best impression of a caring mother right now, rather than her usual manic pixie dream MILF.

Sometimes Sloan was glad she had a mom like Allison instead of a mom like Magda—until she realized if Cherry got an invitation to a celebration of life, Sloan probably did too. Allison must have hidden it. Or thrown it out, more likely.

Sloan leaned closer to read. It was in honor of Kevin's birthday tomorrow. She wondered what Magda meant by "the other day," and was suspicious it was probably more like "weeks ago."

Colleen, Kevin's wife, had been the most organized of all the grieving families. There was no way she had just sent this out now. Especially not to the girls she believed her husband died trying to save.

Kevin had been murdered as he ran out of his office. Sloan didn't remember that, of course, not with her brain, but she had Cherry's version of events, plus she'd read the autopsy reports of everyone involved—had begged the families for them and convinced them it would give her closure, much to her mother's concern—and knew where he had been found. One axe blow had severed his spine, and another had wedged in the base of his skull. He had been one of the last to die.

Sloan remembered his blank eyes staring at her while she hid under the boat. His warm, sticky blood sliding its way around her. The sound of his stupid Nirvana playlist droning on and on . . .

The reporters somehow got ahold of the autopsy reports too, even though they were supposed to be sealed as part of the ongoing investigation. Everyone has a price apparently, even the people in the Money Springs Sheriff's Department.

The press had a field day when they found out Kevin was one of the last to pass. One of the only adults on-site not even seeming to notice what was going on—hiding, potentially, doing something, their articles posited, to live longer than the others.

Kevin was nice, even if Sloan did hate his choice of music and even if he was always a little sweaty, with a haze of bug spray and cheap deodorant clinging to him wherever he went.

But he was more than that. He was kind, welcoming. Exactly what you would want a camp director to be. Whatever happened, whatever he did or didn't do? It wasn't his fault. The human survival instinct is among the most difficult things to kill. Maybe he had hidden, or maybe he just couldn't hear over the sound of Kurt Cobain's screeching through some random live version of "Come As You Are," but either way, Kevin was a good man. He deserved better.

It was bad enough to be part of a mass casualty event, Sloan argued, to be taken out by middle-aged white men with axes and animal masks. Kevin didn't deserve to be humiliated for it. To be called a coward. Or inept. To be mocked for his mortality.

They had to do something.

So, accordingly, Sloan had urged Cherry to help her with a plan. It would come from Cherry first, of course, because she was the only one of them with memories. The only true survivor.

Cherry had—for better or worse—left that night still intact. Her memories, her body, her soul, all in one piece. It was Sloan who was still scraping what little bit of herself that remained into a presentable pile; it was Sloan who begged at the altar of her mind for whatever drips of the past it would deign to bless her with.

When Cherry realized that Sloan was not going to give this up, she posted a lengthy statement in her Snap stories about heroes and the media's rush to judgment, which of course was screenshotted and reposted everywhere just as they'd hoped. Then both girls added matching pictures on Instagram—pictures of them and Kevin from the start of camp that first day, right after they had finished painting the boats—complete with long captions about what had really happened that night.

How the girls had been attacked and were hiding.

How the door wouldn't hold for much longer, the axe splintering the wood as they screamed helplessly, locked in a cabin with jammed windows and no other way out (a detail that Sloan had lifted straight from her worst nightmares).

How Kevin—brilliant, brave Kevin—had shouted at the attackers. Had led them away. Had tried to lead them as far away as he could, in hopes that some of the others would be able to escape. He had died a true hero, the girls said.

The media lapped it up, exactly as Sloan had expected they would. His wife, Colleen, sought them out after that. She thanked them for telling the truth, for sparing her husband's image. She had known all along, she said, that her husband would have fought brilliantly to save all the children.

Cherry had bristled at the term *children*, proclaiming she felt anything but childish after what she had lived through. But Sloan, feeling particularly small and vulnerable, had welcomed the title.

"Do you want to go to this?" Cherry asked, abruptly ending Sloan's reminiscing. "It's only a couple hours from here. I can drive if you want."

Sloan shrugged. "It would probably look bad if we didn't."

"Yeah, given how he 'saved' us and all." Cherry smirked. She was forever amused by the fact a lie could become true if you just got enough people to repeat it.

Sloan didn't mind this lie, really. What Sloan *did* mind, however, was how it had started blending into her own memories. How they re-formed around this new information, accepting it as fact, like new skin on an old wound.

It was the blurriness of it all that bothered her, even if Beth said that was a perfectly normal phenomenon.

"On that note," Magda said, "I'm going to lie down and try to get some sleep. I can't sleep at night when you're not home."

Neither girl bothered to point out that Magda couldn't sleep when Cherry *was* home either.

"You need to get some flowers, then," Sloan said as soon as Magda left.

"You want another masterpiece?"

"Yes, but festive this time. No calla lilies—it's a birthday party."

"Even if it's for a dead man?"

"Especially if it's for a dead man." Sloan sighed.

It had kind of become a thing during the seemingly endless parade of funerals that had haunted them in the early days. Cherry's floral masterpieces. Each one had grown bigger than the last. By the time they had gotten to the last few, the arrangements had turned into wreaths so large that both girls had to carry them in.

"You want to come with?" Cherry asked, her eyes almost giddy with the thought of an afternoon full of flowers.

"No way." Sloan laughed. She had learned her lesson when Cherry had dragged her to three different floral shops before their sixth funeral. It was Hannah's, and Cherry had wanted it to be perfect. Sloan had just wanted a nap and someone to take the itchy stitches out of her arm. "You go on and do that. I'll read through the rest of these clippings and then have my mom pick me up. She'll be ecstatic."

"Are you sure?" Cherry asked, suddenly looking very nervous about leaving Sloan alone.

"Of course." Sloan smiled. "Go. Have fun. Seriously!"

Cherry hesitated but then grinned, seemingly reassured, and leaned closer on the bed. She rested her forehead on Sloan's shoulder and breathed her in dramatically—like she was about to embark on a long and dangerous quest and wanted to memorize everything about her girlfriend before she did.

Why did everything always feel so weighted?

"I love you so fucking much," Cherry mumbled and pressed a kiss to Sloan's neck.

Sloan was tempted to say, "I know," just go full Han Solo on her, but Cherry needed the words today. She could tell.

"I love you too," Sloan said and leaned into her. "Now get out of here."

Cherry's mouth turned up in a smile. "Yes, ma'am." Another quick kiss and Cherry was gone.

Sloan went back to gathering up the clippings and photocopies and putting everything back in neat piles.

She had meant to stop there. She had. But then her foot snagged on the book they had hastily shoved under the bed once they had gotten to Cherry's house. The one they were both supposed to be taking a break from. The one Cherry had asked Sloan not to read without her, in case it triggered her again. Sloan had reluctantly agreed, but still she pulled it out and flipped through it, her eyes dancing across the drawings inside.

It wasn't technically reading, was it? If she just looked at the pictures. And besides, shouldn't she get to decide for herself what she was and wasn't ready for?

Sloan turned to the first picture. This one looked more like a fable than a ritual. An origin story for the evil that eventually killed her friends. The words THE BREAKING POINT were scrawled across the top in big bold letters, a looming city, biting into the edge of a forest, depicted beneath its title. There were all sorts of animals—bears, deer, rabbits, even dogs and cats—and all of them were dying. Choking on pollution, being hit by cars, being shot with guns.

It was a gruesome scene, their faces twisted in pain as the humans in the picture laughed and carried on. Even the trees were dead and gnarled, failed sentries against the onslaught of mankind. In the corner, on the very edge of the page, there was only darkness—so black and so thick the page had rippled beneath the weight of the ink.

Sloan took a deep breath as her eyes skimmed the page beside it. The words jumbled together, forming a rant about the "great unbalancing" and how humans had become a blight on the world. It made Sloan's head hurt, her heart too. She was not a blight; her friends were not a blight. The people who killed them were not maligned animals despite how they saw themselves. They were people, just like Sloan, but worse.

Because Sloan had never killed anyone, would never kill anyone.

She tried to take a break, absentmindedly flipping through the pages while trying to remember the grounding exercises that Beth had given her once. She stopped on a particularly worn page, the spine cracked either by Cherry or someone before her, a sentence underlined in the wall of text.

We will find the fated ones, the destined soulmates, who together form a single vessel to bring unto mankind its just dues and unto earth its rich rewards.

And then, on the next page, she found this, both starred and underlined: *Fear not; there will be comfort in the darkness, and the earth shall rejoice.*

Comfort? Rejoicing? It felt like a load of bullshit to Sloan. But she couldn't look away. She dug her toes into the carpet, bracing herself against the onslaught of pain in her head as she read page after page.

She studied each chapter, soaking up the knowledge of Morte Hominus and their beliefs as best she could. Parts of it were a testament to this Marco person: how he had found them, how they were the special chosen ones, how others had failed in the past, but this time would be different.

The book served as both an instruction manual to unleash the apocalypse and a diary of what the group had done. The parables at the beginning gave way to a series of rituals, each designed to bring the group closer to finding these soulmates, who had both supposedly been "marked at birth," and reuniting them. The cult, as Sloan thought of them, believed each soulmate could only contain half of the darkness, its power stripped and divided by strange, influential men intent on ruling the world, on ruining it for their own personal gain. Only Morte Hominus could restore the darkness, and only the darkness could restore the earth.

And at the front of the group, in every illustration, was the rabbit, always the rabbit, leading the flock.

Sloan ran her finger over the final drawing. The rabbit's head bent in prayer, its large ears resting in the grass, as the darkness washed across the page, emanating from two little girls—the fated soulmates, Sloan supposed—and she couldn't breathe. She couldn't breathe. She stared at the rabbit, and she couldn't breathe.

Sloan wished, as she shoved the book back under the bed, Sasha's since-forgotten photo fluttering out, that she had stuck to the plan. That she had done exactly what she had told Cherry she would. Review the clippings. Clean up the mess. Smooth the bed and head home. Maybe she would have walked part of the way to get some energy out—Beth said it was important for her healing that she move regularly. Or maybe she would have called her mom and waited patiently to be picked up.

Sloan wished she had done any of that. Because now, with the sound of Magda softly snoring upstairs, and Sasha's photo now firmly in her pocket, she found herself once again face-to-face with the closet at the bottom of the stairs.

It was sick.

She was sick, she chastised herself, to get stuck on this again.

She wished she'd never touched that box. Never seen the lid. But still, that nagging voice whispered in her ear, *If there's nothing in it, then what's the harm? And if there is? Oh, if there is!*

With her hands clenched, and the echoes of the drawings in her head, Sloan stared at the dingy brass doorknob. She knew this would likely be her only chance. Magda barely slept, and Cherry never left her alone. Wouldn't it really be best for everyone if she could finally put her suspicions to rest? If she could finally move on? If the rabbit in the book and the rabbit in the box were just similar strangers, with nothing to do with each other?

She could text Connor, and they could laugh about how off she was about everything.

Or not. She and Connor had gone back to silence between them. She imagined he was relieved about that. She would have been, she thought, if the roles were reversed.

Before she could change her mind, her fingers were on the handle. It gave way easily under the pressure of her palm. Almost too easily.

Sloan's first thought as the door swung open was that the box was gone. Fear clenched her stomach as she shoved things around, but no, no, it was still there, behind the coats and under a pile of plastic Marshalls bags now, but in the same spot.

Gingerly, Sloan moved the bags and coats out of the way and slid the box forward. She ran her hands over the soft cardboard and knelt in front of it. The truth would spill out the moment she opened the box, for better or worse. But she couldn't keep wondering. She couldn't keep suspecting. She had to know.

With a deep breath, Sloan pulled the cover off and peered inside, turning on the flashlight on her phone as she leaned forward. She picked up the rabbit, the rough wood scratching at her palm as she studied it from every angle. It was jagged, angular; it reminded her of her mother's horrible art deco phase, when everything in their house looked like it had stepped out of a cubist painting.

Sloan set the rabbit down and reached back into the box. She pulled out a small slab of pine next—the outline of several rabbits in a meadow carved into its rough surface. On the edge of the board, a wolf crept toward them. It was unfinished, just a hint of what it would become.

Sloan could relate; she was just as stalled out and full of dead promise as the half-finished wood in front of her. She wondered if this was what Cherry's dad had been working on when he passed.

She set the slab sculpture beside the rabbit and dug back into the box. Next came a stack of papers, mostly receipts and old, overdue bills. National Grid. Spectrum Cable. Nothing of use. Nothing good. Nothing that told her one way or the other if she was in the presence of The Rabbit or just her own overactive imagination. She supposed it wasn't outside the realm of possibility that she could be in the presence of both.

Finally, her fingers felt the familiar soft, slippery sensation of Polaroid pictures. Her heart was in her throat as she pulled them out, as she drew them closer, as the truth of the truth finally, *finally* came into view. She would see who it was. She would see—

The blare of a ringing phone sliced through the stillness of the house, and Sloan dropped the pictures in surprise. She had almost forgotten someone was home besides her, but Magda's ringtone— an awful beeping sound that made Sloan think of submarines and scanners for some reason—reminded her quick.

"Hello?" Magda said sleepily. The floor creaked as she climbed out of bed and started to pace.

If Sloan had been calmer, if she hadn't already been so keyed up that she couldn't think straight, she probably would have closed the box and shut the closet door. She would have walked to the kitchen and gotten a glass of water and texted her mom. And if Magda had come downstairs, Sloan would have acted surprised and said she was just waiting for her ride.

Which would have been true, technically.

But Sloan was not calmer. Sloan was a hare in a trap, stuck in the meadow of doom just like the rabbits hiding from the wolf in the carving. So instead, she scrambled forward into the closet and pulled the door closed behind her. She turned off the phone's light and wedged herself behind the old coats—the box clutched to her chest, the bunny sculpture in her hand, her breath coming in quiet, terrified pants—as Magda came down the stairs.

"You know you can't be calling me when I'm home," she said, stopping in front of the closed closet door.

Sloan held her breath, watching through the slats. If Magda opened it now, she would never be free. She would be, as Ronnie had loved to say back when he was still breathing, "totally fucked."

Magda threw her hand up in exasperation. "We've been over this. She can't be involved. And she's always got her little girlfriend over. It's like living in a commune, I swear to god."

Sloan brought her hand up to her mouth and willed herself to be quiet. As quiet as a mouse.

As quiet as a rabbit.

She clutched the rabbit in her hand, squeezed it so tight that the splinters bruised her palm. She would bleed, she thought, if she kept going, but it was fine. It was fine. She had bled for the rabbit before—what was one more time?

Sloan shifted forward, just a little, just enough to see through the gap in the doorframe. Magda walked into the kitchen and pulled open the fridge but then shut it again. She took a glass down from the cabinet, inspected it, and then promptly discarded it on the counter and went back to pacing. Magda was antsy, Sloan realized, nervous even.

"It's going to be up to her what she wants to do and how she wants to handle it." Magda snorted. "Seriously? You think I have that much control? I'm just along for the ride, baby; this is her circus."

Who was the "she" that Magda was talking about? Cherry?

Sloan's heart thrummed in her chest. She fought the urge to claw at her neck, her shirt, to get it off, to get space, to get air, to breathe deep.

"My daughter? No. Of course she's not involved. What kind of mother do you think I am?" Magda asked as she crossed back over to the stairs.

Sloan jerked back, silently cursing herself as the hangers rustled and smacked against one another. Thankfully, Magda seemed too preoccupied with her own conversation to notice the quiet commotion on the other side of the door.

"I don't know, Sash," Magda whined as she climbed back up the steps. "We'll have to figure this out. Everything else is going according to plan. We're on track. We just have to get all the pieces right where we want them, and then, bam, we're off to the races. I'd rather have it take a little longer if it means getting it right."

Magda's bedroom door clicked shut, her voice becoming an unintelligible muffle behind it. Sloan exhaled slowly and tried to steady herself. She couldn't make sense of what she'd heard, but she clung to one thing: *My daughter? No. Of course she's not involved.*

Cherry didn't know. Cherry was just as in the dark as Sloan was.

But Magda *did know.* She knew a lot. She'd said "Sash"—Sasha? Had the whole visit at the diner been a setup? Had Magda wanted them to have the book? Had she somehow torn the pages out herself?

Sloan set the box down in front of her and reached in deep to grab the first Polaroid she felt, shoving it into her hoodie beside the photo she got from Sasha without looking. She set the rabbit sculpture back in its place, its roughest parts tinged a fresh rusty red. Next came the lid, trapping whatever else remained in this Pandora's box.

Sloan leaned her ear against the closet door, listening closely for any signs that Magda had gotten up again or left her room.

Hearing none, she slowly crept out. Sloan made it all the way to the front door and, finding it locked, shoved the dead bolt roughly to the side. The sound echoed across the empty apartment, and she waited a beat before pulling on the door. It still didn't budge. She tried the lock again, not even caring about the noise this time, but still nothing. She was trapped, just like she was in her nightmares.

Sloan's heart stuttered in her chest. It felt like choking, like drowning, like being stabbed.

But there were no footsteps running down the stairs. No slammed doors or shouting. Magda hadn't heard her and Cherry was still buying flowers—if Sloan could just get the front door to unstick, she would be fine. She would be fine! She would be—

"Hello?" Magda's voice called down from her now-open door. "Is someone there? Cherry, you back?"

With one final yank, the door pulled open. Sloan held her breath as she slipped outside. She imagined Magda rushing down the stairs, the phone still in her hand. Would Sasha still be on the line? Would they kill her? Would they tell her what was on those missing pages?

No. Not today. Not now.

Sloan ran, and when she couldn't run another step . . .

She hid.

NINETEEN

SLOAN DIDN'T BREATHE again until she was back in her room with two locked doors between her and the outside world. At least she didn't think she did. How could she when all the air had drained right out of the entire universe at the sound of Magda on the phone?

Without wasting any time, Sloan pulled the wrinkled photographs out of her hoodie pocket and stared down at them. The picture she had stolen wasn't the same picture from move-in day; she knew it was a long shot. But this one, the one she'd grabbed instead? It was a nothing picture, less than nothing. Baby Cherry running free in a meadow on a sunny day. There was a man there, sure, but it was only the back of his head. Behind Cherry was another man, but he was out of focus and unable to be identified. Unless . . .

She slid it closer to the photograph she had gotten from Sasha. They were equally yellowed from age, both beat-up Polaroids—unlike the sticky five-by-sevens she was used to in Allison's old photo albums—but besides that, it was impossible to say if the back of what she assumed was Cherry's father's head matched the front of Marco's.

The man in the background wasn't The Fox; she could tell that definitively. People could dye their hair, she supposed, but they couldn't change their shoulders. The build was all wrong.

Still, Sloan felt like she knew these faces. And not from news reports or crime scene photos or mug shots. She knew them deeply, in her bones. There were connections here, somehow. She could feel it.

A knock on her door made her jump, and she quickly shoved the photographs under her mattress. She spun around to see Simon in her doorway, a grin pasted on his face. "It's flautas night!" he proclaimed.

Simon was missing his two front teeth, and it gave him a goofy, gangly look, like a puppy romping around the world without a care. There wasn't much of Sloan's past life that she still clung to, but her love for Simon was part of it.

"Whatcha doin'?" he asked when she didn't make any move to follow him downstairs. He took a few more steps into the room but paused before he got too close. She had snapped at him one too many times for him to trust her completely anymore.

"Reading," she lied.

"You don't even go to school," he said, like that was the only good reason to dive into a novel.

"You don't read nearly enough"—she snorted—"if you think school's the only time you can pick up a book."

He huffed. "I read tons. It's just boring."

"Then you're not reading the right books," she said, and this was easy, so easy. Talking to Simon like this was muscle memory. It left her brain free to fixate on the pictures beneath her mattress.

Simon took his time settling on a comeback. "You're weird," he said finally.

"Undoubtedly."

"Are you always gonna be weird?" he asked, his voice sounding more serious than Sloan expected.

"What?" He had her attention now. All of it.

"Dad says you're not right. That means weird, right? I don't care if you're weird or anything, but Dad does, and Mom won't stop crying. Can you just be regular again like you used to be? I'm sick of everybody being mad."

That was a hard question to answer, even though Sloan wished she could. Knew Simon needed her to. Desperately wanted her to.

She considered saying something like *some people stay weird, and that's okay* or *when a scary thing happens, it changes you* or even *get out, Simon*, but she knew he would be unsatisfied with the first two and would tell on her for the third.

In the end, she said nothing. She just reached out her hand and let her little brother pull her up from her bed, the smell of flautas and the soft beep of the oven timer drawing them downstairs into the comfort and mundanity of family dinner.

It was nice.

The Scrabble her mom insisted on playing. The poorly cooked excuse for Mexican that her father made (which she loved anyway). The low-stakes existence of a family enjoying their evening playing games around the dinner table.

She didn't even mind when she ended up with both the Z and the Q.

Later, when she was back in her room, even with the weight of the Polaroids hanging heavy beneath her head, she still felt calm. Peaceful in a way that she thought she had forgotten.

She tried to ignore the nagging feeling that it would all go to shit soon. That this peace was fleeting, impossible, hard to grasp, and easy to lose. That it wasn't meant for her. Not anymore.

The knocking on the glass of her bedroom window all but confirmed it. Sloan forced a smile as she unlocked the window and let Cherry shove it open.

"Hey," she said.

"Hey," Cherry said, worry evident on her features. "Your front door was locked, and the window too. Is everything okay?"

"Just my mom trying to keep out the riffraff," Sloan lied. She had locked the door herself, dead bolt and all. The window too.

Cherry crawled inside—a physical embodiment of Sloan's past coming to haunt her. Even if Sloan had played *qi* on a triple word score, even if she had shoveled rice into her mouth and laughed at her brother, even if she had texted Connor an apology that he hadn't bothered to answer yet.

"It's going to take a lot more than a dead bolt to keep me out," Cherry said and brushed some tree bark off her legs. Sloan remembered when that had been comforting instead of suffocating. When had that changed?

Was it with the box? Or before that? Sloan had wanted Cherry to move here, desperately, so it must have been after.

After, after, after—she was so fucking sick of the *after.*

"Are you okay?"

Sloan flashed her best smile. "Aren't I always?"

Cherry had a dubious look on her face that Sloan didn't want to think about.

"Have you been googling more?" Cherry asked.

"No," she replied honestly. "I've mostly been eating terrible-yet-delicious home-cooked meals and playing Scrabble with my mom and Simon."

"Wait." Cherry laughed and took in the sight of her. "Are you . . . are you in a good mood? That must be what's throwing me."

Sloan considered sending a pillow flying at Cherry's face but decided that was too hostile. Because yes, somehow, she was in a good mood. It was weird, and Cherry could tease her about it, but she didn't care. She just wished she could shake the feeling it was all pretend. Like she was cosplaying her old life.

"Do you think I'm weird now? Well, weirder than I was when we first met?" Sloan clarified. She grabbed two sets of pajamas out of the closet and tossed one to Cherry. It was clear the other girl planned to stay.

"It's hard to say," Cherry answered and took the time to consider it.

Sloan pulled off her shirt and sports bra and then slid her sleep tank over her head. A second later Cherry followed suit.

"I think we're both different than we were before. But I don't know about weirder. Why?"

"Simon." Sloan sighed and traded her ripped jeans for the soft fleece of her pajamas.

"Ah," Cherry said. "What do you think he was really asking?"

"He heard Dad say that I 'wasn't right,' which Simon kindly

174

interpreted as me being weird. And the thing is, I'm not right, am I?" Sloan swallowed hard. "I'm definitely not getting any better about dealing with this. Am I getting worse, though, you think?"

Cherry came up behind Sloan and wrapped her arms around her. "What does 'better' even mean?"

Not hiding in closets for one, Sloan thought. Not spending all day convincing and unconvincing herself that her girlfriend, or at least her girlfriend's family, was part of the cult that ruined her life. Not eavesdropping on a conversation that basically confirmed it.

But Sloan wasn't ready to admit any of that. So instead, she asked, "Do you think it's weird that we lived?"

"What do you mean?" Cherry tried to lace their fingers together, but Sloan stepped away.

She picked a random hoodie from the piles of them around her desk and tugged it over her head. She carefully pushed her thumbs through the thumbholes in her sleeves so that her scar, and the birthmark it sliced through, were hidden away.

"Sloan?" Cherry said, and the sound of her voice had Sloan turning back around with renewed determination.

"How did you live? How did I?" she asked.

"We've talked about this a hundred times. I went to your cabin while they were . . . busy . . . with the others. I got you out of there. You were panicking and hiding next to your bed. I dragged you away, we hid up a tree, you fell coming down, and that's how you got hurt. I remembered seeing in a movie once people hiding under overturned boats to escape a bad guy. So I hid you under the broken one by Kevin's office."

"But why don't I remember it?" Sloan growled.

"You were out of it. I don't know. If I held your hand and told you to run, you would run, but if I didn't say anything, you would just stand there. You were blank. It was terrifying. You huddled against me all night. I wrapped my shirt around your arm to make it stop bleeding. I tried to keep the blood off you."

"Tell me again how the police knew to come?" Sloan asked. She had asked it a thousand times before but still didn't believe the answer.

"Kevin must have called them before he . . ." Cherry lifted her chin. "Before he saved our lives leading the killers away."

"Don't do that," Sloan snapped.

"Don't do what?" Cherry asked, obviously upset.

"Don't mix me up! That isn't what happened. That's what we're pretending happened for his wife."

"Okay," Cherry said. "Okay. I left you under the boat. I'm not proud of it. But I did. I went back into the office, and I called them myself. When I came back, I realized I had left you in a pool of Kevin's . . ." She trailed off, eyeing Sloan warily. "What is this really about?"

I don't trust you. Your mom is one of them. You might be one—

"Nothing," Sloan said, swallowing the rest of her thoughts. "Were you talking to someone outside my cabin that night?"

"What? No! I was trying to be as quiet as possible because there were men in animal masks murdering all of us! Remember?"

"Are you sure? I thought I heard someone, you, maybe," Sloan said and tried to press herself back into the memory.

"You said you didn't remember that night, and now suddenly you're sure you heard someone? Are your memories coming back? Was this some kind of test? How did I do, Sloan? Did I pass?" Cherry's voice was hard, rough, and maybe also a little hurt. "Are you trying to catch me in a lie or something? Because you won't. That's what happened."

Yes. "No."

Cherry dropped onto the bed. "Do you remember more of that night?"

"Not really. Not any more than usual. I would tell you if I did. And it wasn't a test. I just—"

"Then what do you mean, you 'thought you heard me'?"

"It was just something that came up when I was in a session with Beth. It's nothing."

"It doesn't sound like nothing."

"I just want the truth. I want to know what happened." Sloan bit her lip. This wasn't supposed to be so hard, so confusing. What was right and wrong. What was real and not real. Where was the line, and why did it keep moving?

"That *is* what happened. Well, except for the Kevin thing, but that was your idea to begin with. And tomorrow is his 'celebration of life' or whatever. I don't think we should be talking shit about him right now, do you?"

"I think Kevin has a brain full of maggots and earthworms at this point and doesn't care if we talk shit about him or not."

"Fair enough," Cherry said slowly. "So when is your next appointment with Beth?"

"Why? Because you think I'm crazy?" Sloan snapped.

"No," Cherry said and held up her hands. "Dude, relax. If I was really worried about that, Beth is not the person I would be rushing you to. I was just asking because maybe next time you'll remember something more."

"I did remember more, though. I remember—"

"Something that really happened—not me talking when I was just trying to hide. You'll feel a lot better once you have your own *real* memories back." Cherry rolled her eyes. "Then maybe you won't doubt mine so much." She popped up from the bed and headed to the window.

"Wait, where are you going?" Fear prickled up Sloan's spine. If Magda was involved, she didn't want Cherry going back home.

"I'm not going to sit here and be called a liar."

"I didn't call you a liar."

Cherry paused her climb out the window long enough to shoot Sloan a glare. It was rare to see Cherry this mad, especially this mad at *her*, and it shook Sloan more than she expected. "You don't have to come out and say it. It was implied by everything else you said. If you don't believe me, then what are we even doing?"

"What does that mean?"

"I mean you've been acting so strange around me lately. It's gotten even worse since you talked to that Reddit woman."

"Sasha."

"I don't fucking care what her name is!" Cherry shouted. "You're supposed to be my safe place, and I'm supposed to be yours, and suddenly you're second-guessing everything. If you don't want me anymore, if your road trip with Connor has somehow spoiled you on our relationship, then fine. So be it. But you're not gonna drag me into your drama, and I'm not gonna fucking beg you to care."

"Drag you into my drama?!" Sloan shouted. "Mine? *You* dragged *me* into it when you pulled me out of my cabin and shoved me under a boat!"

"What would you have had me do? Leave you there?"

"Yes!" Sloan cried. She was tired. So tired of all of this. "Maybe I wasn't supposed to live. Do you ever think about that?"

"Jesus, Sloan." Cherry rushed back and grabbed her girlfriend's shoulders, her face, cradled her head, pulled her into a hug so tight Sloan felt like Cherry was trying to tuck her inside of herself and keep her there forever. Hot tears pressed into Sloan's skin, and for once they weren't her own. "Don't say things like that," Cherry whispered through shaky breaths. "I couldn't stand to be here without you. Don't . . . don't ever say anything like that again. You were supposed to live. You *are* supposed to."

Sloan's eyes widened at how pitiful Cherry sounded. Cherry wasn't the weak one. The one who needed comforting, the one who fell apart . . . was she? Sloan wriggled back to face her. She took in the sight of Cherry's puffy, red eyes, the snot she wiped at in embarrassment.

"Don't," Sloan said and tugged her back into a hug. "I'm sorry, okay? I'm sorry. I won't say that again. I promise."

"Don't think it, even. You can't even think it. Promise?"

"I'm not good at controlling what I think about these days, but I'll try." Sloan offered a weak smile.

Cherry looked away. "I couldn't take it, you know. I mean it. If you ever . . . You'd be killing me too."

"I'm not . . . I wouldn't," Sloan said. This was not how she expected this night to go. She had been happy. And then she'd been mad. And now all the anger and frustration and suspicion drained out of her at the sight of Cherry hiccupping through the force of her own tears. "I wouldn't do that to us. Never ever, ever."

"You swear?"

"I swear," Sloan said. "We survived, right? We can't blow it now."

Cherry nodded as if she was trying to convince herself. "Going back for you was the best thing I ever did."

Wait. "Back?" Sloan asked, confused. "What do you mean, *back*?"

Cherry looked away guiltily. "Nothing. Forget it. I just meant going to your cabin."

"Don't do that," Sloan said. "Don't hide things from me. Because if I find out on my own, if my memories come back and ours don't match, it will be so, so much worse. Please."

Cherry wiped her eyes with the palm of her hand. "I didn't want . . ." She shook her head. "I don't even know."

"What?" Urgency cracked Sloan's voice. "Whatever is going on, I can take it. Are you . . . Cherry, did you *know* them? Did your mom know them? Did they let you go? Is that what you meant by going back? You were safe?"

"What the fuck, Sloan?" Cherry gritted out.

Sloan gnawed on her lip. She had gone for it. She had asked the real questions, the hard ones. Except instead of an amazing, cathartic reveal, Cherry stared dumbfounded.

Sloan lifted her chin. "I need to know."

"You really have to ask that? Seriously?"

"I—"

"I knew this would come up. I even had the same thoughts about you a few times. But I just hoped by the time the idea crossed your mind, you would know me enough not to actually need to ask. Just like I never needed to ask you if you were involved. But I guess that didn't happen."

Sloan ran her hand through her hair. She didn't know what to say, or do, or think, or feel anymore.

"I'm too tired for this shit." Cherry leveled Sloan with a fresh glare, but this one had less bite.

Still, Sloan noticed, Cherry hadn't answered the question.

"If you *had* asked me, it probably would have hurt me too. And I'm sorry. I'm sorry! But I can't get it out of my head. It's been bothering me since . . ."

"Since when?" Cherry asked.

"Since the box," Sloan mumbled.

"Fuck me," Cherry said. "We're on that again?"

"And then you said 'back' just now. You said you came back for me. What does that mean? Were you with them? Did you know them? Or maybe you didn't, but your mother or your father—"

"You're so fucking paranoid!" Cherry shouted. "I just need you to be okay. I *need* you here with me, but lately it feels like you're slipping farther and farther away every single day. I don't know what is going on in your head, but it's not good. It's not. Maybe you do need to see someone, someone who's actually trained in this sort of thing."

"But you said . . ." Sloan trailed off, more confused by the second.

"I said I came back for you *because I did*. I don't like thinking about it, okay? And it's my memory, not yours! There's nothing to match up, because it happened before I got to you. Jesus, you expect me to rip myself open for you whenever you need it, but I'm a person too, you know. This is my story too." Cherry shook her head. "Fine. You want the truth? I was already outside when I heard the first scream. I left my cabin to sneak into yours when I heard Anise crying and Shane screaming. I came around the corner—it was dark, and no one could see me, but I saw what those men were doing to them. I watched the blade go into Shane. Sweet, shy Shane. And I ran. I'm not proud of it, but I ran. I ran just like Kevin tried to, except I got away. I was safe in the woods; they never would have found me. I was gonna run all the way to that little gas station outside of camp and call for help. Maybe I should have. Maybe if I had, I could have saved some of the others . . . but I didn't care about them. I was sick over you. The thought of what would happen to you while I was gone. So I stopped. And I ran back as fast as I could. I crept behind the cabins until I got to yours. I found you and, well, you know the rest from there."

Sloan wiped at her eyes at the sincerity in Cherry's voice. Cherry had saved Sloan's life, and she repaid that by doubting her, gutting her. Forcing her to share something she was ashamed of, no matter how much she shouldn't be.

"You came back," Sloan said, stepping closer so the girls were face-to-face.

"Only for you. And I would come back a thousand more times. Even if it still meant everyone else died. Even if it meant I had to die. I will always, always come back for you."

Cherry wove her hand through Sloan's hair and pulled her closer, the taste of tears on their lips when they met. They kissed like the world was ending. Like it was the last breath of air before the asteroid hit, before the darkness came, before, before, before.

They kissed so hard, and so long, that Sloan almost forgot that Cherry had never answered her other question, her bigger question, her *were you involved?* question.

Much later, when the sheets were as tangled as their bodies, Sloan thought she already knew. It was deliberate. And it was fine.

They had lived in the end. Maybe they would live forever.

TWENTY

THE MORNING WAS awkward.

The girls tiptoed around each other, pretending last night's argument had never happened, as they got ready for Kevin's "celebration of life." Sloan wished Colleen had just called it what it was—a macabre birthday party for a dead guy.

She wondered, as she pulled on her socks, if Allison would have continued to celebrate Sloan's birthday. She could picture Simon marching forward with a creepy cake of doom, a fake smile pasted on his tiny face. Would there have been a slideshow? She thought there would probably have been a slideshow. She frowned, realizing that there would also probably be a slideshow at Kevin's memorial.

Sloan hated slideshows. Had gotten her fill of them eight times over.

Although she hated them slightly less for someone like Kevin, who at least had been grown when he died. The slideshows and retrospectives for the victims her age were depressing as hell. Baby pictures to toddler pictures to kid pictures to teen pictures to . . .

nothing. A wooden box on a stand. A shiny urn with a framed senior photo beside it.

Awful. All of it.

"Ready?" Cherry asked, her hair still wet from Sloan's shower. She smelled like Sloan's shampoo, and Sloan liked that. Even if Cherry was a maybe killer. Even if Magda was probably involved.

"Yeah," Sloan said. She grabbed her bag off her desk and slung it over her shoulder. She was wearing a dark dress, blue, not black. Black felt inappropriate for a birthday-funeral or whatever this was. The dress was muted, quiet, like she felt today. If Sloan's mood could materialize as an object, it would be this dull dress.

"I need to stop at home to grab the flowers, and I want to change my shoes."

Sloan glanced down at Cherry's feet. She had her Chucks on. On the carpet. Sloan's mom was going to kill her.

"Sounds good."

"Where are you off to so early?" Sloan's mom called as they reached the front door.

"Kevin's thing," Sloan said.

"Kevin," Allison said, as if she was trying to place the name. "Is that someone from school?"

"It's our dead camp counselor," Cherry said, in a more cheerful tone than was called for. "Remember?"

"How did you . . ." Allison started to ask but then stopped herself. Sloan suspected she was going to say *How did you find out about that?* Or maybe *How did you find the invitation wherever I hid it or threw it out?* Something along those lines. One look at Allison's face told Sloan that her mother had certainly been very instrumental in the invite *not* making it into her hands. "Well, have a good day, I guess," she said finally. "I'll pick you up from Cherry's later. Make sure you're back before your appointment with Beth. I'm driving you today. I need some refills on my homeopathic mixes."

Sloan rolled her eyes. The only thing worse than going to Beth's was going to Beth's with her mother lurking around trying to eavesdrop. But there wasn't any use in arguing. Sloan might technically be an adult, but she had no job, no money, and—while she'd once daydreamed about escaping her house to live with Cherry—no interest in potentially moving into The Rabbit Household after hearing Magda's call, even if her mother decided to cut her off.

"Don't roll your eyes at me," Allison said. "I'll pick you up at four."

"Sounds good," Sloan said for the second time that day.

Beside her, Cherry frowned.

THERE WERE MORE people at Kevin's celebration of life than Sloan expected. When they first stepped into the giant firehouse that Colleen had rented for the occasion, Sloan thought its size would be overkill. But now, as all the people started to flood in, she worried that maybe it wouldn't be big *enough*.

How many people did Kevin know? Sloan supposed there were plenty of lookie-loos here, people who had met him once or twice and now wanted to play a little role in the tragedy under the guise of paying their respects. "I knew him; I went to his celebration of life" probably won you bragging rights in certain social circles.

Then there were the local news reporters, but Sloan was careful to stay far, far away from them.

"Ginger ale," Cherry said and handed her a cup. Cherry had

been worrying over her all day. It was unsettling. In the car, during the nearly two-hour drive to this firehouse in the middle of nowhere, Cherry had been fidgety and restless and kept sneaking peeks at Sloan. When Sloan sneezed, Cherry had snatched a tissue out of the center console so fast the car swerved on the highway. There was a desperation to her care now, one that hadn't been there before.

And now this ginger ale that she hadn't even asked for.

Sloan remembered when she loved the doting, when it hadn't made her feel so claustrophobic. She guessed it was harder to appreciate when the person doing it might be the reason she was so fucked up to begin with.

Maybe.

Stop, she reminded herself. *Make peace with not knowing.*

"Thank you," Sloan said finally and sipped from her cup.

Colleen chose that moment to appear in front of them. The crowd parted around them in hushed whispers as the widow embraced first Cherry and then Sloan. The girls had survived because of Kevin, after all, at least everyone thought so. Colleen seemed to think this made her their de facto aunt. Or no, something closer, more personal than family blood. Sloan didn't think there was a word for it, for the way tragedy bonded people, but she thought there should be.

"Girls! Girls, I am so glad you made it," Colleen said, clutching both of their hands. "There are so many people here I don't even know. It's nice to see a familiar face. How are you holding up?"

"Fine," Sloan said automatically.

"It's been hard," Cherry said. Sloan smirked at that. Since when was Cherry the honest one?

"Of course, of course." Colleen patted their hands with a grim smile. "I'm just so glad you both are here." The way she said it, Sloan knew that she didn't just mean here, as in at the party. She meant here, as in on earth. She meant she was glad they hadn't shuffled off this mortal coil the way so many of their peers had. The way her husband had.

Sloan pulled Colleen into another hug, meeting Cherry's worried eyes and looking away quickly. She didn't know why she had done that exactly, but as the older woman dabbed her eyes and flashed them a watery smile, Sloan understood it was the right thing.

"Thank you for that, honey. It's been a day already. This morning, of all mornings, that ADA woman finally gets back to me to say that Edward Cunningham is refusing to see me. Can you believe that? Apparently, that invitation was only meant for 'the survivors,'" Colleen said bitterly. "I'm a survivor too! He killed me just as surely as he killed Kevin that day."

"What?" Sloan asked. She flicked her eyes back to Cherry, who was suddenly looking very guilty. "What invitation?"

"I'm sure it's for the best," Cherry piped up. "What else have you been up to, Colleen? The decorations are lovely. I'm sure Kevin would have adored them."

Lovely? Adored? Sloan looked at Cherry like she had two heads. This was not a subtle subject change. Cherry was getting sloppy.

"You wanted to see The Fox?" Sloan asked, because she would not be pushed out of this conversation. "Edward Cunningham, I mean?"

"Well, yes, dear. I need to forgive him like Jesus would want me to. It's hard to do that if he only wants to see the two of you. I know some of the other parents have the same concern. We need to tell him he's forgiven. We want to look him in the eye and let him know he can still be saved."

"You could write it in a letter," Cherry said. "I'm sure that would still count. But seriously, where did you get this ginger ale? Sloan is a bit of a fiend and—"

"Oh yeah, I get that. I am definitely looking forward to looking him in the eye." Sloan shot Cherry a glare. Sloan seemed to be the only one surprised by this revelation, which meant Cherry already knew. Cherry had been notified somehow that The Fox wanted to see them. As usual, Allison must not have passed that information on.

But then Cherry had kept it from her too.

"It will be so good for you. Healing, I'm sure. Will you give him one message for me?" Colleen grabbed both of Sloan's hands. "Will you tell him that I forgive him? Will you help him find Jesus's light, or at least ask him if he'd like me to come and read the good book with him? There are ladies from our church who have done that before at the women's jail there. They said it can be done. If there's ever a soul that needs saving, it's his."

Sloan pulled her attention back from Cherry and stared down at the woman's hands, shaky and raw, around Sloan's own pale fingers.

She wanted to scream.

She was so tired of people keeping things from her.

But she knew Colleen needed this. That Colleen was maybe the only true victim here. "Of course." Sloan smiled. "Of course I will." She pulled her hands back and clasped them in front of her. "If you'll excuse us, though, we have to get going. We just had a few moments, and I wanted to sneak in and give you that hug," Sloan lied. "We have a long drive ahead of us, and I have an appointment this afternoon."

"Oh, but we didn't even get to the cake! My cousin made the most wonderful cherry cake. And my niece even made a slideshow set to his favorite music; it's a Christian rock band! Kevin always loved his rock and roll."

Sloan was pretty sure Kevin's favorite band was Nirvana, but she wasn't about to rat him out for whatever double life he'd been leading with his playlists.

"That sounds wonderful, but we really must be going," she said instead. "Thank you so much for letting us be a part of this. I'll check in with you again soon, okay? You get back to your friends and family. Tell everyone I said hello." Sloan smiled again.

"Alright, dear, if you're sure." Colleen pulled them both into another group hug. Cherry's body was rigid against Sloan's. Leaving this early had not been part of the plan, and Sloan bet her girlfriend was already dreading whatever was going to come next.

Two Tupperware containers full of pizza and garlic bread, and at least five more hugs goodbye later, and the girls were finally back in Cherry's truck.

"Are you going to say something?" Cherry asked, after twenty minutes of silence.

Sloan huffed out a laugh. She had been saying quite a lot, she thought, with her crossed arms and her body angled as far away from Cherry as she could get it.

"You're scaring me," Cherry said, but Sloan just stared out the window, the betrayal burning up her veins until she couldn't take it another second.

"You knew," Sloan sneered. "What about *no secrets, no lies*? I could forgive you for the box, maybe, but not about this."

"What are you talking about?!"

"You lied. And don't say you didn't, because I saw your face when Colleen said The Fox wanted to see us. It wasn't shock; it was guilt. How long have you known?"

Cherry's jaw ticked, her eyes still fixed on the road as she talked. "Sheridan reached out to my mother. It was the day of the press conference. She wanted to let my mom know that the announcement was forthcoming, but also that Edward was requesting to meet with us."

"And you didn't think to mention this to me?"

"You should have gotten the same call. I assumed—"

"Stop lying! You knew my mother wouldn't tell me. You're so full of shit right now! Why did you cover it up? We could have seen him days ago!"

"That's why I didn't tell you!" Cherry said, her fingers white as she gripped the wheel tightly. "Because I knew you would want to go, and we are absolutely not going to sit down with that murderer."

"You don't get to decide that! I'm so sick of people thinking they can decide for me. I get a say too! I'm not made of glass. I lived through it the same as you did!"

"No, you didn't," Cherry spat.

"Fuck you."

"We have to stop kidding ourselves, Sloan. You are *not* okay. You're not. We might have both survived the attack, but you're not living. Not even a little. Last night you said I should have left you there to die, and now you're all guns blazing wanting to run back to the person who left you catatonic for days. I *do* get to decide. Your mother *does* get to decide. You are not well, Sloan. You're scaring me more and more every day. You actually accused me of being a part of Morte Hominus last night! You're not thinking straight!"

"Because of you. Because of you and your secrets! You're constantly keeping things from me. And I'm not just talking about the stuff in your closet. But also this! The Fox! Would you have even told me about Kevin's thing if I hadn't been there when Magda gave you the invite?"

"Stop calling him 'The Fox' like he's some magical movie villain or something! He's not. He's just a regular man in a creepy mask. We are not the babes in the wood. He is not a cunning fox. This is not a fucking fairy tale. His name is Edward Cunningham, and he lived in a goddamn van! He's forty-three years old and never had a job or a family or contributed to this world in any way, and I wish he'd fucking fry."

Sloan went very still. "How did you know that?"

"What?"

"How did you know that he never had a job or a family? I didn't tell you. It wasn't in any report, and it's sure as hell not on our wall."

"I'm tearing that fucking wall down as soon as we get home."

"How do you know those things?"

The truck went quiet, the only sounds the asphalt beneath the wheels and Sloan's heartbeat thrumming hard, so hard the whole world could hear it.

"I followed you, okay?"

"What?"

"I followed you and Connor to the diner. I used the Find My Friends app again. I noticed an emergency exit by the bathrooms, and there didn't seem to be an alarm, so I snuck in the back. You guys were already all talking. I sat in a booth a little behind and on the other side of you. You couldn't see through the frosted divider. Not that you would have noticed anyway; you were so wrapped up in what that woman was saying."

"You WHAT?!"

"I was worried about you! I knew you weren't going anywhere good or else you would have let me take you. How do you think I got to your house at almost the exact same time as you? I was a couple cars back the whole way home. It was killing me not to go get you at every red light—you were so upset on the phone—but I didn't want you to be mad at me. I waited at the end of your street for a minute when you got there—that was as long as I could stand—and then I rushed to your driveway. I couldn't see the book or pictures or anything obviously, but I heard what that woman told you. And I knew the second she said Marco was the rabbit you were thinking of my father."

"And then you took the pictures of him out of the box so I couldn't prove it?"

"What are you talking about?"

"I heard your mother on the phone with her."

"With who?"

"Sasha! Your mom was talking to Edward's sister. How are you two involved with all of this? Please. Will you just tell me what's going on?"

"Jesus, do you even hear yourself right now?"

"Your mom told Sasha that you weren't a part of it." Sloan shook her head. "You and your mom need to have a conversation, then. Maybe you're the one out of the loop, not me."

"You're not making any sense. When was my mom on the phone

with anyone? What pictures? I don't know what you're talking about!"

"I heard Magda on the phone with someone, and she called them Sash—like Sasha. You were buying flowers, and I was still at the house. She thought she was alone. I don't know if you're trying to cover for her or if you just don't know, but I'm positive about what I heard."

Cherry veered the truck into the next lane, narrowly avoiding missing the exit for their town. "My mom isn't involved at all, and she's certainly not talking to Edward Cunningham's sister. I don't know why you keep . . . Oh. Oh! Not Sasha. Stosh. You heard her say Stosh. It's her manager." Cherry glanced at her. "He's always trying to get me to do events and stuff with my mom—capture the youth demographic and all that. It's so gross," Cherry said bitterly. "But why didn't you just ask her who was on the phone? She would have told you. We can probably even call him if that would make you feel better."

"I'm not gonna tell your mother I was sneaking around eavesdropping on her!"

"You were what? Sloan, you have to get a grip. This isn't some slasher movie with a big plot twist. This is *real life*! We've been through hell, yeah, but now we need to come out the other side, whatever that looks like. I promise you didn't hear what you thought you heard."

Sloan wiped fresh tears away angrily. She knew what she heard. Didn't she? Didn't she?!

"Stosh, not Sasha," Cherry continued softly. "I swear. He's setting up some new collaborations with her and some burlesque shows or something. I try to tune it out because, ew, that's my mother." Cherry faked a shudder. "I'm not even going to ask you what you meant by 'sneaking around' and 'eavesdropping,' but I promise, my mom can't even stomach killing a bug. She's not going to be lining up to join a cult full of axe murderers. Sometimes a rabbit is just a rabbit, and a coincidence is just a coincidence."

Sloan wanted to believe her. Sloan wanted to believe her so bad. There was just one problem.

She didn't.

She couldn't. She was done trusting people. She was done with other people telling her what she knew or lived or heard. She was *DONE*. She would untangle this all herself if she had to. If that meant reliving that night in Camp Money Springs a thousand more times to do it, she would.

Because she needed to remember, and she needed to remember now, before this went any further. Before she lost a sense of who she was and who Cherry was, and reality as a whole.

But it wasn't just Beth who could help her unlock the answers. Or Cherry who could share memories. There was one other survivor.

Three people came out of the forest alive that night.

"I'm going," Sloan said and turned her gaze out the passenger window. "You can come or not, but I'm going."

"Sloan," Cherry said, "that's a terrible idea."

"You don't get it, and that's fine. But you won't stop me. Not you or my mother or anyone else. The Fox wants to see me, but I want to see him even more."

"Sloan—"

"Just drive, please."

TWENTY-ONE

"I'M GOING TO see The Fox," Sloan said. She hadn't intended for those to be the first words out of her mouth when she sat down across from Beth for her session after Allison left—her hands full of fresh homeopathic mixes—but they were, nonetheless.

"I wasn't aware that your mother had discussed this with you."

"She didn't, but it sounds like you and her sure did."

Beth had the good sense to look guilty for a second before catching herself. She pasted on her professional hypnotherapist smile and jotted something down in her notebook. Sloan resisted the urge to look. She suspected that if she did, she would see some variation of *oh shit oh shit oh shit* scribbled across the page.

"Do you make a habit of discussing personal information about your clients with other people even though they are legal adults, or, like, was that a onetime thing? Isn't that, like, a HIPAA violation or something?"

"I'm not technically a doctor, as you love to point out," Beth said. "And your mother was my client first."

"Sounds unethical," Sloan deadpanned.

"Probably is." Beth leaned back in her chair. "Are you going to report me? Or can we get on with it?"

"Get on with what?"

Beth folded her hands on top of her desk. "I'm assuming that the reason you came here wasn't to yell at me for allowing your mother to pick my brain about what was in your best interest. And if it was, I have disappointing news for you. Your mother is also my client. I didn't share any information about you or your mental state with her. I didn't betray your trust, and I didn't break HIPAA. I did, however, allow your mother to fully explore her feelings when she was notified that you would have the opportunity to speak with Edward Cunningham before his transfer to a federal penitentiary."

"And what were her feelings? Let me guess: to keep me locked away in my bedroom until the end of time."

Beth tapped her lips. "You came in here, guns blazing, about a supposed violation of your trust and privacy, and now you seem to expect me to violate your mother's trust and privacy. No. I don't speak to her about the things we discuss or the progress you are or aren't making. Just as I won't discuss with you the things that I talk about with your mother or her progress as my client. Now that we've reestablished that, shall we get on with it?"

"With hypnotizing?" Sloan asked. She had been knocked off-balance. She was prepared to be angry with Beth; she was prepared for Beth to apologize or maybe backtrack into a lie. She wasn't prepared for Beth's honesty or a session still being on the table.

"No, today I think we should explore your planned visit to Edward Cunningham, the man who slaughtered your friends and tried to do the same to you. What do you expect to get out of your visit? What's motivating you to go see him?"

Sloan scoffed. Beth should know this more than anyone. "I just want the truth."

"And you trust him to give it?"

"I don't trust anyone to give it at this point," Sloan said. "But I figure he has less to lose than anyone else I know, so why would he bother lying?"

"That's an interesting perspective."

"Well, he's already pled out. All his friends are dead . . ."

"Do you relate to him?"

"To The Fox?"

"To Edward Cunningham," Beth said. "You may refer to him as The Fox outside of here, but I would prefer if we could use grounding language during our sessions. Regardless of what you call that man, do you relate to him?"

"No, sorry, I'm not a masked psycho killer. Wait, is this supposed to be some metaphor? Like I'm locked in a cage of my memories while he's locked in jail? Come on, Beth, do better than that."

"We can get philosophical if that's how you relate to him, but I was thinking more along the lines of the fact that you're both the last of your kind. He's the last of Morte Hominus as far as anyone can tell, and you are the last of the counselors. It must be lonely."

"I'm not the last, though. I have Cherry."

"How is that going?"

Sloan lifted her chin and glared at the wall. She didn't like this line of questioning.

"You know, Sloan, it's completely normal for trauma bonds to weaken over time. Especially in cases like this where your mind is protecting itself from its own memories. Cherry became a shield for you, both in reality and in your thoughts and feelings. She protected you that night, and she's filled in the gaps of what you can't remember. It's only natural that—"

"If you believe her," Sloan interrupted.

"Pardon?"

"If you believe Cherry's version of events, then yes, she's the hero and the keeper of my memories apparently, since you can't get the door unlocked for me."

"It was never up to me to unlock the cabin door in your memories, Sloan. I'm here to facilitate the opening of the door, but you're the one who has to do it. But let's set that aside. Cherry—"

"Let's not. Put me under. I'm ready."

"That's not how this works. I won't perform a session when my patient is already highly stressed."

"So, what? I'm paying for you to sit here for an hour and pretend you're a shrink?"

"Technically, your mother is paying me. And we can do whatever you want for the next hour. You can run out that door right now if you want to, into the pickup truck that's waiting across the way. She's always waiting for you right outside that window, isn't she?"

"Cherry likes to stay close. She worries," Sloan said, but even as the words came out, she didn't fully believe them.

"Is that all?"

"What else would there be?" Sloan asked, chickening out. Because saying what she really thought about that truck always waiting, what she was most scared of: the idea that maybe Cherry wasn't worrying about her, really, but keeping tabs . . . Sloan couldn't.

Saying it out loud would make it feel real in a way she wasn't ready for.

"It seems like you're questioning your relationship. Would you say that's accurate? You're doubting her version of events, which is perfectly healthy, by the way. It's a normal progression while you're healing, and I'm hopeful that soon we can unlock those memories and you can see for yourself. But in the meantime—"

"In the meantime, I'm going to see The Fox, and you can tell my mother I said that." Sloan grabbed her jacket off the back of the couch and stood up. "If we can't do a session today, then I think we're done here." She tugged her jacket on as she walked to the door.

"Sloan," Beth said, in a tone that made her turn back around.

"Yeah?"

"Be careful with yourself."

Sloan waited a moment to see if Beth would say anything else, but she had already gone back to jotting notes in the file.

Be careful with yourself, Sloan thought as she walked out the door. She didn't even know what that meant anymore.

TWENTY-TWO

"I WANT TO go home," Sloan said the second she crawled across Cherry's lap and landed in the passenger seat.

"How did it go?"

"If you don't want to bring me home, I can just call my mom."

Cherry sighed and pulled out of her parking spot. "I didn't say I wouldn't take you home. I asked you how it went."

"Why? So you could tell me what I can and can't do and what I should and shouldn't know?"

"No, because I'm trying to be supportive. That's it. Fuck, Sloan, I don't know why you're so determined to make me the enemy all of a sudden. Did you talk to Beth about that?"

Maybe you are the enemy, Sloan thought, just before her brain flooded her with memories—happy, cozy memories of the two of them. If Cherry was the enemy, then maybe Sloan was too. But no, she couldn't think like that. She shouldn't.

Cherry dropped her hand, palm up, on the seat between them. In the past Sloan would have rushed to grab it, Cherry's hand a jolt of comfort in a painful world. But right now, it felt like an accusation. Sloan looked away.

"Is this it, then?" Cherry asked, moving her hand back to grip the steering wheel so tight that it had to have hurt. "You just woke up one day and decided to hate me for saving you? I know survivor's guilt is a bitch, but warping things to make me into the bad guy is a new low, even for people like us."

"I don't hate you for saving me."

"Then what is it? Because you used to be in love with me, didn't you? And today you won't even touch me. You look at me like I repulse you. If you need me to be the villain in your story, then I will, but I'm not going to apologize for doing everything I could to save you that night."

Sloan didn't know what to say to that. She didn't know what to say to any of this. Everything was so jumbled up and confusing. Their entire relationship had been a great and terrible thing, from the second their universes collided.

"Maybe this *should* be the end," Sloan said, and the words shocked her. She hadn't expected them to come out. She wasn't sure she even meant them. The gasp from the seat beside her made Sloan's heart thunder to take them back.

Cherry poked her tongue into the side of her cheek and stared ahead at the road. Sloan knew that look well. It was the same look she had whenever she was upset with her mother, the same as when Kevin had screamed at her for turning off his Nirvana playlist and replacing it with one of Sloan's to be sweet. It was the face of someone trying to swallow their words—and choking on every single one of them.

"Cherry," Sloan said, quiet, quiet, quiet.

"Don't."

"I—"

"Don't. Say. Another. Word." A tremble ran through Cherry's otherwise very still body. And oh. Oh. Sloan had done that. Sloan had hurt her. A lot. And in doing so, she had hurt herself even worse.

Why did everything feel so suddenly out of control?

"I don't actually want that," Sloan blurted out, even though Cherry raised her hand up in the unmistakable gesture of *please, shut up*. But Sloan wouldn't. She couldn't. "Pull over. Stop the car."

"Why? So you can jump out?" Cherry sneered. "We're almost to your house. Despite what you think, I'm not an asshole. Let me get you there safely, and I'll be out of your hair."

"Cherry—"

"Don't make me leave you on the side of the road," she said, her voice pathetic, a near whimper. Sloan had never heard anything like it. "Please, Sloan, I can't. I'm going to be worrying about you for the rest of my life, missing you too. Don't make me start yet. Just . . . give me a minute. Let me drive you home. *Please.*"

"Pull over, Cherry," Sloan said again. This time her voice sounded gentle. "You're shaking."

Cherry sighed and dropped her head before pulling into the very edge of a gas station parking lot. "I didn't have getting dumped at Sunoco on my bingo card for the day."

Sloan shifted to face her, but Cherry kept staring out the window, her eyes fixed on the bright yellow sign.

"Look at me," Sloan said softly, like Cherry was a scared animal about to bite. When Cherry still didn't move, Sloan decided to try another approach. "It's not like I can jump out anyway. Your truck sucks, and this door doesn't open."

"I knew there was a reason I didn't fix that." Cherry huffed out a breath that could almost have sounded like a laugh if it wasn't so sad.

"So you could kidnap unsuspecting girls?" Sloan teased, realizing too late how bad of a joke it was.

"Well, I am part of a killer cult, aren't I? Me and my mom. Probably my dad too, right?" She crossed her arms. "I'm sure you consider kidnapping just part of my job."

"I don't think you're—"

"Don't you? Or at least my mother? My dead fucking father?"

"I don't know. Everything is so mixed up."

"What do you feel, Sloan? Because it isn't love, right? You couldn't love someone like that."

Sloan rolled her eyes. "People fall in love with serial killers every day. Half of them are married, some more than once. It's not that."

Cherry looked at her in disbelief. "Do you even hear yourself right now?"

"That came out wrong," Sloan groaned. "I'm just saying me loving you isn't contingent on . . . I don't even know."

"Was that your really fucking demented way of saying there's still hope I'll find love even if I am a mass murderer? Jesus, Sloan."

"I don't know what I'm saying," Sloan said. "I just . . . I thought we were forever."

"We can be," Cherry said.

"No secrets, no lies. You said that from the beginning, and now suddenly it's like all we have are secrets and lies. You've been keeping things from me, like The Fox wanting to see us—sorry . . .

Edward. You know, *you* were the one who started calling him The Fox in the first place."

"That was before," Cherry said sadly.

"There was nothing before," Sloan said and crossed her arms. "There was just after. We've *always* just been after. I knew you for literal days at Money Springs. We had a couple great nights and *one* kiss before we were covered in blood. No matter how much we want to pretend we had some great love or something, we had *days*, Cherry. Days. If none of this had happened, who knows where we would have been when summer ended."

"But it did happen, and we're here now," Cherry said. "It doesn't matter if it would have been different."

"That's my point! You saved me. And you want me to be here, and you want me to *want* to be here, right? Then we have to start doing things my way. You can't decide what to keep from me and what I do and don't deserve to know. People have been doing that since I was four years old, and I'm so sick of it!"

"I'm not trying to be like that. I'm just trying to figure out what's best for you."

"It's not on you to figure that out. God. If it's not you, it's my mother. If it's not my mother, it's the adoption agency and my sealed records. I don't know what happened this summer. I don't know what happened fourteen years ago. I don't know what's happening now! Do you know what it's like to not know where you came from? All I know is that I have this birthmark." Sloan yanked up her sleeve and shoved it in Cherry's face. "And a fucking Polaroid of two strangers who . . ." Sloan trailed off, her eyebrows pinched together.

"Sloan?"

Sloan tilted her head, remembering being four and so scared and clutching the photograph. A woman—her birth mother—had pressed it into her hand with a whispered plea, "Remember who you are."

Then she was gone, and Sloan was left with a strange woman who smelled like the hospital but had a warm smile. "Your new mommy is waiting for you. Someday you'll see this is for the best."

Sloan had screamed. She'd clung to the Polaroid like a lifeline, a promise. They'd gotten off to a rocky start, and Allison insisting on being called "Mom" from day one didn't help. Sloan knew it wasn't always like that for other children. She had been to many child therapists and adoption support groups in her young life. So many other children loved their adoptive parents like their own from the start, or at least soon after. You didn't need to be blood to be family. But maybe their birth mothers hadn't begged for them to remember. Didn't haunt their dreams in little flashes.

She hadn't felt the tug of her birth parents in years. It had taken time, but she had settled into a routine with Allison and Brad. Had thought of them as her parents for more years than she hadn't, had instantly loved Simon as hard and as true as any blood brother. She thought she'd locked up that particular trauma, the loss of her birth family, in that little box up on her dresser . . .

But as Sloan sat there—Cherry still calling her name—she realized there might be another reason that the man in the photograph with Marco and The Fox looked familiar to her.

Maybe he was her father.

That could be why her birth parents had given her up. They were trying to protect her, but the cult had found her anyway. It made sense, in a weird way. Another puzzle piece was clicking into place, and her veins thrummed with excitement.

"Sloan! You're scaring me," Cherry said.

"Can you still give me a ride home?" Sloan asked as she snapped back into herself. She needed to see all three pictures side by side. She needed to see the truth.

"Are you okay? I thought . . . I thought you were gone again. Like you were that night. I've been—"

"I'm fine." Sloan smiled, and this time it wasn't forced; it was relieved.

"Sloan . . ."

"I'm fine. You're fine. *We're* fine," she said. "We can still be forever if you want. I just need to check something at home. I'm sorry I scared you. I was just trying to think things through."

"What did you remember? Was it about that night?"

"I'll tell you once I'm sure."

Cherry sighed and pointed her truck toward Sloan's house. "I feel like if I keep asking, you're going to shut me out again," Cherry said softly. "Don't shut me out, please."

"I'm not. I won't. I just, I got really mad that you didn't tell me about The Fox wanting to see us. I didn't handle it well. I was really caught off guard, and I'm sorry." Sloan was only half lying when she said that. She was getting closer to the truth; she could feel it. Even if she couldn't unlock all those memories in her head, Sloan could still figure it out from the outside.

It was just a matter of time.

"Can we . . ." Cherry trailed off as she pulled up in front of Sloan's house. It was a family night, as usual. Cherry wouldn't be allowed in, even if Sloan had wanted her to be. But tonight, Sloan didn't want her there.

She waited for Cherry to finish anyway, knowing she had pushed the other girl too hard today, too far. Sloan had been too angry and too loud and too confused, and if she didn't pull it together, then it was likely that people would start to worry more one way or the other. Cherry had been protecting her, after all.

Cherry shook her head and set her hand on the lever to pop the door open.

"Wait," Sloan said, her face softening. "What were you going to say?"

Cherry hopped down from the truck, making room for Sloan to come out. She didn't answer, so Sloan crawled forward. She flashed Cherry a soft, crooked smile when she got to the door. Their faces were level like this—Cherry standing outside the truck, Sloan still in it.

"What were you going to say, Cherry?"

"Nothing. It's stupid."

Sloan sighed and hopped out. She stood close, close, close. "There is nothing stupid about you, Cherry. I'm sorry I hurt you, and I'm sorry I lashed out. This is hard."

And you don't even know the half of it.

"I just want . . ." Cherry shook her head. "I just want to know if maybe tomorrow we could be normal. Even if we have to pretend for the day. Can we just have a normal day? Because I think I forgot what those feel like, and that scares the shit out of me."

"Last time I tried to do normal, I ended up with a massive panic attack and iced coffee everywhere."

Cherry flashed a small smile. "That's because you didn't have me."

Sloan huffed out a laugh. "So, what? You wanna go get ice cream and walk around town like everyone else?"

"Would it really be so bad?" Cherry asked, her eyes going glassy before she could look away. "Just one day, one, where we don't talk about what happened or think about what happened or wonder about—"

Sloan tipped forward on her toes. The height difference didn't make surprise kisses easy, but Cherry had her head hung low enough that Sloan found her target without any trouble at all.

"Yes," Sloan said when they broke for a breath. "We can be 'normal,' if that's what you need. We can get lunch and go for a walk and stop at Target."

"Target?"

"I don't know. Isn't that what people do?"

Cherry grinned. "It sounds utterly mundane."

"Downright boring even," Sloan agreed.

Cherry kissed her again.

"I can't wait," Sloan said, because she knew that was what Cherry needed to hear, and as much as she loved Cherry—because she still did somehow, even in this emotional hurricane—she needed this conversation to end even more.

The sooner she could get up those steps and into her house—into her room—the sooner she could compare those pictures.

TWENTY-THREE

SLOAN MANAGED TO dodge Simon's plea to play Scrabble and ignore her mom's disappointed sigh when she declined a request to help with dinner. And so she found herself alone in her room, rethinking the events of the day.

Sloan wasn't sure what to make of the conversation with Cherry—the argument, really. And she definitely didn't know what to think about its resolution either, if you could even call it that.

But if Cherry needed Sloan to smile and be normal, whatever that meant these days, then she would do it. Because if there was one thing Sloan had figured out for sure, it was that Cherry was not as strong as she thought. There was a sadness to her that Sloan had somehow missed, that Sloan had helped put there, probably, if she was being honest.

But none of that mattered right now.

Not as she flicked the lock on her door and then reached up to the top of her dresser to pull the small wooden box down. It was made of pine, because of course it was. Sloan almost laughed when she realized.

She set it down carefully in the center of her bed before dropping down to fish the two Polaroid pictures out from under her mattress. For a moment, she worried Allison had found them and gotten rid of them, but she soon felt their gentle poke against the pads of her fingers.

Sloan set them on the bed and gingerly climbed up next to them. She swallowed hard and reached for the box. The unstained pine pressed into the meat of her thighs when she finally unlatched its tiny gold clasp and pushed it open.

It was almost funny, Sloan thought, that this little five-by-eight box held the entirety of what she knew about her life before she'd been adopted. She had barely been conscious at that age. A little lump of meat who had even less control of her life than she did now.

Sloan reached in and pulled out a folded-up photocopy of a birth certificate. It was heavily redacted, nothing visible except her first name and date of birth. Even the town had been blacked out and removed. Connor had been the one to add it to the box when Sloan couldn't bring herself to put it away. Connor, who still hadn't texted her back and probably never would.

Allison didn't even know Sloan had it. That she had photocopied it once, when Allison had left the safe open and Sloan had walked into the office to grab a pencil. There it was, tucked away with her passport and her newly reissued social security card—the one that called her Sloan Thomas instead of whoever she had been before.

Next came a tiny beaded bracelet. Sloan had invented hundreds of stories about this particular item in the box. Had Sloan made it herself? Had her birth mother? Had they made it together? She had refused to take it off until her wrist grew too big. That was what prompted this special box in the first place—at a therapist's suggestion, of course.

Allison had intended for little Sloan to color it, had encouraged her, with new paints and markers, to make it into anything she wanted. A special place to keep special things, like the bracelet that was cutting off her circulation and the crumpled Polaroid she slept with every night in her tiny fist.

Sloan knew what Allison had really wanted. Allison had wanted them to be put away. To be done with "the before," the way she wanted Sloan to be done with "the before" now. *Forget your birth parents. I'm your mother,* Allison's eyes had always said. *Forget your trauma. You have me. Why aren't I enough? Why aren't I ever enough?*

(Sloan understood, in that moment, that perhaps Cherry and Allison were more alike than either of them realized.)

Little Sloan had picked up the paintbrush, right in front of Allison's eager eyes, and placed a large black circle on the top of the otherwise unfinished box. Because that's how she felt about her "before" even as a preschooler. It was nothing. It was a void. A flash of antiseptic. A promise of a new mommy. A whispered plea not to forget.

When Allison asked about the black dot, Sloan simply said it was her old mother. Allison was worried by that point. Sloan wasn't doing the appropriate things. She wasn't drawing stick figures and smiling and all the other stuff that perfect daughters did. She was painting voids and calling them Mommy, and that was good for no one, least of all Allison.

Sloan didn't realize how wrong she felt until Simon came along years later. He was an emergency placement that turned into a long-term foster, that turned into foster to adopt. Sloan loved him, she did, but a teeny-tiny part of her was jealous. He came to them at two days old. His birth mother hadn't even held him. She was too high, too confused. Couldn't deal with his screams as he writhed his way through withdrawals. Didn't want him to begin with and couldn't wait to see him go. Allison was the only mother he ever really knew, ever really had. His birth mother hadn't begged to be remembered; she couldn't wait to be forgotten.

It was a kindness. A blessing, if you wanted to get mystical about it.

Sloan set the bracelet aside. Downstairs, she heard Simon whining that no one wanted to play Scrabble. She could hear her mother banging pots on the stove, her father promising to play after dinner, which made Simon cry because that would take too long.

They were the sounds of the life she should have. The life she should be grateful to still have . . . and it never felt farther away.

Sloan looked down. There was only one item left in the box. It was facedown and crumpled. Other kids had lovies or taggies or blankies, but not Sloan. She had a faded yellow Polaroid that dug into her fist and left creases on both her heart and palm.

She picked the Polaroid up and set it in her lap facedown as she reached for the other two, lining them up in front of her. She studied each photo carefully, first the one she took from Cherry's, and then the one Sasha had given her. Then she stared down at the crumpled mess in her lap. She smoothed it flat as best she could, still without flipping it over.

Here it was, the moment of truth. Well, the first in what she hoped would be many moments of truth. Maybe *unraveling* was a better word for it, because god knows, now that she had tugged on the string, she wouldn't be able to stop until she tore it all apart.

Sloan flipped the Polaroid in her lap and set it down beside the others. She didn't dare look at them all, not yet, her eyes transfixed by the sight of her parents. Or what she had always assumed were her parents. She pressed gently, smoothing the crinkled plastic a bit more and rubbing her fingers over the heavily scratched-up surface.

She soaked up the image, letting the feelings of familiarity wash over her and dump their endorphins into her brain. It had been years since she last pulled this photograph out. Too many years.

Sloan knew some adoptees searched out their birth parents, and she had intended to, secretly, once she was eighteen. She had thought she could do it when she was away at college, privately, without having to worry about Allison or her feelings or Simon's prying eyes. That was the plan before.

It was just that . . . everything was wrong now. All her perfect plans had slid off track.

She took a deep breath and moved her eyes to the photo from Sasha. To Marco and The Fox and the mystery man. And then to the third photo, the one of Cherry playing in the yard, the back of Cherry's father, and the other man, blurry, his head thrown back as he laughed.

Back to her own picture. Then Sasha's again. And Cherry's.

Sloan's eyes rolled over and over them, her breathing panicked. They looked the same. All three of them. The same faded yellow. The same clothes.

The same people.

It was Sloan's father standing beside Marco and The Fox. Her father playing monkey in the middle with Cherry. They were the same person.

They. Were. The. Same.

Adrenaline surged through her, horror, elation, her body a confusing tangle of everything and nothing, the serpentine sensation giving way to butterflies giving way to a hurricane giving way to—oh god, she was going to be sick.

She ran to her door and yanked it open, nearly tripping over Simon on her way to the bathroom.

"Mom," he shouted as he ran back down the stairs. "Sloan pushed me!"

Good, she thought, *good, let him be mad.* Let him tattle. Let Allison yell at Sloan and tell her to stay in her room. Let her spend eternity curled up around those three Polaroid pictures that contained something so beautiful and perfect.

Let everything melt away.

Everything but them.

TWENTY-FOUR

UNFORTUNATELY, ALLISON DIDN'T ground Sloan for supposedly pushing Simon. She sentenced her to more family time instead. Which meant it took two rounds of Scrabble and helping with the chicken pot pie before she could escape back to her room and to her pictures.

It was all so regular, so boring, that after placing T-H-E on the Scrabble board for the second time in one night, Sloan had started to doubt herself. Was her mind running away with her again? Was she concocting a fantasy, one where her birth parents were wild and powerful, if she believed what was in Edward's book? People determined to help the world, to restore it, in a way that Sloan's metal straws and dedicated recycling bin never could.

Once she got back to her room, safely locked inside again—her parents and Simon satisfied that she wasn't losing her mind, that she was, in fact, fine—Sloan could see she wasn't.

The proof was in the pudding, as her grandma used to always say. Well, in this case, the proof was in the pictures.

As she woke the next morning, her alarm blaring that it was

time for her "normal day" with Cherry to start, she was even more sure of it.

She knew it to be true, just like she knew no one would believe her. Sloan needed confirmation, and there was only one man who could positively give it to her. That man was sitting in a jail, hours away, just a few miles from Camp Money Springs, waiting for his transfer.

And he wanted to see her. He could confirm everything that Sloan already knew.

Because it was all coming together.

Beth was wrong.

There was a reason all of this happened.

Sloan had worked it all out during the night, jotting little notes to herself on a piece of paper she later stashed in the tiny pine box along with the three pictures. No one would ever look there.

She wished she could tell Cherry how it all made sense now. How it wasn't a random attack; they had been looking for her. Maybe Cherry was telling the truth and she didn't know anything, but Magda definitely did. Stosh, her ass. Sloan knew what she heard. If Magda was involved, that meant Morte Hominus *wasn't* completely dissolved after all. Which meant maybe her parents were still—

"Hey, your mom let me in," Cherry said, knocking on Sloan's open door. "You ready?"

Sloan checked her reflection. She took care to wipe the guilty expression off her face as she turned to greet her girlfriend. "Can't wait!"

Sloan smiled.

She would pull off "normal" if it killed her.

How fast can you die of exposure in semi-moderate temps? Sloan wondered as she licked her ice cream cone on a sticky bench outside the shop. It was cold out, way too cold for this, and she wished she had thought to wear gloves on her aching fingers.

Even if the ice cream *was* pumpkin spice, that didn't make it cozy. It was, in fact, the opposite of cozy. Cozy implied warmth. Sloan supposed the name of the shop itself, Cozy Creamery, was a misnomer of epic proportions.

Beside her, Cherry wrinkled her nose. "Brain freeze," she said around a massive mouthful of hot cocoa–flavored ice cream. "Oh god, oh god."

Sloan smiled. Despite the cold, the sun was catching Cherry's hair just right, lighting it up like a halo. She was beautiful.

Sloan had always known this, had felt it deep down in the warmest parts of her from the moment their eyes first met, but this was different. There was a lightness to Cherry that hadn't been there in a really long time. Sloan assumed it probably had to do with today's embargo on talking about The Fox and everything that they'd been through.

It was killing Sloan not to tell Cherry what she had puzzled out, not to show her the photographs, not to poke at all her weak spots, hoping for a confession or at least a hint that Sloan was on the right trail.

If Sloan's birth parents had been friends with Magda—if their parents had all been a part of Morte Hominus—then Sloan thought maybe her relationship with Cherry was more than just trauma bonding or two queer girls who couldn't let go of a summer fling.

Maybe their bodies remembered each other, their souls—a shared childhood, at least a sliver of one, a time when it was safe and warm and content.

"I'm freezing my balls off," Cherry said, if not ruining the mood, then at least changing it a little. Sloan didn't bother pointing out that Cherry didn't have balls. Mainly because she shared that sentiment.

"What's next? Target?"

"Do you really want to go to Target?" Cherry asked doubtfully.

"No, but I figured we ought to. We could go buy paper towels or something. Isn't that what regular people do during their normal days?"

Cherry laughed, loud and real. It did things to Sloan. It had been a while since she'd heard it.

"I love your commitment to the cause." Cherry grinned. "But we don't have to go quite that far. We could do something more fun."

Sloan liked the gleam in Cherry's eye. "Oh yeah, like what?"

Cherry smirked and looked Sloan up and down in a way that made her stomach clench and go all warm. "We could go bowling," she said, once the blush had reached Sloan's neck.

Sloan miraculously resisted the urge to shove Cherry right off the sticky bench. She pinched her lips together instead and tried very hard not to smile or look disappointed. She wasn't going to let Cherry win this round, no matter what. "Bowling?"

"Yeah," Cherry said. Sloan thought she was trying to look thoughtful, but really it came off more like the teasing they both knew it was. "I'll even let you use bumpers."

"Bumpers," Sloan said dryly.

"Or," Cherry said, and leaned in closer, so close that Sloan could feel her breath, warm and smelling of chocolate, against her neck. "We could go back to my place and make out until my mom gets home from the studio?"

"The second thing. Definitely the second thing." Sloan laughed. Cherry grabbed her hand and pulled her up from the bench, their ice creams forgotten in the trash bin as they rushed to the truck. The lightness, the laughter, it felt good.

She wished it could last.

"YOU REDECORATED," SLOAN said as she pulled her shirt back on. Magda had loudly announced her presence a few minutes ago as if she had known the girls would need a warning before she came upstairs.

"I did," Cherry said and waited.

Sloan wasn't sure what to say next, but she could feel the tension bleeding into their otherwise perfect day.

Cherry had torn down the collage. In its place were fresh posters, still slightly curled at the edges from being shipped in cardboard tubes. There were no hints of what the girls had been through—no news stories or Reddit posts or carefully cut-out photographs. The Fox was nowhere to be seen, and neither were the headlines. If someone had met Cherry today and walked into her room, they would have never known that she was *the* Cherry, the one with her picture posted under *Survivors* on The Fox's Murderpedia page.

Sloan looked at the wall that used to hold their shared history and then back at Cherry. She wasn't sure what to do next. It was impossible to ignore the obvious change, the giant bellowing elephant in the room, but they were trying so hard to be someone else today, anyone else, and calling attention to the missing reports on the wall would surely shatter the illusion.

"I like your new posters," Sloan said finally.

Cherry visibly relaxed. "I thought you might be mad."

This was tricky. Because a little part of her was mad, or at least betrayed, but she couldn't go on saying that if she wanted the rest of the night to stay good.

"It's your room," she said. Sloan was proud of that one. It neither confirmed nor denied how she was feeling.

"So you are mad, then." Cherry frowned.

"Do you want to be normal, or do you want to talk about our feelings?"

"Isn't talking about our feelings normal? Shouldn't that be what we're doing?"

"Not about this." Sloan slid her legs back into her pants. She fussed with the button on the denim, feeling Cherry's eyes on her the whole time.

"Probably not," Cherry said.

"Are you hungry?" Sloan asked at the same time Cherry said, "Are you really going to go see him?"

Both girls sat in silence after that. Sloan didn't think either one of them had any idea what was going to come out of their mouths just now until it did. She wasn't hungry, wouldn't want to eat even if Cherry was starving. As for Cherry, she all but clamped her hand over her mouth. Maybe she didn't really want to know, after all.

"What are we doing?" Sloan asked after another beat of silence.

"What do you mean?" Cherry looked at her warily, as if this was going to be another fight, but that hadn't been what Sloan meant at all.

Sloan sat back on the bed and ran her finger gently over the small birthmark on Cherry's hip that matched her own. Cherry said it tickled but in a good way whenever Sloan touched it, so she tried to touch it a lot. "Do you want to continue to pretend we're more boring versions of who we used to be, or do you want to talk about who we are now? I'm good either way. I just want you to be too."

"Why do you have to go there? Why do you have to see him?" Cherry asked, her voice a thin whine.

Sloan would be lying if she said she hadn't expected this to come up. She had. She had prepared for it even, the small pine box resting snugly at the bottom of her backpack just in case. The box had waited, watched, while they ate ice cream, while they consumed each other, and now it called to Sloan, urging her to show it to Cherry, its patience worn as thin as its tiny gold clasp.

"Are you sure you want to talk about this?" Sloan asked.

"Is there anything I can do to change your mind?"

Sloan shook her head.

"Fine. Fuck, at least let me drive you."

"What?" This caught Sloan entirely off guard.

"I want to be the one to take you. I thought about it last night. Allison would make it worse, and it doesn't seem like you've been talking to Connor at all since . . . you know, so I'm not sure if he would even be an option. I don't want you to drive yourself, because what if you're upset and can't drive safely home after talking to him?"

"I thought you didn't want to go."

The blankets pooled in Cherry's lap as she reached for her bra. "Oh, I am definitely not going in," she said. "But I know I'll lose it if you're in that town alone. If I can't talk you out of it, then I need to be there, even if I'm just outside being useless."

"You're not useless," Sloan said, her palm against Cherry's cheek. "Don't say that."

"I'm not strong enough to go in," Cherry said. "It's too much. Even the idea of being in the same town as him makes my skin crawl. I can't."

"We could do it together, though. We could."

Cherry shook her head. "There is nothing you can say to get me in that room with him. It'd fuck me up too much. It's probably going to fuck you up too, even if you won't admit it."

Sloan nodded, but she couldn't shake the niggling feeling in the back of her brain, the dark, vicious voice. The one that had helped her survive. *Is that the only reason?* it wondered. Or was Cherry worried about something else? Being recognized maybe? Or was she worried that The Fox would let something slip about how he knew her or had known her once? How her father was The Rabbit, even if she didn't know it. (Even if she did.)

"What?" Cherry asked, and Sloan realized she had been mumbling to herself.

"Nothing," she said. "I was just thinking it through. What it'll be like to sit face-to-face with him."

"Traumatizing," Cherry said. "Which is why I don't want you to go."

"I need to go," Sloan said.

"Why? Why put yourself through that? You talk about pretending to be who we were, but that's not what I was doing. I wasn't pretending to be someone I'm not. I was trying to figure out who I am *now*. I want to be someone with posters instead of news clippings. I want to be someone who eats ice cream and lives their life and is more than just a fucking survivor. Don't you?"

"Yeah, and I know the only way I can be that is if I get all the answers."

"What fucking answers?!" Cherry shouted as she struggled back into her hoodie. The hood rested gently on her head, creating a shadow over her face that made her look even more tired than before. "Why do you think he has any answers? He's a fucking psychopath who killed all of our friends and then tried to kill us! There is no deeper meaning here, even if his sister gave you some bullshit book that says otherwise. He's delusional. They all were. That's it! That's your big secret answer."

"Everything okay in here?" Magda popped her head in as she knocked on the doorframe.

Perfect timing, the darker part of Sloan thought. Just in time to make sure Cherry didn't blow their cover.

"Yes," Sloan said, at the same time that Cherry shouted, "No!"

Magda looked between the two girls and sighed. "I used to fight with your father like that, you know. He said we couldn't get so mad if we didn't love each other."

"What did you do?" Sloan asked. She wondered if maybe she could soothe Cherry the same way Magda had soothed The Rabbit years ago.

Magda laughed. "I gave him space. I let him carve his little animals and talk to everyone in the group, and then when we calmed down, we'd have the best make-up s—"

"Seriously?" Cherry shouted at her mother. "Stop there. Stop."

But Sloan couldn't focus on that. She was too hung up on what Magda had just said. Carving his little animals—she supposed that meant the rabbits—but talking to everyone *in the group*? What group? Morte Hominus?

Maybe it wasn't Cherry who needed to be monitored. Maybe it was Magda who was the true wild card. Sloan would have to talk to her later, as soon as she could get her alone.

"I'm sorry, Magda," Sloan said and put on her perfect parent smile. The one that always put them at ease and made them think that Sloan was a "good girl." The best girl. Perfect for their kids to date. "We'll keep it down, I promise. You're right—we couldn't get this mad if we didn't love each other. We need to remember that."

Cherry rolled her eyes in the corner, but Magda was beaming too hard to notice. She stepped into the room and kissed the air twice in Sloan's direction. "I knew you were good for my girl." She turned and headed back out. "I'll be downstairs if you need me. With the music on, very loud." She winked and closed the door. Cherry let out a groan that sounded like she wanted to disappear.

"So that happened." Sloan laughed.

"It sure did," Cherry grumbled.

Sloan didn't want to go back to fighting. She wanted things good between them. No matter what the truth was about Cherry or Magda, she knew she wanted to keep her girlfriend. Cherry was hers in a way that no one else could ever be. It was like they were two sides of the same coin.

"We could skip the fighting and just make out," she teased. "Er . . . make up. I totally meant make up."

Cherry rolled her eyes again, but this time there was no heat behind it. "You're infuriating," she said. She slithered down the bed and tugged Sloan with her. "I just want you to be safe. I want you to be happy. And I don't think that going to that jail and talking to that monster is going to get you closer to either one of those goals."

"Shhh," Sloan said. She pressed her finger to Cherry's mouth and then leaned in for a kiss.

Cherry kissed back, but it was slow and sad. Gone was all the urgency of before, when they were trying to have the perfect normal day. It was all ruined now, and Sloan couldn't shake the feeling that it was all her fault.

She would keep the pine box in her bag. She would wait to talk to Magda more. She would be better for Cherry, whatever that looked like, as much as she could.

But she needed the truth. Was willing to die finding it.

TWENTY-FIVE

SLOAN COULDN'T SLEEP.

She lay in bed beside Cherry and puzzled over what to do next. Cherry wanted happiness; she wanted fresh starts and smiles. Or at least that's what she *said* she wanted. It was hard to know what was true and what wasn't anymore, harder especially in the dark of the night.

The Fox would hopefully be able to clear that up for her soon. Sloan just had to hang on for a little while longer.

Sloan was still staring at the ceiling when she heard Magda head downstairs to the kitchen, followed by the telltale sounds of mugs scraping off shelves and beans being ground. Coffee was officially on.

It was barely 5:00 a.m., and Sloan still hadn't slept yet. Beside her, Cherry snuffled softly against her pillow. She looked so peaceful. Calm and content and warm.

She would have liked that side of Cherry, she thought, if she had gotten to know it for more than a week. Sloan wondered if she could dig that out of her girlfriend still, if it was there in Cherry, waiting . . . Cherry would probably leap at the chance to show her, if only Sloan would drop the rope with her investigation, her plans to meet The Fox.

Except Sloan needed answers in an all-consuming way. A way that Cherry didn't understand.

Sloan pulled the covers back gently and slid her legs out. She pulled on one of Cherry's hoodies—an old high school one with a tiger mascot roaring on the front—as she slipped through the apartment in search of Magda and, more importantly, coffee. With any luck, they would have a few hours alone before Cherry woke up. A few hours during which Sloan was hoping to interrogate— no, she couldn't think of it like that—*have a conversation with* Magda.

"You're up early." Magda was sitting at the kitchen table reading, a steaming coffee mug in her hand and one of her legs propped up on the seat beside her. It made for a welcoming, relaxed look, which Sloan didn't trust.

"Late, actually," Sloan answered. She filled a mug of her own and then took one of the empty chairs at the table.

"Nightmares?" Magda furrowed her brow. "Cherry thought they were getting better."

"No, they are, sort of, when she's there." Sloan shrugged. "I just couldn't sleep either way. I gave up trying a little while ago."

"Mmmm." Magda set down her mug, spilling some coffee in the process. Cloudy white rings appeared in the cheap varnish of the table—spreading even more as she tried and failed to soak it up with her sleeve. "Goddammit."

When Magda rushed to grab a towel off the counter, Sloan's eyes snagged on the book she had been reading.

At first, she thought it was a second copy of the book Sasha had given her, and a thrill rushed through her. Finally! Proof that Magda was involved. But when she looked closer, she realized it was the same one she had gotten from Sasha. Same pages torn out. Same bend in the exact same spot on the cover.

"Where did you get that?"

"Oh." Magda dropped the rag on the table like it was no big deal at all. "Cherry gave it to me."

"She *gave* it to you?"

Magda wiped a little harder. She would ruin the varnish permanently if she didn't stop, but she didn't seem to care. "Well . . ." Magda went quiet. She dropped her rag onto the table and sat back down. "You're going to tell her I was reading it, aren't you?"

"So she didn't give it to you, then?"

Magda sighed. "Cherry doesn't want me looking at this stuff anymore, but I found it in her room the other day and couldn't resist."

Sloan frowned. This didn't fit the narrative at all.

Magda was supposed to already know what was in the book. Magda was supposed to be a part of it. Magda and Sasha and Cherry and Sloan's own birth parents and god-knows-who-else. They'd been looking for her, all of them. They had to be. And then when they'd found her, they attacked. It made sense.

It was the only thing that made any sense.

So why did Magda look so upset and confused?

"She doesn't want you looking at it?" Sloan repeated, but the words came out like a question.

Magda rubbed her hands together and looked away. "I can get

carried away sometimes. I spent hours trying to figure out who these people were who tried to hurt my baby. It was bad."

"Define *bad*," Sloan said.

Magda pushed the rag farther away from her, a slight blush of embarrassment on her cheeks. "I got so wrapped up in what happened—what almost happened—that I stopped making content for a while. And when I went back to it, everything centered on it. My fans didn't like it as much. I started losing subscribers, which meant bills went unpaid, and the landlord threatened to evict us for back rent.

"As much as I'd love to say I moved here for you and Cherry and your puppy love, we would have been homeless if we'd stayed out there anyway. I promised Cherry when we left that I'd work on letting it go. And I mostly have," she said firmly, as if Sloan had accused her of lying. "I've been putting out tons of fresh, unrelated content for my fans so we could stay current on things. Cherry was pissed she had to put the electric bill in her name. That was a big wake-up call to get my life together. I've got another art installation coming up next month that should put us firmly in the black. I shouldn't have taken this book—I get it—but please don't tell Cherry. I don't want her worrying over me anymore."

"No," Sloan said, because none of this was right. None of it. Magda wasn't supposed to be trying to find answers like Sloan; she was supposed to *have them*.

Magda pulled Sloan's hands into her own. "You can't tell her, please."

"But you already knew," Sloan said. She couldn't help it. "What about the pictures? What about talking to Sasha on the phone? I heard you! I was in the closet when—"

"You were what?" Cherry's sleepy and confused voice scratched out.

Both of the women in the kitchen went ramrod straight and turned to look at her. Their conversation must have woken her up.

Cherry dropped her hand from the doorframe where she had been leaning and took a step toward them with a disappointed look.

"What are you talking about, hon?" Magda said as she tried and failed to hide the book beneath the damp rag. Cherry beat her to it and yanked it away.

"What is the matter with you two?" Cherry asked, but instead of sounding angry, she just sounded sad. "You're stealing my stuff now, Mom? And you're what, Sloan? Hiding and eavesdropping? Do you two even hear yourselves?"

Magda looked away, ashamed, but Sloan lifted her chin to meet Cherry's eyes. "I need answers."

"What. Answers?" Cherry seethed.

"I . . . I have pictures. Your dad might have been . . . I think your parents knew my parents. I think they were friends."

"I can definitely tell you that Magda and Allison were never friends."

"Not Allison. My birth parents."

Cherry looked confused. "I thought you didn't know your birth parents?"

"I didn't. I don't. But I have this picture, and it matches the other pictures. I think they're all from the same time. I don't care if it's you or Magda or The Fox, but somebody needs to tell me how this all fits together."

"Honey, I don't know any more than you do," Magda said.

"She thinks Dad was a part of Morte Hominus," Cherry snorted.

"Peter? My Peter?"

"Yep, she's decided he was a cult leader because she found a rabbit he carved when she was helping us move in. She thinks it has something to do with the masks those men wore."

Sloan clenched her jaw as Magda patted her hand. "Peter did love rabbits, but it had nothing to do with . . ." She waved her hands as if to say *all of this*.

"Tell her why, Mom," Cherry said, angrier than Sloan had ever heard her.

Magda's eyes went glassy. "I don't think—"

"Tell her why," Cherry gritted out. "She's like you. She's not going to give up until she knows it all. Just get it over with."

"Peter," Magda started and then stopped to take a few shaky breaths. "Peter and I met at a county fair when we were seventeen. He was there with a 4-H club. He raised these funny rabbits. They had some French name—I don't know. They were these pure-white things with the blackest eyes I'd ever seen. They looked like they had eyeliner on—it was ridiculous. Peter was changing some of the hay, and he was hot in this kind of sad farm boy way. And I mean smokin' hot. He—"

"Mom."

Magda smirked at Cherry. "Well, he was."

"Just stick to the story," Cherry said.

"Fine, fine." She took a sip of what was left of her coffee. "Anyway, I wanted to get his attention, so I made this awful joke and asked him how much My Chemical Romance he had to play to make his bunnies grow up looking like that. He said he didn't know who that was because he was more of a Tim McGraw kinda guy. I gave him my number and said, 'Why don't you give me a call sometime, and I'll play them for you.' And he did, and I did, and that was that."

Sloan narrowed her eyes. "And what? He just carved rabbits all the time because that's how you met?"

"Tell her the rest, Mom. Don't sugarcoat it. She obviously *needs* to know. Right, Sloan? Who cares if it hurts anyone else as long as you get your answers?"

Magda looked between the girls and then slumped back against her seat. "Cherry, I don't think this is a good idea."

"It's a great idea." Cherry crossed her arms.

"You don't have to—" Sloan started.

"Oh no, she does. She definitely does. Maybe once you have all the goddamn answers, you'll let it go."

"Okay, just . . . okay," Magda said as she futzed with the edge of the rag. "I'll tell her the good, bad, and ugly of it all—if you're sure?"

Cherry nodded.

"I fell for Cherry's dad and his nerdy little emo bunnies pretty quick." Magda laughed. "His parents hated me, but me and Peter loved each other too much to care. We started making all these plans, right? He was already accepted to college for environmental science—you know those rabbits were technically a threatened species? Wild. I was going to move with him and get a little place near his school . . . but I didn't have any money. He was still breeding bunnies, and he started selling some of his stock off here and there to save up. People would pay a couple hundred for them, you know. Even I started getting into it, made more than waitressing, honestly. But then just before we graduated . . ." Magda sighed and wiped beneath her eyes. "We found out we were having Cherry."

Sloan glanced at her girlfriend, who stood stiff-lipped beside the table. "It's okay, Magda. If you don't want—"

"No, it's not that. I . . . I haven't talked about Peter in a while. It's nice, in a weird way." Cherry rested her hand on her mother's shoulder, and Magda patted it. "His parents were, of course, furious when we decided to keep the baby. Peter was so excited even though it meant turning down college and getting a job. One of the other 4-H families had a little farm with an in-law apartment and said we could stay with them cheap if he kept helping the kids with their 4-H stuff. We could even bring the bunnies if we let the kids raise a couple and show them—it was almost too good to be true. Everything was working out, you know? We moved all our stuff in, set up the new hutches, and went to get our rabbits . . . but they were all gone."

Sloan leaned forward in her seat. "What happened?"

"They were dead. All of them. Peter's father was sitting on the porch, grinning away as I started crying. He said we must have left the pens open when we fed them that morning, and the dogs got in. But we didn't. He let them in. He probably sat on that porch smiling while those dogs tore our poor bunnies apart. There was just blood and . . ." She wiped at her eyes again and then sat up straighter. "I bawled the whole way home. I don't know if it was the pregnancy hormones or just seeing those beautiful things that meant so much to Peter be reduced to meat and fur. Peter felt like it was all his fault somehow that I was upset, even though it wasn't. He took me home and got me settled into bed and disappeared into the yard. He came back a while later with a chunk of pine and started carving away. By the next morning, I had my little rabbit, and I was done crying."

"That's what you found in the box, Sloan," Cherry said, her voice hard. "The rabbit he carved her that day. Now you know."

Magda smiled. "We took that little rabbit everywhere we moved. And after that, he carved me rabbits every time I got mad at him until he . . . until he died. It was too hard to look at them after that, so I gave some away, and I packed up the special ones, and that was that. Our whole marriage, just shoved in a box in the closet."

Sloan shook her head. "No, but I thought . . . There has to be more to it."

"Honey, there just isn't. Peter was a good man, a great husband, and an even better father, who just happened to love rabbits. It's not—"

"I don't . . ." Sloan swallowed hard. "I don't know."

"Sloan." Cherry looked at her sadly, the way one might look at an orphaned kitten or a bird with a broken wing. Is that what Sloan was to her now? Or worse, Sloan realized, is that what she'd always been? A broken bird. Something to pity. Something to save. Something that wasn't right.

"Don't look at me like that." Sloan slid her chair back. It nearly fell over as she rushed out of the room. She needed to get out of here. She needed to be away. Someplace quiet. Someplace where no one was looking at her or telling her stories that didn't make sense.

She nearly made it to the front door before she realized that she had left her bag upstairs. Her bag with the pine box. She couldn't leave that. Slowly, she turned and marched up the stairs. Cherry barked, "I'll deal with you later, Mom," before running up the stairs herself.

"Leave me alone," Sloan called. She couldn't, wouldn't, didn't want to face Cherry or her pitying eyes. But it was no use, Cherry was right behind her.

"What pictures?" Cherry asked as she cut in front of Sloan and blocked the door to the bedroom.

"Don't," Sloan said. "You don't believe me anyway."

"I want to."

Sloan looked up and searched for any signs Cherry was lying. She found none, but that didn't mean anything. Her girlfriend had always been impossible to read. "If you want to believe me, then why don't you?"

"Because it doesn't add up, Sloan. It doesn't. I would love for there to be a whole big conspiracy that made it all make sense, but there just isn't one."

"How can you be so sure?"

"I almost lost my life to these people." Cherry looked down. "Then I almost lost my mother to her obsession with them. And now I feel like I'm losing you the same way. Can you blame me for wanting it all to go away? Can't we just move on and be happy? I wanna crash in your dorm at NYU next year until your roommate hates me. I wanna travel around the world before the people in charge blow it all up. I want us to—"

"I need to go back before I can go forward, Cherry." Sloan looked away. "You lived through that night, but I only have stories from other people. You remember things before, during, and after that I can't even imagine. It's like I'm drifting through life now, ping-ponging from one second to the next. All I'm trying to do is find my footing and make it make sense. I'm not going to go to NYU like this because I can't. I can't start my life until I have my past back. If you don't understand that, then I don't know what to tell you. *I need this.*"

"Let me see the pictures. Maybe they'll make sense to me or spark something from my memories. I don't know. I'm willing to try if you want me to." Cherry reached for the bag and Sloan let it fall into her hand.

"In the pine box. At the bottom."

A bitter smirk formed on Cherry's lips. "Fitting."

"What?"

"A pine box? Like a coffin?"

A shiver ran through Sloan as Cherry pulled out the box and carried it over to the bed. She hadn't thought of that.

Cherry took a deep breath, locking her eyes quick with Sloan's before pulling it open. She winced as she did, like she thought something would come flying out and attack her. Just the truth, Sloan thought, just the undeniable truth.

Sloan reached inside to pull out the photographs. She laid the first one down in front of them.

"This one is from Sasha. This is The Fox. This man is The Rabbit—we know him as Marco, but I think that's a fake name. And this one . . . this could be my father." Sloan hovered her finger over each man in the first picture until Cherry nodded.

Sloan set the next picture down. This one would be harder to explain. "This one I found here."

Cherry's face pinched. "How did you *find* it?"

Sloan braced herself. If she wanted the truth, she had to be willing to give it right back. "The reason I overheard the conversation your mother had was because I was hiding in the closet."

"Wonderful," Cherry said, clearly annoyed. "Why were you hiding in our closet again?"

"I couldn't stop thinking about what Sasha said. About how Marco was The Rabbit. And your dad had all those rabbit carvings."

"Jesus, Sloan." Cherry ran her hand over her forehead.

"Look," Sloan said and pointed to Marco and the back of the man in the photograph with baby Cherry, her father. "Same shirt."

Cherry dropped her head back. "You can't be serious. It's a white business shirt with the sleeves rolled up. Half the men in the world probably own a shirt like that. You can't think that my father was Marco based on a white shirt and the back of his head. My mom told you about the rabbits! It has nothing to do with—"

"Look at the other man in the photo." Sloan pointed to the blurry man laughing in the background of Cherry's baby picture. "I think that's my dad again."

"What?!" Sloan yelled. "Where are you even getting that *anyone* in these pictures is your father? You don't even know your father! It was a closed adoption! You said it yourself!"

"Because of this." Sloan set down the final picture. The missing piece to all of Sloan's puzzles. "These are my parents. I came with this picture when I was adopted. I used to sleep with it."

"May I?" Cherry asked as if she sensed how important it was. Sloan nodded. Cherry held it up close to her face. "This is wild. I didn't know you had a picture of them. Maybe we can find them. My mom knows somebody who could probably help actually. That could be a great—"

"Do you get what this means, Cherry? I think my parents were in Morte Hominus, and I think yours were too. I know your mom says it's nothing, but everything else points to your dad being The Rabbit."

Cherry let out a heavy sigh, her eyes wide.

For a second, Sloan thought she had finally gotten through to her. But then that look was back. That pitying look, and Sloan's stomach flipped. "You don't believe me."

"Sloan, these pictures . . . I mean, the one from Sasha isn't bad, but the one from the box in the closet is blurry, and yours is so wrinkled and scratched. My dad isn't Marco. That's not him in Sasha's photo. His name was Peter. He didn't run a cult; he worked at a gas station, filling tanks and changing oil. You heard my mom—the rabbits were a 4-H thing. He was such a nerd, I promise. And that's not your dad throwing the ball with him. It's my uncle Jared. And that's definitely *not* Jared in the picture with Marco or the picture with your birth mother. I'm sorry. I wish it were true. I wish I could give you that kind of closure."

"Well, what about this? Don't you think it's weird they're all Polaroid pictures? I know phone cameras weren't really a thing back then, but most of my mom's old pictures are regular photos. They aren't self-developing Polaroid pictures! It would make sense, though, for Morte Hominus to do that. Anti-capitalist doomsday cults aren't exactly going to rush to invest in smartphones or expensive cameras. Not to mention the fact that they probably don't want outside people developing their film and potentially being able to identify them. Plus, it fits the whole retro hippie vibe they had going on. Think about it!"

"Oh my god, lots of people take Polaroid pictures! Your own brother has an Instax! Do you think he's in on it now too?" Cherry held up her hand. "Wait, do *not* answer that."

"I knew you wouldn't take this seriously."

"I'm trying to, but this isn't it!"

"Fine, say it is all one giant weird coincidence. Isn't it strange how close you and I got, like, right away? It was like we knew each other already. And I think we did. I really think we did!"

"Sloan, we didn't. We grew up on opposite sides of the—"

"I don't know where I was before I was adopted! I could have been anywhere. I could have been right next door to you. You told me you guys traveled a ton."

"For my mom's shows!"

"How can you be sure?! How do you know that the people you traveled with weren't—"

"Because I remember. I was there."

Sloan winced. Those words felt like a knife through the gut. *Cherry* remembered. *Cherry* was there. Something Sloan could never say.

"How nice for you. How nice that you can remember. How nice that you weren't ripped from the life you had and dropped into another one."

"Baby," Cherry said as her eyes welled with tears. "I know this is hard but—"

"Don't." Sloan picked up the pictures and shoved them back into the box, closing herself off as quickly as she closed the lid. It was fine. It was fine. It wasn't the first time she'd lost something she loved. Something she thought she couldn't live without.

"Sloan, please."

"You read the book, same as I did! You know that they believed there were soulmates chosen at birth. They were destined to find each other; they'd usher in the reset. You saw those rituals, at least the ones that weren't torn out. What if it's us?"

"Wait, now we're involved too? Everyone's just part of some big conspiracy?"

"What if it's not a conspiracy? What if it's a prophecy?"

"Holy shit, Sloan. I take it back. You don't sound like my mother; you sound like *them*. There is no prophecy! Come on, come lie down. You're not making any sense right now. Did you even sleep last night? You look like shit. You need to rest."

"What if it's us, Cherry?" Sloan said, louder. "What if we're the soulmates?"

"Are you . . . Do you honestly believe what was in that book?"

"No, but . . ." Sloan sighed. Because she didn't. *She didn't.* But she didn't know how else to explain it. "I get how they could think it was us. It's a lot of coincidences. We even have the matching marks."

"Matching marks?"

"It said in the book they'd be marked at birth." Sloan pushed up the sleeve of the hoodie and held out her wrist. "I have this one." She put her hand on Cherry's hip. It was almost as if she could feel it there, under her clothes. "And you have this one."

"Sloan. Let's be real. Yours looks like a cigarette burn. That's probably why you ended up in foster care in the first place. And mine's not a birthmark either! I fell off one of those pony rides when I was, like, five and tore my hip up on a rock."

"Maybe that's what you want to believe."

"It's what I know."

"No, Beth said that memories can be transient. If they told you that lie enough, your mind might build a memory around it. You don't know any more than I do who is in those pictures and how we got these marks. What if we were little together? What if we loved each other from day one? You'd be more than just my girlfriend. You would be family. My soulmate."

Cherry brushed some hair out of Sloan's eyes. "Baby—"

"Is being fated to find each other really that bad?"

Cherry pressed a gentle kiss to Sloan's forehead and pulled her close.

"No, Sloan," she said softly. "I would love that, but not like this. You're mine and I'm yours, but not because of some book or matching scars or stupid trauma. If we're fated or soulmates or whatever you want to call it, it's because I love you, and I want to keep loving you. It has *nothing* to do with anyone but us. It doesn't."

Tears ran hot and sticky down Sloan's face as she buried herself in Cherry's neck, confused. Overwhelmed.

"Do you hear me?" Cherry said, this time more firmly. "It doesn't."

Sloan nodded between shaky breaths. A thousand questions and doubts ran through her head, but Cherry was so sure. She sounded so sure.

"But—" Sloan said, not even bothering to lift her head.

"No buts. Anything that I need to know about us and our relationship, I already know." Cherry squeezed her tighter. "The next time you tell me that I belong to you, and I'm your soulmate, you better be fucking smiling, okay? We better be happy, and this whole thing better be behind us. We deserve that."

Sloan nodded, numb with a brain full of bees. Everything was so cold. She was so cold.

Cherry grabbed a heavy fleece blanket and walked her toward the bed. "C'mere. Let's pretend this was all just a bad dream."

A bad dream.

Sloan was used to those.

TWENTY-SIX

SLOAN WOKE WITH an ache in her chest that hadn't been there before and a sense of dread that hadn't left her for months. A dark, sick feeling lay thick on her tongue and bloomed down throughout her limbs.

She missed the numbness. The nothingness. She wished her brain would switch off again like it had that night; she wished for a break. She wished Cherry's arms, warm and heavy and wrapped around her, were enough.

She wished everything inside her didn't feel so weightless, like she was drifting through the world, through her body. A tiny atom surrounded by countless others, all rudderless and lost.

Cherry had been an anchor for her, a crutch, a lifeline, and now she had ruined it. She was sure she had.

Her outburst, her insistence that they were soulmates marked at birth, that they were part of The Great Reset, that everyone had been involved—a conspiracy leading all the way back to her adoption—it all felt thin in the light of day. Flimsy. A spiderweb tether that would break in the lightest of breezes.

And god knows Cherry was always more of a roaring thunderstorm.

Sloan sat up, stretched, and tried hard to swallow down the growing fear. Everything had made sense for a minute, and then it all got blown to bits.

"You're thinking too loud again," Cherry mumbled into her pillow and then pushed herself up to sitting. She eyed Sloan warily. "Are you . . . are you feeling any better?"

Sloan knew what the real question was: *Have you pulled yourself together? Have you figured out what's real or not? Have you gotten a grip?* Sloan rubbed at her eyes and looked back at Cherry. She wanted to find just the right words—something that would fix this or tear it all apart, she wasn't sure. But either way she couldn't find them.

Whatever Cherry saw on her face must have been enough, because she pulled Sloan into a tight hug, burying her nose in Sloan's hair and breathing in. "I just want us to be okay," she whispered.

Sloan nodded and leaned into the hug. The words *I love you* dripped from the tip of her tongue before she could catch them. Sloan wasn't sure if that mattered anymore, or if it ever had. It was probably wrong of her to even say them. But the way Cherry's whole body relaxed into hers was worth it.

She wanted Cherry to be happy, even if it was fleeting. Even if Sloan couldn't stay. Couldn't eat the ice cream on benches. Couldn't hold hands and walk down the street and smile.

Because the little part of Sloan that wasn't still trying to tape the ruins of her relationship back together was sure that she had found the truth.

Had found it in the book despite its torn-out pages.

Had found it in the blurry photographs, even if Cherry couldn't see it.

She needed to follow the thread, not let Cherry break it, no matter how much easier it would be to stay wrapped up in this bubble. No matter how much safer.

"I have to go," Sloan said. She pulled away from Cherry to check the time on her phone. "I have an appointment with Beth soon."

"I can drive you," she said. "We'll get coffee, and then later we can—"

"I'd rather walk." Sloan didn't miss the hopeful desperation in Cherry's voice. It hurt. It hurt deep in places that Sloan had forgotten she even had. In all the places that she thought had been killed that hot summer night, when the mosquitos lingered and the blood smelled like copper.

"You're not gonna let go of this, are you?" Cherry asked, resigned.

Sloan gingerly placed the pine box in her bag and slung it over her shoulder. "I need to follow this through as far as I can. And then whatever happens, happens. It'll be done. No matter what." She hoped it would be enough. She hoped this tenuous promise of "maybe" would be enough to hold Cherry over for the next two days.

She had Beth today, one last stab at getting the door unlocked in her mind. And it would be the last. She could feel it in her bones, that everything would be different once she talked to The Fox, once she heard his secrets, once it all came to light.

The way she had it worked out, it could go one of two ways. One, The Fox confessed all that he knew. It properly aligned with everything that Sloan had already discovered. Sloan and Cherry were fated in some weird cosmic way—not that they would finish what Morte Hominus started. She had no interest in any of that, didn't believed in the rituals. Just knowing she was right would be enough.

Or two, she would find out that everything she thought she knew, everything she thought she had discovered, was complete and utter bullshit. And then what would happen? Then she would go home and learn to love eating pumpkin spice ice cream on sticky benches and get on with things. She would come to terms with the idea that she wasn't special. That she was given up for adoption because her parents didn't want her or couldn't handle her or something. That she had survived a mass murder because of a random roll of the dice. That it could just as easily have been Anise or Rahul or Dahlia sitting here with Cherry. That realization made her stomach churn with jealous, possessive thoughts.

"What do you mean, *done*?" Cherry's voice pulled Sloan out of her head. She looked worried, and Sloan realized how that must have sounded.

"Not . . . not what you're thinking. I mean it'll be over. I'll either have the answers, or I'll have exhausted every lead. There won't be anything else to do."

"You sure you're not gonna find some other wild-goose chase to go on after all this? It can just be over? For real? We can move on?"

Sloan nodded. "Either way, it's over tomorrow."

"Promise? No matter what?" Cherry looked so sad, so pathetically sad, it made Sloan's heart twist.

"Yeah, there's nothing else left after this. We've hunted down every lead we had. If you're saying your mother isn't involved—"

"She isn't," Cherry said firmly.

"Then it's The Fox or bust. I hope you can understand why I have to do this, or at least accept it."

"Yeah, I get it. You don't know your history, and you don't remember that night, but instead of buying a 23andMe kit and laughing when your results come back part Neanderthal or Swedish or something, you decide to walk yourself right through hell as some kind of confused penance for surviving." Cherry stood up and shook her head. "Did I get that right?"

"I need to do this."

"I know," Cherry said and took Sloan's hand. "But I don't have to like it."

Sloan squeezed their fingers together with a sad smile before pulling back and shoving hers into her pocket. She felt the loss immediately, deep in her heart. But it was better this way. Ripping Cherry off like a Band-Aid, instead of slowly and painfully prying themselves apart.

Cherry was right; Sloan did need to walk through hell.

And it looked like she would be doing it alone.

"You seem very relaxed today," Beth said, her fingers steepled in front of her chest.

"Isn't that the goal?" Sloan asked. But she wasn't relaxed; she was resigned. This would be her last visit with Beth. She knew it as surely as she knew that the sun rose in the east, the world was round, and The Fox held the key to everything.

Sloan had considered skipping the appointment. It wasn't strictly necessary, but she wanted to go back one last time, into her memories, to see if she could get the door unlocked herself, if she would remember something that would help her at the jail tomorrow. A clue that would lead her to asking all the right questions and getting all the right answers.

"My goal is healing," Beth said. "In my experience, the process of making oneself whole again is very rarely relaxing. Would you like to talk about what changed?"

"No."

"Does it have something to do with your trip tomorrow to see Edward Cunningham?"

Sloan couldn't remember if she had told Beth when her trip to the jail was, but if it hadn't come from her, it probably came from Allison—who, by the way, was still worried sick and wringing her hands over the whole thing.

Sloan had stopped at home to shower and change her clothes before going, and she'd had to practically shut the door in Allison's face to get her to stop wailing about what a bad idea this visit would be. Sloan wasn't much surprised by the idea that her mother had most likely called ahead.

"I don't like to place my own expectations on my clients," Beth said, "but I anticipated your stress level being higher than usual today."

"What can I say?" Sloan asked. "I'm an anomaly. I'm just glad to be getting some closure."

"Closure?"

"Yeah, when I talk to The Fox—to *Edward* tomorrow."

"Perhaps it would be helpful to do some expectation setting," Beth said and wrote a note in her file.

"Look, we both know you aren't a real shrink, right?" Sloan leaned forward in her chair. "We don't have to do this whole, like, pseudo-therapy thing. I just wanted to go under one last time."

"One *last* time?" Damn, Sloan hadn't meant to say that part out loud.

"I don't know. One *more* time. I feel like we're getting close, and if I can get my memories back before tomorrow, that would be ideal."

"How would that help you, Sloan? You would be walking into an emotionally charged situation in a very vulnerable state. It isn't like flicking a switch; it's more like opening floodgates. It can be very traumatizing. That's why we do it here in a controlled environment where I can monitor you."

"Right, and here you are, and here I am. Monitor away. Let's go." She tried for a cheeky smile, but her voice sounded desperate even to her. This wasn't part of her plan, her quest for closure. Beth was supposed to help her. Beth was supposed to want to help.

"You understand that honesty is an integral part of our relationship, right? I can only help you if you want to be helped."

"I do want to be helped." Sloan crossed her arms against her chest.

"Are you sure about that, Sloan?" Beth asked. Her voice was even, gentle and calm as always, but an undercurrent of accusation was there. When Sloan didn't reply right away, Beth shook her head. "You know I'm required to report if I find you to be a danger to yourself or others."

"Oh my god, do you think I want— No. No! Sorry, I fully get that's probably what someone would say if they *did* want to, like, shuffle off this mortal coil, but I swear, I'm not thinking about it.

That's not even on my radar. Scout's honor." She held up her hand despite having never been a scout. "That's not what this is."

Beth arched an eyebrow. Sloan figured none of this was reassuring, but she didn't know how to convince her otherwise.

"Okay, expectation setting, then," Sloan said. "That's what you wanted to do, right?"

Beth looked apprehensive but nodded. "We could do that."

"Okay." Sloan wasn't sure where to begin. It wasn't like she could admit the truth about her hopes for tomorrow. Based on Cherry's reaction, it probably didn't sound the most logical. "Closure," she settled on finally. "Closure is all I'm after here."

"What does *closure* mean to you?"

Sloan paused to choose her words carefully. "I think I'll know when I see him."

"How so?"

"I feel like I've tried to understand everything I possibly could. I've tried to unlock my memories and research everything and learn about the cult and all these different things. And none of it led anywhere real, or if it did, it was just more confusing."

"And you're hoping that Edward Cunningham has the answers."

"Yes."

"And what if he doesn't?"

"Then I'm going to have to get a real shrink and move on from this, aren't I?"

Beth laughed. "Despite what you think, I can help with that too. We don't have to work on reprocessing your memories. I can help you heal in other ways."

"I would like that, I think," Sloan said and realized that she meant it. No matter what happened tomorrow, she would have to put it to rest, just like she had said to Cherry. "But . . ."

"But," Beth said with a small frown, "you want to do a session today anyway."

"I do. And I know you're worried, but this is the best place that I've been in since we started. I want to try one last time. I want to see if there's anything left to see, when I feel really ready to see it in a way I never have before."

"What changed for you?" Beth asked. "What put you in this positive headspace?"

Sloan shrugged and shook her head. "I'm just . . . I'm ready."

Beth took a deep breath. Her eyes searched Sloan's, and she nodded. Seemingly satisfied with whatever she saw there.

"There is a trigger we could try. I was hesitant before because you were . . . let's say, sensitive."

"Anything."

"We can use this." She held up her phone. The Nirvana album cover glared at Sloan from behind the glass screen. "You said this was playing while everything happened. Specifically, when you were hiding near Kevin's office. I can take you under, make sure you feel safe, and play this at a low volume. We'll see if it triggers something. I'll be beside you the whole time. You will be safe. I'll end the session if your distress levels become unmanageable."

"'Come As You Are,'" Sloan whispered.

"Hmm?"

"That's the track we heard when he . . ."

"I'm willing to let you see what happens if I play it when you get to the door. Only if you feel comfortable. Like I said, we don't have to do any of this today."

"No, it's a good idea. I can do it. I want to do it."

Beth nodded, but otherwise remained stoic. "Alright, Sloan. "Let's see what happens."

THE WOOD DUG hard into Sloan's knees. She opened her eyes slowly, the haze fading to crystal clear, leaving just the tiniest blur on the edges, just enough to let her know that this wasn't real. That this world didn't exist when she wasn't looking at it.

But this was new.

This wasn't where she had started before. This wasn't right. Sloan was supposed to start in the bathroom. Was this before the bathroom? She reached up and touched her face. Warmth and wetness coated her finger. Blood, no, tears, she realized when she pulled her hand away. This was after. After? Before? She was hiding, though. She must have heard the screams, she thought. That must have already happened. She tried to push up to standing, to move, to get the wood out of her knee. To find somewhere else. Safer. Darker. Not the middle of the floor. Not waiting for The Fox to find her.

The music started. The familiar thrum of the guitar opening.

And the screaming. So much screaming.

They were being murdered to dad rock. She remembered thinking that. The wood dug deeper into her knee, and she let it, waiting, waiting, waiting for her turn.

Her throat burned, and a hard hand clamped over her mouth. It was her own. It was her own screams she had been hearing, and now she was being dragged backward, and the wood was still digging, scraping against her skin. A flash of silver. A knife?

The splinters in her legs burrowed deeper as she struggled. She tried *to focus on them, let them ground her. But they were gone. The feeling was gone. Everything was blending and blurring around her. Her arm was bleeding, and the wood of the floor dug, dug, dug into her skin again. No, not the floor. A tree. There was a tree. The wood of a tree. The hand on her mouth was gone, and she fell.*

Her throat hurt. Her throat hurt. Cherry's face. The music. It was all spinning so fast. The cabin, the canoe, the tree, the knife, the blade, the skin, the skin, the skin, what was she forgetting about the skin?

"Sloan!" the voice was loud and hard, as loud as her scream.

And her throat burned. It burned so bad. Hands were clamped around her mouth, no, her face, as her unfocused eyes took in the spinning room. Gone was the cabin and the canoe and the pines. The pines. The pines!

In their place was a very, very worried-looking Beth. Beth was younger than Sloan had realized. Up close, without her glasses or her folded hands or the notes she wrote in her file. Sloan wondered how old Beth was exactly. She didn't even look thirty. Sloan wondered if they could have been in college at the same time in another life. If Beth had had a college degree on her wall and if Sloan hadn't postponed attending, that is.

"No more music." Beth leaned back. "We're not trying that again."

"I was getting somewhere." Sloan pushed herself up to sitting. "I saw things I hadn't seen before. My memories were coming back. They were just out of order, just little snips."

"That happens sometimes, but it can't be so out of control," Beth said and pushed up to stand. "The point of these sessions has always been to safely reprocess memories, not traumatize you all over again. I'm worried about you, Sloan, and I apologize for add-ing to your stress level."

"I'm fine," she insisted. "Let's go again."

"Absolutely not." Beth walked back to her desk. "You were right about one last time. Which we have now done. Your next appoint-ment will be a debrief of your visit with Mr. Cunningham, and then we move forward from there. Forward, Sloan. Not backward. We're done looking in the past for now. You need to be in a much more stable position. You misled me today, and it won't happen again."

"You can't cut me off like that."

"I'm not a drug dealer," Beth said, her voice hard. This was clearly not up for debate. "I've given you a substantial amount of leeway in this process. More than most. And I need to maintain my professional integrity. Frankly, I shouldn't have even brought you down today."

"Why not?"

"This isn't healthy for you. You're not trying to reprocess any memories; you're feeding off them. It's doing more harm than good right now. I know you want answers, but sometimes there is no good reason why things happen. We need to accept that."

"Let go and let god?" Sloan sneered.

"There are worse things." Beth shut the file. "I want you to take it easy tonight. I'd like you take it easy tomorrow too, but I know you won't. We made progress today in a way that I'm not comfort-able with. You got through it, but not safely. I'm worried that your visit tomorrow could trigger a resurgence of these memories and I won't be there to help you process them."

"But I want my memories back." Sloan raised her chin. "Any

way I can have them. I don't need you or anyone else to help me process them. If they come back tomorrow, all the better. I'll have all the puzzle pieces at least for once in my fucking life."

Beth's eyes narrowed. "Is there something else you'd like to share?"

"Not that we haven't already covered, *Doc*," she said, enjoying the frown that passed briefly over Beth's face.

"I'm not a doctor, Sloan, as you love to point out. I think perhaps you've outgrown your use for me."

"Are you firing me?" Sloan laughed. Of all the possible outcomes, this one was unexpected. "That's not very *live, laugh, love* of you, Beth."

"Of course not," Beth said. "But our sessions are changing from here on out, should you wish to continue. If you believe I may still be of service to you, I'm always a call or text away. But I think you need to evaluate what you want to get out of this, and what I can offer you, in light of my refusal to continue with sensory regression."

"Isn't that your job to figure out?"

"I can only bring you as far as we can safely go. After that, I may be doing more harm than good."

Sloan shook her head and grabbed her jacket off the hook. "Fine, bye. *Doc*."

"Sloan," Beth said, and Sloan paused in the hall, her hand still holding the door open. "Be careful tomorrow. Regardless of whether you decide to move forward with me long term, call me if you need me these next few days. I'll have my ringer on. Seeing Edward Cunningham again may prove very triggering for you. You don't have to go it alone."

Sloan nodded once and walked slowly out the front entrance as she had a hundred times before. Down the steps. Across the sidewalk.

She was about to cross the street when she realized Cherry's truck wasn't there.

For the first time, Cherry hadn't come.

TWENTY-SEVEN

AT 4:00 A.M., Sloan got up and paced.

She had managed to doze once or twice during the night, but only for a few minutes. She hadn't woken up with Cherry beside her like she had expected, just with a few half memories and the sensation of wood biting into her skin. The pine of the floor, the bark on the tree, the swinging sensation as she fell.

Chaos. Her head was chaos.

Plus, there was now the problem of a ride, she realized.

Cherry hadn't shown up after Sloan's appointment with Beth. She hadn't crawled through Sloan's window in the middle of the night. She hadn't done any of the things Sloan had expected her to do, which meant there was a strong possibility she wouldn't show up today either.

Sloan didn't need to leave for hours. A noon departure for a 4:00 p.m. appointment. It was a three-hour drive, but she wanted to be early, always early. And now she didn't have a way.

Maybe she would steal her mother's car. Or she could probably call a taxi. Her town was too small, and too far from any major city, to offer Ubers or Lyfts with any sort of regularity, and too stuck-up for a functional bus line.

Sloan would find a way, even if she had to run. She needed to know why the pine bit like a blade. Whether it was steel she remembered in her skin or slivers. She would run forever to find that out. She would.

Her mother left for work early, around six, refusing to even make eye contact with Sloan. She had taken to that lately, going to work early and staying late. Her father wasn't far behind Allison, always rushing Simon off to visit their grandma, or his friends, or for extra batting practice, but Sloan understood what they were really doing.

They were running. Running away from the monster in their house, the memory of what was lost. The shell of what remained. They ran from Sloan . . . and now Cherry was running too.

It was fine, Sloan thought, it was fine.

She opened her bedroom door and got ready for the day. She would have to find her sneakers.

SLOAN HADN'T EXPECTED to hear the familiar rumble of Cherry's truck when she stepped downstairs, about to call the phone number for the taxi service she had looked up earlier. As expected, her mother had ignored her repeated texts pleading with her to come home. Sloan had even considered texting Beth for half a second, before deciding she would just eat the cost. Simon's piggy bank was disturbingly full, even with Sloan running up a tab. She knew he wouldn't even notice.

But now her ride had arrived, right on time. Cherry hadn't run after all. Sloan bit her lip, determined not to cry.

Today was not about being emotional.

Today was about being fine. Getting answers. Being cold and detached and pretending this had happened to someone else. She was a reporter on a fact-finding mission, nothing more, nothing less. But now Cherry was here, the door to her truck held wide open, and Sloan felt *almost* like herself again. Almost human again, instead of a ball of questions covered in skin.

"You came." Sloan's voice was soft and breathless.

"I said I would," Cherry said, without even the barest hint of a smile in her voice. She was blank, neutral, and Sloan hated it.

Sloan wanted Cherry to kiss her or slap her, yell at her or hold her tight. Something. Anything would have been better than this.

"Thanks" is what Sloan settled on instead, and then she climbed over to the passenger side.

Today is not for emotions, she reminded herself.

Cherry didn't say anything. She took her place behind the wheel and sighed as they pulled slowly away from the curb. Sloan wondered if Cherry had hoped she would change her mind, tell Cherry that she had thought it over and didn't want to go to the jail anymore. Or maybe Cherry was hoping that Sloan would kiss her or kick her or a thousand other things. Anything to prove she was still in there.

Sloan dropped her hand onto the seat, palm up, and waited to see what Cherry would do. She left it there, stone still, for nearly ten minutes, staring out the window as the roads flew by, pretending it didn't hurt like hell. The empty space where Cherry's hand should've been was cold and cavernous.

And then, as suddenly as it wasn't there, it was. Warm skin, light pressure, followed by a squeeze and a shaky breath from the girl on the other side of the seat.

"It ends today, right?" Cherry asked, and Sloan turned her head to face her.

She studied Cherry's expression: the tense jaw clamped shut, the eyes locked on the road even though they were practically the only ones on it, the one-handed grip so tight around the wheel that her knuckles had gone white.

"It ends today," Sloan said.

Cherry nodded, just once, so slight it was almost imperceptible.

They sat in silence for most of the rest of the drive. Sloan would almost have forgotten that Cherry was even there were it not for the way the truck slowed, her grip on Sloan's hand tightening as they passed the locked and chained front gate of Camp Money Springs.

They had to drive past it to get to the jail, a fact Sloan hadn't realized, and icicles spiraled dizzily through her veins.

The camp looked deserted in a way that it hadn't ever, even on the first day of prep last summer. Bits of crime scene tape flapped in the wind, knotted around the pines, seemingly forgotten when the rest had been sliced away and tossed. The front gate was closed; a heavy padlock secured two large, crisscrossed chains, sealing it shut. It was probably meant to keep things out, but Sloan couldn't shake the feeling it was really keeping something in—the truth? Her memories from that night?

All of it?

Cherry accelerated, and the sight of the camp gave way to a

couple miles of pine trees and brush. They were deep in the forest now. The grip on Sloan's hand loosened and then pulled away, as if Cherry needed both hands on the wheel now, both hands to keep them pointed straight.

"You can still change your mind," Cherry said as they passed the gas station. They had gone there together once before when they were still at camp. Cherry had tried to use a fake ID to buy them some White Claws and had failed spectacularly. The fact the clerk still let her pay for her Red Vines and peanut butter cups spoke volumes about how nice the people in this town were.

"I won't," Sloan said. "We should get Red Vines on our way home," she added. Cherry smiled at that, just for a second, and Sloan wondered if she had remembered the same thing.

They kept driving, past the main street where they liked to get coffee, past the post office and the YMCA and the little car wash, until finally they reached the sheriff's station and the jail behind it.

It wasn't much to look at, Sloan thought as she stared at the gray building, at the fences, razor wire looped in giant circles over the top. It seemed so simple, so basic a container to hold someone who Sloan suspected might hold the key to her entire existence. It was almost disappointing.

Cherry seemed to be having the opposite reaction. She stared up at the big building in front of them with wide, scared eyes and a tremble in her hands.

"Are you coming in?" Sloan asked. "ADA Sheridan said you could wait in the officers' lounge. There's good Wi-Fi. She wouldn't make you sit in the regular waiting area where anybody could see."

"I can't," Cherry said, not *wouldn't* or *don't want to. Can't.*

Sloan put a hand on Cherry's arm and then reached over to pop the door handle. "It's okay."

She paused in Cherry's lap and waited for her to look up, and when she did, Sloan kissed her. Long and hard and sad. Like she would never have another chance. Like this was not only the end of a quest for answers, but the end of them too, fate be damned.

Cherry stopped first, her eyes squeezed shut, her fists at her sides, like it was taking all her willpower not to grab Sloan. Not to deepen the kiss. Not to hold Sloan against her, keep her trapped in her lap, in the truck, in the parking lot, anywhere but in the looming gray building with its razor-wire mouth.

Sloan pressed her forehead against Cherry's, but just for a moment. Then she pushed the door open wider and climbed out.

The air was crisp. Autumn had murdered summer completely, the warmth just a memory beneath Sloan's boots. She stepped back and took one last look at Cherry. She couldn't shut the door behind her, she couldn't. Cherry would have to do that on her own. Maybe before she drove away.

And Sloan was sure Cherry would drive away. That she would come out after this to an empty lot and an empty heart. There was no coming back from this, probably. Sloan could only hope getting a head full of answers would be worth it.

Before she could take another step, Cherry's hand wrapped around Sloan's wrist and tugged her back. Back against the truck, back against Cherry, who had gotten out after her. She pulled Sloan tight, tight, tight against her, like she could keep her there, absorb her, keep her safe inside. Sloan felt Cherry's heart, its strong, steady rhythm now replaced by a trilling beat of fear.

"Promise me," Cherry said, and she sounded like she was on the edge of tears. "Promise me we'll get the Red Vines."

Sloan stepped away, still holding Cherry's hands. She wanted Cherry to see her eyes. To be sure. To feel how sure Sloan was. "I promise," she said, and then she let go.

TWENTY-EIGHT

ASSISTANT DISTRICT ATTORNEY Colleen Sheridan was a tall Black woman with impeccable taste in pantsuits, who somehow managed to look serious even when she smiled. She stood waiting for Sloan just inside the doors, just as she had said she would on their call a few days ago. It felt like it was years ago now.

"Good afternoon, Sloan," she said. Curt. Efficient. Sloan appreciated it. She didn't want to be met with a hug or a pitying smile. She was done being the victim. She was going to get to the bottom of this, finally. And maybe move on. Maybe get herself some Red Vines after all.

"We're going to go through those metal detectors and down that hall. They'll buzz us in. You can leave your coat in the officers' lounge. Has Cherry decided not to come in?"

Sloan nodded as she stepped through the metal detector and followed Sheridan down the hall.

"I can sit beside you as you talk or be in the room in any capacity if you'd like, or I can give you some privacy. Everything has been signed, and he transfers tomorrow. My main job at this visit is as your advocate. I'm here to support you."

"I'd . . . I'd rather speak to him alone."

Sheridan nodded and waited politely for Sloan to set down her things. "If you're ready, it's right this way."

Sheridan led her to a large room with a cheap linoleum floor. It almost reminded her of her old high school's ugly cafeteria—if it wasn't for the row of phones along the glass partition, and all the bars behind that.

Sloan's side, the visitors' side, had several partitions and a row of hard plastic chairs, although one had been replaced by a comfortable-looking office chair. Sloan looked up at Sheridan, the question already forming on her lips, and Sheridan smiled.

"Chief Dunbar wanted you to be more comfortable," she said. "He brought in his own chair."

Sloan nodded in appreciation; it was nice of him.

Sheridan headed for the door as Sloan took her seat. "I will be right on the other side of this door if you need me, Sloan. You'll have as much privacy as possible. There will be a guard behind the glass with Mr. Cunningham, and there are video cameras in each corner. The visit will be recorded, as is standard. You may stay as long as you wish. There are no visiting hours today. This room is reserved for you for as long as you'd like. Do you have any questions?"

"No." Sloan scooted her chair closer to the glass. She wasn't sure if she should lift up the phone now to be ready but decided it would feel silly without anyone on the other side. Too eager. Instead, she sat and waited.

"If you're ready, I'll ask them to bring him in now."

Sloan took a deep breath. She was ready. She was *ready*.

TWENTY-NINE

THE FOX, AKA Edward Cunningham, aka the boogeyman under Sloan's bed and in her dreams, lumbered into the room, a thin pane of glass all that separated her from her living, breathing nightmare.

Sloan stared at The Fox, confusion coloring her face the palest of pinks. The man in front of her looked . . . so damn human. So ordinary. Even shackled, he looked like someone she could bump into at a grocery store and ask to please hand her a box she couldn't reach off the top shelf. She frowned—how was this the same man who had . . .

He shuffled around and dragged the small plastic chair back with his handcuffed hands. The dark chains stood in stark contrast to the pale blue prison jumpsuit. He was tall, taller than most. The reports had said 6′2″, but in her dreams he was more than that. He was ten feet tall and raging. A monster come to life.

She felt his eyes on her but couldn't bring herself to look up, not quite yet. She was too busy staring at his hands, the same hands that had killed her friends. She cataloged every bit of them she could see: dirty fingernails, dry skin, a red patch of eczema that crept between his thumb and pointer. He scratched it as she stared, either because it bothered him or because he was self-conscious. Either way, it was so human. So spectacularly human. She almost laughed.

Maybe Cherry had been right that this jail would hold nothing for Sloan. Maybe Cherry had been right that Sloan should stop calling him The Fox. This person in front of her was Edward Cunningham. It was an utterly boring name, and as she watched him pick at the skin between his fingers, she realized it fit him.

He raised one of his hands and tapped the glass, which caused Sloan to startle and shove her chair back.

"Quit it," a guard barked beside him, his voice deep and muffled through the divider, a threat in his tone that had Edward setting his hands back down. Sloan locked her eyes on the inmate's. And his eyes? Those were all The Fox.

The mask.

The pine.

The blade.

The screams. The screams. The screams.

Sloan blinked hard at the eyes that had haunted her dreams for so long.

This was what she had come for.

She had to do this. For her, for Cherry, for their families. She needed answers. She needed to put things to rest. She needed so much.

Sloan rolled her chair all the way forward to the little ledge in front of her. The Fox tilted his head, but his eyes never left hers. A full-body shudder wracked through Sloan, and a small smile crept across Edward's cracked, dry lips.

He *enjoyed* that. And no. No, Sloan thought, he had enjoyed her fear long enough. She reached for the phone.

The Fox grinned and did the same. Some of his teeth were gone. She wondered if they had always been or if that was courtesy of the sheriff's office. Sloan had read jails and prisons weren't especially welcoming to anyone who hurt children. She wondered if she still counted as a child. She hadn't felt like one in a long time.

You could murder a woman, and no one would care—you might even turn into a *Dateline* special for thousands of people to watch for fun. But you couldn't kill a toddler or a child or a baby, or the world would eat you alive.

Although, maybe that was his goal, wasn't it? For the world to eat him alive?

The Fox's hand hesitated on the phone, and for one terrible second, Sloan thought he wouldn't pick it up. That he had wanted her to come all this way for nothing. Just to see if she would. And she had. She had.

But then he slowly leaned forward and lifted the receiver on his end.

Sloan didn't know where to start.

She almost said hello but stopped herself. *Hello, how are you?* didn't seem like the appropriate words to greet the man who had changed her life in the worst way.

She listened to the heavy, wet sounds of his breath in her ear and dug her nails into her palm. She shut her eyes and tried to remember: Had she heard it before? Had she? Or was Cherry telling the truth, that The Fox hadn't actually gotten all that close to them, that none of them had? She couldn't be sure.

She tucked the receiver against her shoulder, pinned it to her ear, and took a deep breath, trying to decide where to start.

"What happened that night? Why did you come? Why there? Why us?" The questions rushed out of her, but the man didn't move. Didn't flinch or twitch or even act like he heard her.

Fine. She would try something else. She slowly rolled up her sleeve and exposed the long, jagged scar that ran the length of her forearm, rubbing absentmindedly at the point where it intersected with her birthmark.

"Was this you?" Sloan asked, careful to keep her voice neutral even as her arm shook.

Edward grunted from the opposite side of the glass. The receiver echoed it into her ears.

"Was it?" she asked again, but still he didn't speak.

She slid her finger over her birthmark and pointed.

"Is this a soul mark?"

That at least earned her another smile, this one less menacing and more like the face of the cat that ate the canary.

"I talked to your sister. To Sasha."

At the mention of her name, his face clouded over. His hand squeezed the phone tighter, as if he was willing himself not to react. Sloan knew the feeling. "Sasha gave me the book. She . . . she told me about you. She thinks you're good. Are you good?"

Nothing. No reaction.

"Why did you tear the pages out of the back of the book? The final ritual is gone. Did you realize how fucked up it was?"

Surprise crossed his face, a blink-and-you-miss-it moment, but it had been there. Sloan was sure of it.

"*You* didn't tear the papers out, did you? Who, then? Was it Marco?"

No response, just the sound of his heavy breathing in her ear, slow, steady, menacing.

Sloan pulled her sleeve down, and The Fox leaned back in his chair, watching, waiting.

"If you aren't going to talk to me, then why did you ask me to come here? Why bother doing anything at all?!" she yelled.

The guard behind The Fox shifted slightly. His finger twitched near his gun as if he expected Edward to react in some way, but Edward just sat there. Perfectly still. Staring at her.

"Fine, bye," she said. She tried to force herself to hang up the phone but couldn't bring herself to actually do it.

The Fox made no move to stop her, effectively calling her bluff.

"Why am I here?" she grumbled, not sure if she was asking why she had been called to the prison, or why she was alive at all, or why she had made herself sit here across from him. All of the above maybe. Probably.

"You never forget the one who got away." His voice crashed into her ears, and she jumped. His voice was deep, more of a growl, just as creepy as the rest of him, just as strong.

He smiled again, satisfied. He had wanted to startle her, she realized. He had waited to catch her off guard, had waited for her to settle.

Fuck him.

She angrily hung up the phone, but then slumped in her seat

instead of leaving. She was at his mercy, again. This time for answers and not for her life, but still, she hated it.

Sloan picked the phone back up, and Edward leaned forward, his breath fogging up the glass.

"I didn't get away, though, did I? You let me get away. It was part of the plan. I have the book. I know all about your rituals, about The Culling. You needed eight victims. I would have made nine. I was never in danger."

His face twitched, and the grin was back. "Are you sure about that, *Sloan*?"

The sound of her name coming from this monster's lips made her shudder. Another grin as he watched her react. It was fine, Sloan thought. He could victimize her all over again if he had to, if that's what he needed to give her answers.

"Yes, I'm sure. I read the book. I know what you were all trying to do with the reset. You needed me to live. I'm one of the soul-mates, aren't I? Is Cherry the other?"

"What a waste, what a waste," said The Fox, and his grin turned to a sneer. "What a waste you are. We'll try again. We'll try again in the next lifetime and the one after and the one after and the one after—as long as it takes. The others are already working on it."

"Who? The people in your shitty cult? They're all fucking dead, Edward." Using his name, it felt powerful.

He laughed, and it was a sickening sound. "If you believed that, you wouldn't be asking me about soul marks."

Sloan's breath caught in her throat as she pulled one of the photographs out of her hoodie pocket and slammed it onto the glass. Edward's eyes flicked to the Polaroid of Sloan's birth parents, and then back to her.

"You know them, don't you?" she said. "Where are they? Was my father part of Morte Hominus? Was Cherry's? Tell me what this mark is on my wrist. Tell me why I'm still alive. Tell me—"

"And if you are born of our blood, will you bring the darkness?"

"What does that—"

"Is it in you? Is it in your blood, Sloan? Can you feel it?" he asked, louder and louder. Flecks of spit flew from his mouth and splattered on the glass, yellow and phlegmy and dripping down an inch from her face. "Can you feel it, Sloan? Can you feel us in your blood?" The veins bulged in his neck as he shouted, "Is it in your blood? IS IT IN YOUR BLOOD?!"

Officers rushed into the room and struggled to get him to stand as Sloan watched in horror.

"Is it in your blood? Is it in your blood?!" he screamed as the officers pinned him against the glass and pulled his chains tighter.

Sloan jerked back and dropped the phone. The guards shoved him against the glass once more, his nose hitting with a sickening crunch. Blood splattered on the pane, smearing when he clawed and banged at it, still screaming about her blood, her blood, her blood, even though she had long ago dropped the phone.

ADA Sheridan burst through the door and tried to spin Sloan's chair to face her. "Sloan, Sloan, look at me," she said urgently. "Don't look at him. Let's get you out of here."

Sloan wanted to pull her eyes off Edward, but she couldn't. What did that mean? "Is it in your blood?" Blood like family? Did he just confirm that her parents were involved? Or was this another game?

The officers finally dragged him off, the bars clanking behind him with a finality that made Sloan jump. Sheridan kept trying to get her attention, but she just stared at the smears of blood left in his wake and wondered. She was supposed to leave here with answers, but all he gave her was more questions.

"Sloan," Sheridan said again, and this time Sloan looked at her. "Are you okay?"

Sloan shook her head, the numbness coming back as her adrenaline fell.

This was supposed to be the end. This had to be the end. She had promised Cherry that they'd get Red Vines. They deserved Red Vines. But there were no answers here, and she was tired. She was so tired.

"I sent an officer to get Cherry for you. She'll—"

"No," Sloan said and stood up. She wouldn't do that to Cherry. She wouldn't make her come inside this place. Make her rescue Sloan again. "I'm fine. I was just startled. I needed a minute."

"What you experienced—"

"Is nothing. I need to go. Cherry's waiting."

ADA Sheridan watched her walk out of the room in the direction of her coat. There was nothing else left to do.

THIRTY

IT WAS A quiet start to the drive as Sloan tried to process everything that had just happened. The Fox was vague, yes, but the implication was that the attack had been a part of the The Culling. He didn't deny it. And then there was the insinuation that Morte Hominus was, if not her birthright, at least something her birth parents could have been involved in.

Can you feel it?

She didn't miss Cherry's nervous glances. She didn't miss the way Cherry kept asking if she should pull over, if Sloan needed to talk, if Sloan needed anything. The way she shoved a too-warm water bottle into Sloan's hand and told her to take small sips rankled her—she was so sick of feeling like a small, scared animal. So sick of being something others had to care for.

They were barely a mile past the jail, but they might as well have been on the moon. Everything was tangled now. Sloan tried to make sense of the flashes in her head—the before, the after, the now.

Is it in your blood?

His voice echoed inside her, and Sloan wished she knew the

answer. The only thing she knew about her blood was the way it looked running down her arm. She traced the scar again and looked out the window.

Then there was the matter of the missing pages. He clearly hadn't done it, and even if he only broke his careful neutrality once—one tiny moment of surprise—Sloan thought it was likely that no one else he knew had removed them either. Then who did?

Cherry started to babble, talking about something and nothing all at once. It was nerves, probably, her effort to take up space. She had taken up enough space for both of them the last time Sloan had caved in on herself. She was doing it again; she would probably do it forever if Sloan let her.

Sloan should let her, she realized. She should let Cherry live in a world where none of her deepest fears and theories had all but been confirmed by a madman with a bloody nose.

Sloan was jealous of Cherry's ignorance, of the fact that Cherry had decided this was all bullshit. The fact that Cherry was so sure none of this meant anything.

Sloan wanted that for herself.

Instead, she leaned against the window and wondered how she had been put on a path to live, while almost everyone else who applied to that stupid summer job had been put on a path to die. How had Morte Hominus worked it all out so perfectly?

Is it in your blood?

None of this made sense.

None of it.

Cherry slammed on the brakes, which sent Sloan's water bottle flying out of her hand. It ricocheted off the dashboard and then rolled under her seat.

"Sorry," Cherry said sheepishly and took a hard left turn into the run-down gas station. "But I promised you Red Vines."

Sloan looked over at her. "I think technically I promised *you*."

"Yeah, you did. Do you want to come in with me and grab them?"

"Fuck no." Sloan laughed.

"Fine. I'll tell you what, they're on me this time—but you owe me." She winked. "Sit tight, okay? I'll be right back."

Sloan smiled as Cherry pressed a quick kiss to her cheek before she disappeared out the door. She felt warm and safe now, tucked up into Cherry's truck under the bright gas station lights—good almost, maybe. Cherry had a knack for chasing the monsters out of her mind, even if it never lasted.

Through the giant gas station windows, Sloan watched Cherry make her way to the candy first, her steps fast and eager. She smiled when Cherry yanked the Red Vines off the rack so hard it shook. Cherry looked excited. Cherry looked happy. And maybe that could be enough. Maybe Sloan could keep her promise for once. Forget everything else.

When Cherry made her way over to the giant beverage cooler in the back of the store, Sloan remembered her own water, forgotten under the seat. She bent down and reached under as far as she could go. Her hand grazed the edge of the plastic bottle, along with something else. Something cold and hard. She pulled it out.

It was a large hunting knife.

A flash of steel. The bite of pine.

Sloan barely got it up to the light before she dropped it to the floor and tried to jam it back under the seat.

Why did Cherry have a knife? What else was she hiding? Put it back, put it back, put it back!

There had to be an explanation. She peeked up over the dashboard—Cherry seemed to be trying to decide between Gatorade flavors. Sloan flexed her fingers and reached farther back, just in case, just to be sure. They scraped against the plastic water bottle again, and the knife in its sheath . . . and then they caught on the very edge of something else. Papers?

She squeezed herself down even more and dragged the papers forward with her fingertips, sweeping everything else with it. A flashlight rolled out beside the knife—a giant black Maglite—and then, finally, the papers.

Sloan lifted them off the floor and held them up with shaky hands. She was hoping they were registration cards or receipts or old magazines, harmless things, things that wouldn't hurt. Things that would have them eating Red Vines on the road in no time at all. But no, there was the familiar font, the glossy paper, the promise of magic and restoration.

The Ritual of the Fated Souls, it read.

The final ritual.

There were a dozen pages, give or take—all of which had been shoved under the seat behind a knife and a Maglite big enough to be used as a weapon, her brain helpfully supplied.

All of it resting right under Sloan this whole time.

Cherry had to have put them there. Cherry had lied.

A flash of steel. The bite of pine. A voice outside the door.

"Not this one. This one's mine."

Sloan dug her nails into her palm and forced her focus back to the pages in front of her. Sacrifice, soulmates, resets—it was all there. Another painting was mixed in with the words. One of the girls was killing the other. Ushering in The Great Reset. Reuniting the darkness in a single vessel: the true last girl standing.

A realization washed over Sloan: Cherry was going to kill her. She was going to complete the ritual on her own.

Fear trickled through Sloan's veins like blood. No, that wasn't right. That couldn't be right. Could it? All those nights spent together, for what?

To keep her close until the time was right?

No.

Her eyes snapped to the store window. Cherry was in the checkout line now. Only one person ahead of her. A woman with a dozen cans of cat food and a pile of candy. Voracious toddlers clung to the woman's legs as the she tried to count out cash.

What if this was all part of the plan?

The Fox and Cherry conspiring to bring her here so that Cherry could get her alone and . . . Why else would she have the knife? The pages? Even the broken passenger's side door could have been a setup. Could have been a lie.

Sloan's hands shook. It was now or never. She shoved the papers into her hoodie pocket and snatched the knife up off the floor. With a quick glance to make sure Cherry was still in line (she was) and not looking toward the truck (she wasn't), Sloan quietly popped open the driver's side door. She climbed out slow, slow, slow and held her breath as she pushed it gently shut.

Cherry was at the register now, still oblivious.

Sloan took a few slow steps behind the truck and then bolted. She thought of grabbing the woman, now putting her bags in her trunk, and begging her to drive her somewhere safe . . . but there were children with her. Actual children. She couldn't put them in danger like that.

Sloan ran into the darkness on the side of the building instead. There wasn't much in the way of hiding places, but there were a couple dumpsters and a pile of tires. Sloan's first instinct was to jump in one, but then she realized she would have nowhere to run if Cherry found her. She would be caught. Snared like an animal in a trap just waiting for its end.

No, better to stay outside, the ground firmly beneath her feet. She dipped behind the smaller of the dumpsters, nearly choking on the smell of rotted garbage and something else, something sinister. She gagged when she caught sight of a chunk of fur sticking out from under the lid.

A raccoon, she thought.

Probably got stuck.

Sloan tucked herself beside it anyway. It had to be done. She could see the side of Cherry's truck from her hiding spot. She pressed herself against the dumpster, straining to see, and waited.

She didn't have to wait long.

"Sloan? Sloan!" Cherry's voice echoed across the parking lot. The woman looked up from buckling her kid. Sloan held her breath, but the woman didn't give her up. Maybe she hadn't even seen Sloan sneak out.

Sloan sank back farther into the shadows as Cherry spun in a slow circle, still calling out her name.

Sloan considered her options. The sheriff's station was only about a mile or two down the road. If she stayed in the woods, maybe she could make a run for it without being seen. She could explain to them that she had found the knife and the papers. She would come clean about meeting Sasha and having the book. The people at the station could keep her safe until Allison, until her *mom*, came and got her. She would call her mom as soon as it was safe, tell her to meet her at the jail. Pray that she picked up.

It was a good plan.

The pages burned in her pocket. Maybe she could even read them on her way there. What would be the harm in that? She was safe in the pines if she stayed out of sight, and her mother was hours away at least. Besides, Cherry would probably check the police station first anyway. It would be better if Sloan took her time getting there, she decided.

"Sloan?!" Cherry lifted her phone to her ear, and a beat later Sloan felt her own ringing in her hand. It made a loud buzzing sound against the metal of the dumpster.

"Shit." She lost her balance in her rush to silence it, and instead the phone went flying. It landed in a puddle with quiet splash.

Fuck, that wasn't good. Sloan slunk back farther into the dark, closer to the trees that surrounded them.

"Sloan?" Cherry called. "Are you . . . are you hiding? I got the Red Vines. Are you ready to go?"

Sloan didn't move, she didn't breathe—she just stared at Cherry and wished she were invisible.

Cherry shoved her phone back into her pocket and then whipped open the truck door. She bent over as she dug deep under the seats, and Sloan's heart rate picked up. Cherry was probably looking for the knife. And now she knew Sloan had it.

"Fuck," Cherry groaned and turned around with the giant flashlight. Damn, Sloan wished she had thought to grab that too.

Cherry clicked it on and waved the light over the area around the dumpsters, but Sloan darted quickly around the very edge of the building. The bricks scratched at her arm as she watched Cherry search the dumpsters, even lifting up the lids to check. The dead raccoon fell to the bottom with a sickening thump.

"Sloan!" Cherry called. "I can explain! I know you found the papers. There's a reason I hid them. I promise. A good one. Just come out, please? This place is fucking creepy. These trees—I just want to go home. Come on! Seriously, I want to go home." Her voice came out in a broken whine.

Sloan almost fell for it. Her fingers twitched against the blade in her hand. It would be so easy to believe Cherry, so easy to give in. So easy to believe that the girl with the Red Vines hadn't just gone looking for a knife under the very seat Sloan had been sitting in.

Sloan slipped back around the other side of the building and melted into the light brush of the forest. Cherry's light swept along the tree line—nearly catching Sloan—before Cherry turned her attention to the bathroom door on the side of the building. Sloan hadn't even noticed it. Good thing too, because she probably would have tried to hide there.

Cherry twisted the handle. Locked. She banged on the door. "Sloan, this is ridiculous. Come out. I know you're upset. Let me explain! You always jump to—"

The bathroom door yanked open, and a gruff trucker type shoved past Cherry. "I wouldn't go in there right now if I was you." He laughed and hitched his belt as he walked back to his truck.

Cherry let the door bang shut behind him as she sagged against the building. "Sloan," she said, softer this time, so soft Sloan had to strain to hear her. "If you're out there, I'm sorry for ripping the pages out. Okay? I just . . . I wanted things to be different. I didn't want that in your brain." She hit her head against the brick and then shoved off back toward her pickup. "I'm going back to the station. I'm going to get help. I understand if you don't want to see me right now. Just please, stay where you are. Stay safe until someone . . ." The rest of what she said was lost when Cherry shut the truck door behind her.

Sloan barely breathed, barely moved a muscle until the truck backed out of the parking lot and left. As soon as it was out of sight, Sloan pulled her phone out, ready to call 911, ready to call the police. She didn't know what she'd tell them exactly, but she'd think of something. She had to, and quick, before Cherry got to them.

She slid her hand to the corner of her phone and clicked on the flashlight. It was dark, even at the edge of the pines, and she didn't want anything sneaking up on her. Satisfied she had secured as much light as she could, she turned the phone toward her to unlock it.

The facial recognition failed. She entered her code. Nothing. She tried pressing the emergency call buttons on the side, but they didn't do anything. A tiny bright zap danced across the screen instead, and then it all turned black.

"Shit," Sloan whispered. She must have fried it when it landed in the puddle.

The flashlight beam stayed stubbornly stuck on, a small consolation as she considered her options. She could go back to the gas station and ask them to call. It was right there; all she had to do was cross the parking lot. But what if that was what Cherry was expecting? Cherry could have lied, circled back around and parked just out of sight. Cherry could be waiting. No, Sloan decided, it would be safer to walk the mile or two back to the police station herself. Call Cherry's bluff the way The Fox had called hers.

The woods would carry her the whole way there. She could stay off the roads and keep the flashlight low so no one else would notice. She could do this. She could keep herself safe. She had a weapon now.

It was her turn to be the monster in the woods.

Sloan gripped the knife tighter and smiled.

THIRTY-ONE

SLOAN'S TERRIBLE SENSE of direction didn't help things.

She felt like she had been walking for hours but had no way of truly knowing the time with her phone out of commission. She was getting tired, though, so tired, and very cold.

Sloan wanted to cry, but she knew that was useless. Even more useless than she currently felt, wandering around in the woods, obviously lost. Every sound made her jump. Even if it probably *was* just random chipmunks she'd startled awake or something, she couldn't get it out of her head it was him. The Fox. That he had escaped the razor wire and stalked her. Ready to kill her. Ready to complete the ritual.

The ritual.

Sloan had been so worried about getting away at first that she hadn't yet looked the pages over. But now she was hopelessly turned around in the woods, so what did it matter? If she truly was walking toward the police station, she should have been there by now.

Her foot sank into mud with a sickening squelch that sent her sprawling and reminded her too much of an axe through a belly.

She nearly knocked her head on a rock when she landed. She almost wished she had. Finally, a quick end to a long nightmare.

But no, she was still here. Still alive. And there was still work to be done.

Sloan rolled to her back and let the mud soak through her clothes, cold and wet against her skin, her hair, her ears, her ankles, and her hips.

She was tired. Bone-deep tired. She picked the blade up from the mud where she'd dropped it, and crawled over to a downed tree, finally pulling the damp papers from her pocket.

If she was going to die, Sloan thought, she might as well know what was coming for her.

The first page was a basic rehashing of the idea of soulmates and their importance and how to identify them. She had already read about that in previous chapters.

This one was a little different, though; it went much deeper. The tiny baby hairs on the back of Sloan's neck stood up as she processed the wrinkled words in front of her.

It said that the soulmates would find each other across every lifetime during their eighteenth year. Each of them represented one half of the balance. They were honored and revered by Morte Hominus, typically raised from birth to prepare for their sacrifice each generation.

Sloan's eyebrows pinched together as she ran the flashlight along the page, confused. Cherry hadn't sacrificed her that night; Cherry had *saved* her. And Sloan certainly hadn't felt revered or worshipped by Morte Hominus—she felt terrified. She was eighteen, sure, but that was where the similarities ended.

A part of her, the part that was cold and scared and exhausted, told her to stop reading, to leave it at that, to decide the book was bullshit just like Cherry had. To try to retrace her way back to the gas station before hypothermia set in. To ask the clerk to call Cherry, who was probably worried sick about her. Or the sheriff. Or her mom. Or everyone. To do anything but sit out here and read more about Morte Hominus and their divine plans.

But the bigger, louder part of her wanted her to press on. To read more. To *survive* more. To trust less. Maybe this was the part that had kept her alive during the attack. Maybe this was the part holding her memories back and keeping her safe.

She glanced at the knife beside her again and listened to the wind as it whipped through the trees. She settled her phone's flashlight back on the page and kept reading.

Each soulmate contained half of the world's darkness. Each had half of the recipe for the end of the world, half of the ability to set things right . . . until they found each other.

Then there it was, right on the page in black and white. One had to sacrifice the other—proving their devotion to the cause and reuniting the two halves, absorbing and reuniting the darkness in one body—to trigger the reset. The living soulmate would then act as a conduit for the darkness, a near possession, spreading its will and aiding it to bring about the end of times.

It was the final phase. The final ritual before The Great Reset.

It was also where they had failed, every time.

Throughout the generations, Morte Hominus had weakened. The soulmates hadn't found each other or hadn't followed through, and so the balance of the universe had tipped more and more to one side.

That was what The Fox meant when he said the rest of the

members were working on it, Sloan realized. When they failed in their current lives, steps were immediately taken to be reincarnated and try again, like little secret bombs set to go off across the centuries.

One member was left behind to observe, to see this life through until the bitter end. They would bear the weight of any consequences, learn what could be learned, and then, much later, after they had died and been reborn, find the others in the next life, wiser and ready to lead—like Marco had found them in this one.

The air rushed out of Sloan. It was deliberate, then, that The Fox's cyanide hadn't worked. It wasn't meant to. It wasn't an accident that everyone had died but him; he was left behind as a watcher. Here to see the soulmates fail. Or, she realized, maybe he thought there was still a chance. Marco's time had passed, yes, but it looked like The Fox's had just begun.

Sloan held her wrist up to the light and stared down at it, at the soul mark that bound her to Cherry, and at the jagged scar that dug through the center of it. It marked her as the one to die, she was convinced now. It was the only thing that made sense. Cherry's mark was fine. She had run through all the same places that night— more even—and had never gotten hurt. Her mark was intact, like her memories, like her skin.

It couldn't have been luck.

The bite of steel. The bite of pine.

But Sloan wasn't going to die tonight.

And Cherry wasn't going to be the last girl standing.

That was bullshit, she thought. That wasn't her ending.

Sloan grabbed her knife.

Sloan grabbed her knife, and she ran.

THIRTY-TWO

SLOAN RAN UNTIL she couldn't run anymore.

Until her feet were blistered and raw from her wet shoes. Until her lungs burned and ached, and she thought she might collapse if she had to run another step.

Then she walked, deeper and deeper, the woods urging her on, ushering her to safety, she hoped. The rustling sound of whatever had been following her was long gone when she stepped into a clearing, bathed in moonlight and mud.

She froze.

She knew this clearing. Had kissed Cherry in this clearing. Had wanted to kiss her more, but Kevin had caught them and sent them to their separate cabins.

Sloan knew that if she walked across it to the other edge, she would find a path, and at the end of the path, she would find the first of the buildings at Camp Money Springs—Cherry's cabin.

She hesitated, but only for a moment.

If this was where the universe wanted her to be, this was where she would be.

She had meant to travel in the opposite direction, to get to the police, to bring the pages and prove that she wasn't crazy, that she was *right*. Had been right all along. That Cherry was in on it, and Magda was in on it, and maybe Sasha too.

That they were trying to kill Sloan, not save her. That they needed her. That she was important.

And her birth parents? Her birth parents, she decided as she tromped through the woods, had given her up in an effort to save her, hide her away, stash her someplace Morte Hominus could never find her. Allison had been there to scoop her up and bake cookies and head the PTA without ever realizing that her new daughter housed one half of the darkness set to devour the world. Sloan's birth parents were heroes, she decided. They had saved her life.

Can you feel it? Is it in your blood?

As Sloan stepped out of the pines, the sight of Cherry's cabin directly in front of her, she felt . . . nothing. It was as if this was all happening to someone else, like she was watching a movie, or stuck in a session with Beth.

Cherry's cabin was exactly as Sloan remembered it when she climbed the stairs and pushed open the door. Cherry's quilt was still stretched across her bed, her Sleater-Kinney poster still taped to the wall. Cherry's toothbrush still dangled on the edge of the sink—a deep purple turned blue by the moonlight.

Sloan wanted to lie down. To sleep. To rest.

But she couldn't. She couldn't get caught up in the happy memories—and there were so many memories in this room, even in the short time she was here.

She needed to stay focused. There was nothing here for her now. She headed out, checking the other cabins one by one. She was careful to sidestep the bloodstains on their porches while she counted the ghosts in her head. Eight of them, all lined up behind her.

Those she could feel.

They had haunted her from the moment she opened her eyes in the ambulance with a sore throat from screams she couldn't remember. They were glad she was here now.

Her cabin, the farthest from the woods, loomed above her like a coffin as she climbed the steps.

"This one's mine," she said to the ghosts behind her. "This one belongs to me."

It was locked. No, it was stuck, but as she shoved it hard, her shoulder pressed against pine, it gave way.

Sloan stood in the doorway and stared down at the echo of herself, its silent tears and skinned knees. "We have to go, we have to go," Sloan said as she rushed inside and crouched beside—

No one. There was no one there.

Sloan, real Sloan, was the one on her knees. On the ground. Screaming. Trying not to scream. A million memories flitted through her head at once, but all she thought was, *So this is reprocessing.*

She laughed, and she couldn't stop. Not as steel bit into her arm or the pine bit into her legs or none of it happened at all. She laughed and remembered the way Cherry had dragged her out. The way her arms had hung limp. No, a flash of steel. Of Cherry cutting, cutting, no.

Yes.

Cherry had sliced her arm. She had probably aimed for the soul mark but started too high. Sloan, the little lamb to the slaughter.

Cherry, so sure she would be the last girl standing as she sliced through their bond. Cherry was going to complete the ritual. She was going to kill Sloan.

Sloan stared down at the crinkled pages in her hand. A fresh fear washed over her. What if the ritual wasn't bullshit? What if none of it was? Morte Hominus had never gotten this far. There could be more to this than she even realized.

This wasn't just about saving herself anymore; this was about saving the world. Preventing the darkness. She couldn't let Cherry finish the ritual. She couldn't. She wouldn't. She—

Sloan bolted up at the sound of a loud crash. Small pinpricks of blood formed on the scrape on her knees as she rushed outside.

The bite of the pine.

The sound of a car door.

She shook her head and stepped out of her cabin as Cherry hopped out of her truck and ran up the path toward her. The truck's bumper was a mangled mess. The chains and gate had done a number on it. She must have rammed right through them.

"Thank god! Thank god you're okay," Cherry cried, just as a cloud cracked open above them and sent a heavy rain cascading to the ground. Sloan stood very still, the knife tucked into her waistband behind her back.

Cherry grabbed one of Sloan's hands. "Jesus, have you been outside this whole time? You're freezing. Come on. Let's get you in the truck. Hopefully the heat still works. Everyone's looking for you. Sheridan called everybody out, the whole force. Your mom is on her—"

"I know everything," Sloan said, her eyes fixed straight ahead. And it would be so easy to give in to Cherry's warm, soft skin. Her warm, soft words. If Sloan didn't know they were lies.

Cherry wanted to kill her. Cherry wanted to be the last girl standing.

"Baby," Cherry whispered and tugged on her hand. "We shouldn't be here. This isn't good for either one of us."

"When did you decide?" Sloan asked and finally turned her head to look at Cherry.

"Decide what?" Cherry asked, her hands coming to Sloan's face, her sides, her hips, as if she was checking to make sure her girlfriend was alright. As if she wasn't just planning to kill Sloan herself.

The bite of steel. The bite of pine. It was all such a blur.

"I read the papers you ripped out. I know about your plan."

"What the fuck are you talking about?" Cherry shouted. "Yes, I ripped out the ritual, and yes, I hid them from you, back that first night when you brought it home, but it was to protect you! Christ, Sloan, you were nearly catatonic when I got you back from Connor. Once I read that part . . . I knew what you would think. You were so desperate to find a reason for everything that happened, and it would have given you one. It scared the shit out of me that you might believe it."

"You said we were meant to be," Sloan said. "You knew we were soulmates."

"Because I love you," Cherry said, and her voice broke on the word *love*.

Sloan reached behind to feel the reassuring coolness of the knife. Because it almost, almost sounded like Cherry's heart was broken too. And Sloan couldn't fall for that.

"Why was this with it, then?" Sloan pulled the knife out and held it up between them, her grip hard, unwavering.

Cherry stepped back. "Where did you get that? I haven't seen it for years."

"Nice try. It was under your seat. Right next to the papers you ripped out of my book."

"*Your* book? Didn't you just say it was mine?" Cherry shouted. "It's *their* book, Sloan! Theirs! We have nothing to do with this!"

"Why do you have a knife, Cherry?"

"It was my dad's! He always had it on him for cutting branches when I was little. For kindling or marshmallow roasting. That sort of thing. It must have been in his truck this whole time."

"Carving?"

"What?"

"Did he use it for carving?" Sloan smirked. "Little animals . . . or masks?"

"You and the fucking rabbits! My dad died, Sloan. You know this. He had a heart condition—a shitty mitral valve issue that was never caught. He died at the fucking gas station he worked at. Just dropped dead and left us all alone," she sobbed. "He's not Marco. He's not secretly still alive. And he definitely didn't take a cyanide nap. I took a summer job at that camp to help my mom cover bills. And for whatever reason, I didn't die. There is no conspiracy. Sometimes bad things just happen. That's it. It's just a fucking stupid random thing."

"But you read the ritual. You know about the marks and being eighteen. You cut mine. You—"

"Sloan, no. I didn't cut you. No one cut you. You fell. I don't know if it was the branch or a rock or what, but it wasn't a person who cut your arm. You're getting confused. I hid those pages because you're confused."

"I'm not."

"It's like you've been *trying* to believe them. And that scares me so much. We don't have soul marks; we have scars. And if you really were my soulmate, you'd believe me, wouldn't you? You would know I was telling the truth. If we aren't soulmates, then this whole ridiculous ritual doesn't matter anyway, right? Let's just go home."

"No."

"Being back here doesn't help us at all. It doesn't. Sheridan will be here soon, or her cops or whatever. We've been searching the woods for you for hours. Think about it! If I really wanted to hurt you, would I have gotten help?"

"This doesn't make sense. You had the pages. You had the knife. You—"

"If you don't trust me," Cherry said, "at least take my phone and call someone. Your mom, Connor, Sheridan—I don't care." She tossed her phone onto the ground and backed up toward her truck. "Call someone and tell them to come get you. I won't come near you. I'm not trying to hurt you, Sloan, I promise. I'll stay in my truck with the doors locked, or better, you stay in it with the doors locked and the heat on, please. You're so cold, baby. You have to know I would never fucking hurt you. I almost died trying to keep you safe. I almost died for you, Sloan Thomas. Now will you please just fucking live for me?!"

Sloan was so confused. This wasn't . . . Cherry wasn't . . . Why was she trying to help her? Oh god, what if she was wrong? What if she was wrong about everything?

"Cherry?" Sloan shook her head and held out her hand. "I don't know what's happening. I'm sorry. I'm sorry. I don't—"

"It's okay. It's okay." Cherry rushed back. She grabbed Sloan's face and kissed her lips, her cheeks, her eyelids, her forehead, her nose. "We're gonna go. We're gonna get you help, and we're gonna get me help too." She let out a soft, sad laugh of relief. "We'll get through this together. We will."

Sloan's brow furrowed as things reshuffled in her brain again. *The bite of steel. The bite of pine. Slivers in her knee.*

"But no, wait, what if they're right? Then aren't we just like them?" She searched Cherry's eyes. She was confused, so confused. Nothing made sense anymore.

"Who?"

"All the others before us. They didn't do it, so things just kept getting more and more out of balance. And they are out of balance. Aren't they?"

"Baby, no. This is . . . that's pretend. This is all pretend."

Sloan stiffened. "But you would say that, wouldn't you? Because you're supposed to be last. You're supposed to be the vessel—"

"No. I'm not. We're not." Cherry kissed her hard and pressed their foreheads together. "I promise you."

The rain was still pounding down around them, and Sloan felt like the whole world was weeping. Like she was weeping. She tipped her head back and let the rain—the world—wash the mud off of her face. She was so tired. "It's too many coincidences for it not to be true. Our parents, the Polaroids, even the marks . . . And I remember a blade. I remember something . . ."

Cherry shook her head. "I found stuff out about your parents, Sloan. Your birth parents."

"What?" Sloan snapped her eyes up.

"They're—they're definitely not involved. You're looking for connections that aren't really there."

"You—"

"One of my mom's clients is a private investigator. She was willing to barter with him." Cherry sighed. "I wasn't expecting anything, but he came through right away. He doesn't know if your birth parents are still alive. But he found out they didn't *willingly* give up custody of you. You don't have a soul mark. You were never even near Morte Hominus. I didn't read your records—it felt like a violation of your trust—but the PI did. He said it was . . . he said it was bad what you went through with them. Like, your-parents-were-charged kind of bad. It's no wonder your memories are all jumbled. You've been through so much even in just the eighteen years you've been—"

"How do I know anything you say is real?"

"Because you know me. You love me," Cherry said, stepping closer.

Sloan rubbed the rain out of her eyes with her free hand. The knife dangled in her other. She was getting a headache.

Cherry seemed to take this action as an agreement. With a whispered "I'm so sorry, baby," she ran her hand down Sloan's arm and tried to wrap her own hand around the knife.

Sloan jerked back and took a few steps away. She tipped the blade toward Cherry, her eyes flashing in warning. "What are you doing?"

Cherry held her hands up. "Put the knife down, Sloan. We can . . . we can go back to the station. I'll have the PI email the records he found on your birth parents to us, or Sheridan can probably pull up their arrest records herself. Whatever you want. Just put down the knife, please. Put down the knife, and let me prove to you that this isn't real."

"I can't trust you. I can't trust anyone right now!"

"Okay." Cherry put her hands together like she was praying, like she was pleading. "Okay, you don't have to trust me, then. How about this? I'll leave right now, if you promise to stay put so the sheriff can find you. You're freezing, Sloan. You need help. And if it can't be me, tell me who you want, and I'll get them for you. I'll get them right now. Because I love you so fucking much. I just want you to get through this."

"You love me? Still?" Sloan shook her head.

"I said it, didn't I?"

"Yeah," Sloan said softly, and then everything went quiet for a minute, both girls just watching each other. Sloan still loved her too. She did. "Cherry? I don't . . . I don't know what to believe. I love you. I do. I'm just so . . ."

A corner of Cherry's mouth edged up in the saddest smile Sloan had ever seen. "You know, if you didn't want Red Vines, you coulda just said so. You didn't have to be such a drama queen about it."

Sloan let out a watery laugh and wiped at her nose, her face, her tears. "I was always more of a Twizzlers girl, now that you mention it," she said in a shaky voice.

"Baby." Cherry took a deep breath. "Put down the knife. Please. This isn't you. We can get help. We can figure this out."

Sloan nodded. Maybe this *was* just paranoia. A desperation to find where she fit. To never let it go. To make sense of what she'd been through. Soulmates and prophecies and . . . She set the knife down on the picnic table beside them. It was where Ronnie had died, she realized, and she had stood next to it this whole time like it was nothing. Like it didn't matter.

She rubbed her hands over her face and turned around to take one last look at the cabins. It was over. Or it would be. She just needed to—

A twig snapped behind her, and she spun around just in time to see Cherry scoop up the knife.

"No!" Sloan rushed toward her, feeling stupid for believing Cherry, for falling for all her pretty lies. Cherry would have said anything, probably, to get Sloan to put down the knife. To make sure *she* was the last girl standing.

"I'm just—"

Sloan grabbed Cherry's arm and shoved it up and away. "I'm not dying here tonight! I won't!"

"Stop," Cherry said. "I'm not—"

But everything went blurry then.

The bite of steel. The bite of pine. A flash of metal in the moonlight.

Sloan was here, wrestling with Cherry, and then there, kneeling on the floor of her cabin that night, over and over, like a flickering light. Everything colliding into one confusing timeline in her head.

They were running. Sloan held Cherry's hand as they raced through the woods.

They were—

"SLOAN, STOP IT!" Cherry yelled.

"Sloan, stop it," Cherry whispered. "Stop crying. They'll hear us!"

And Sloan did. Sloan stood beside her, quiet as mouse, and listened. They listened to screams around them. And Cherry smiled at her. Cherry smiled. No. She cried. She was crying.

"Up," Cherry said. "We need to go up." And then they climbed. They climbed, and Sloan's hands were sticky with sap, but they were quiet as little mice in the tree.

A broken twig. The bite of pine. A flash of steel beneath them. Beneath the tree. The Stag. The Stag with his giant blade dragging behind him. A man, a beast, a menace, a threat, but he was down, and they were up, and then he was gone. Cherry said they would be okay. She said they would be safe. That she needed Sloan to believe her. That Cherry needed her.

Needed her—

"You needed me safe to finish the ritual," Sloan gritted out, her rain-soaked hands slippery as she tried to wrestle the knife away from Cherry. She cut her palms in the process, but it barely registered. "You've been planning this the whole time!"

"Fuck you," Cherry spat. "Fuck you for even saying that."

"I'm not dying for you. You won't win." Sloan shoved herself forward. "They won't—"

Moonlight danced across the blade as Sloan lunged with all her weight.

There was no sickening squelch.

There was nothing really, just a blade slipping into something soft and staying there. It wasn't like cutting meat. It wasn't like meat at all when the knife plunged into Cherry's belly. Soft and warm. Warm and red as the blood covered Sloan's hands—the blood and water and mud mixing in a little pool around them.

Cherry staggered back and fell to the ground. Her hand pressed hard around the knife in her torso as she looked at Sloan with wide, stunned eyes. "Baby?" she choked out.

Sloan dropped to her knees. *The bite of pine.*

She cradled Cherry's head in her lap and scooted forward so their eyes could meet. *The bite of—* What had she done? What had she done?

"I'm here. I'm here," Sloan said between shaky breaths. "You're going to be okay. Stay with me, Cherry. Stay with me."

"It hurts," Cherry whimpered. "Get my phone . . . Call . . . call the station."

Is it in your blood? Can you feel it?

"Shhh, shhh," Sloan whispered to the voices in her head. "It's over now, it's over."

"Call for . . ."

"Yeah, I will. I will! Where is it? Where the fuck is it?!" Sloan frantically scrambled through the mud trying to find where Cherry had tossed her phone, but it was no use. It was too dark; the ground was too muddy and overgrown. Sloan crawled back, sobbing as she pulled her girlfriend onto her lap. "It's gone. It's gone. I don't . . . I can't . . ." Sloan brushed the rain-soaked hair out of Cherry's face, and the girls sank deeper into the mud, like the world itself was trying to drag them under.

To bury them.

To become one with them.

"You did this," Cherry said and coughed up something red.

Can you feel it? Is it in your blood?

Sloan wiped the red from Cherry's face as a realization washed over her. There was no way to get help. No one knew where they were. Cherry was dying.

Cherry would die tonight.

And then, when she did, the ritual would be complete.

In trying to save herself, Sloan had lost. In trying to save herself, she had ended the world.

She had ended the world just like Morte Hominus had wanted. Just like the book had said. No. No!

"Don't you leave me," Sloan begged and curled over, pulling Cherry as close to her as she could. "If you go, it'll be done. They'll win. You'll unleash the darkness, Cherry. You can't. You can't. I was trying to save us. I was trying to—"

"I hate . . ." Cherry coughed.

"Hate me, please hate me, just don't—"

Cherry's face scrunched up in pain. "You killed me . . . for a fuck . . . a fucking fairy tale."

"No. I didn't kill you. You can't die. You won't. The darkness. The darkness will come if you do. I'm sorry. I'm sorry. You have to live, please. Please, Cherry."

Cherry grew impossibly pale, her eyes drifting shut longer and longer between each blink. She was fading; it was obvious to anyone.

Sloan dropped back in shock, and Cherry's head slipped back down.

The ritual was almost complete. Her love was dying, dying, dying, and it was all her fault. It was too much.

It was too much.

There was a rustling sound at the edge of the clearing. Sloan let her eyes drift over in time to see a lone white rabbit hop out into the moonlight. Its black-ringed eyes stared up at her.

"It's over," Sloan whimpered. "I ruined it. Now the darkness will come for us all."

Or have you saved it? the rabbit's eyes seemed to say.

Had *they* saved it?

The rain roared in Sloan's ears at this revelation. She blinked, and the rabbit was gone.

The Rabbit.

No one had ever gotten this far. No one had ever completed the final ritual. Maybe something good *could* come out of all this horror. It had to. *It had to.* Sloan wouldn't let it all be for nothing. No. This had to be fate. Prophecy. Destiny. It had to be true. It needed to be true. Sloan *had* to believe. Sloan *would* believe.

She bent over and brushed the hair and blood off Cherry's face.

"It hurts," Cherry choked out.

"Shhh. It's okay. It's all okay now. We did it." Sloan smiled down at her. "I know you thought it would be you, but I'm strong enough. I won't let you down, I promise. I'll restore the balance. I saw the rabbit. I saw—"

"S . . . Sloan—"

"It's okay. It's okay." Sloan leaned over and gently pushed Cherry's hands away from her wound. The other girl struggled weakly at first, and then gave in, let Sloan lace their fingers together and bring them up to her mouth for a bloody kiss.

It wasn't the first.

There was no going back. There was no *point* in going back. In untangling the before from the after, the fact from fiction. Sloan was trapped in the cabin, and she was witnessing the final sacrifice. She was home and gone. She was a baby being reborn. She was everything and nothing. She was.

"What . . . are . . . ?" Cherry asked, confusion on her face. Sloan kissed her properly then, long and hard, in the rain, letting her fingers trail lower and lower until they found the handle of the knife. She hoped Cherry didn't feel her slide the blade down and out. Didn't hear the apocalypse roaring to life inside her as they kissed. Didn't hear the blade land in the mud beside them.

And there, finally, was the sickening squelch of the earth receiving its price.

"I love you. I love you," Sloan said and tugged Cherry against her chest, holding them both still as Cherry's blood mingled with the water above them and the earth below.

It was as inevitable as they were.

The sirens in the distance came closer. Red and blue flashes between the trees just like before. But they were alone with their ghosts, just like before.

"Can you feel it? Can you feel it?"

"You killed . . ." Cherry said. Her eyelashes fluttered against her cheeks as they quietly closed.

"I love you," Sloan sobbed. "We did it. I'm so proud of you. I love you."

Cherry coughed one last time, and there was so much red. Too much red for talking. Still, Sloan held her. Listened to each ragged breath. Kissed her. Kissed her again and again and again until Cherry went quiet and still.

Just the sound of rain. The sound of the darkness brushing against their skin. Everything quiet, even the wind. The earth waiting, listening, hoping.

Sloan took a steadying breath.

It was over. Cherry was safe now. Cherry was *holy* now. Cherry was everything and nothing, just like Sloan. She was whole again, just like Sloan was whole. Just like the universe would be soon.

And it was so quiet.

Quiet . . .

Quiet . . .

Quiet . . .

And then it was loud. It was bright. The sirens, a searchlight, the slam of a door. A man walked toward them, his gun drawn at the sight of the knife beside them, inches from Sloan's fingertips.

"Easy, easy," the officer said.

Sloan thought she remembered him from that afternoon. Sloan thought he was the one who had stood next to The Fox when they met. She smiled. He was a part of it too. Had to be. He knew what was coming.

The officer talked into the radio on his shoulder. Called for backup. Called out some numbers. Said some words, but words were meaningless. They wouldn't need words where they were going.

"Sloan Thomas?" he asked, his gun still pointed. She shook her head. Because she wasn't Sloan anymore. She was the darkness. She was the darkness, and Cherry was the light, and now there was only one of them left.

She smiled. "We did it," she said. And then again, louder, "We really did it."

"Yeah, you did it, alright," the man said. "Now put your hands on your head and step away from the victim."

Sloan tilted her head. She hesitated, but then realized it didn't matter.

Cherry was just a body now.

Even Sloan was just a body now.

It was fine. It was fine. She did as she was told, and the man led her away. She got lost in the bright blues and reds as more and more police cars appeared. People shouted; people ran to Cherry's body, her empty, empty body.

Sloan let herself be shoved inside the cop car. She smiled at the bite of steel around her wrists. The bite of pine in her knees. She was used to it by now.

It had to be like this so they could be together again when things were balanced. When they never had to die again. For the future, and the future, and the future. She would find Cherry there, and she would never let her go.

Sloan leaned back in the seat, her head pressed against the cool leather. The radio was a mess of static and shouting and confusion. But it was quiet. It was so quiet inside of Sloan.

Because she could feel it.

She could feel it in her blood.

ACKNOWLEDGMENTS

I'M FOREVER GRATEFUL to my agent, Sara Crowe, for encouraging me while I explored the spookier side of my writing and to my editor, Stephanie Pitts, for believing in me and giving *The Last Girls Standing* such a great home.

While they were its first cheerleaders, they were far from the only ones! This book would not exist without an entire brilliant team of people standing behind it!

My eternal gratitude to:

The amazing Matt Phipps, who always keeps everything rolling. The entire crew at Penguin, including my publisher, Jen Klonsky, and my publicist, Lizzie Goodell, along with Felicity Vallence, Alex Garber, James Akinaka, Shannon Spann, and everyone at Penguin Teen. Cindy Howle, Bethany Bryan, and Janet Rosenberg, my awesome copyeditors and proofreaders, as well as Natalie Vielkind, managing editor.

Michael Rogers and Kelley Brady for illustrating and designing such an eye-catching cover.

Joe, Rory, and Kelsey for joining me on my constant quest to find the perfect horror movie, and Dylan for ensuring that every-thing is crisp and I am not accidentally set to 720p. Erik J. Brown, even though you overhyped *Skinamarink* by A LOT (although you were dead on about *Halloween Ends*; let's co-write some fanfic).

Heather Kassner for rush reading when I was panicking I couldn't pull this off.

The Coven, The Zachelor Crew, and all my friends and family for keeping me going every day.

And to all the readers joining me on this journey, I wouldn't be here without you.

JENNIFER DUGAN is a writer, a geek, and a romantic who writes the kinds of stories she wishes she'd had growing up. She's the author of the graphic novel *Coven*, as well as the young adult novels *Melt With You*, *Some Girls Do*, *Verona Comics*, and *Hot Dog Girl*, which was called "a great, fizzy rom-com" by *Entertainment Weekly* and "one of the best reads of the year, hands down" by *Paste* magazine. She lives in upstate New York with her family, their dog, a strange kitten who enjoys wearing sweaters, and an evil cat who is no doubt planning to take over the world.

You can visit Jennifer at
JLDugan.com
Or follow her on Twitter and Instagram
@JL_Dugan